The
Spiderweb

BY JOSEPH E. PERSICO

The Spiderweb

Joseph E. Persico

CROWN PUBLISHERS, INC.

.New York

© 1979 by Joseph E. Persico

Inquiries should be addressed to
Crown Publishers, Inc.,
One Park Avenue, New York, N.Y. 10016

Printed in the United States of America
Published simultaneously in Canada by
General Publishing Company Limited

Designed by Shari de Miskey

Library of Congress Cataloging in Publication Data

Persico, Joseph E.
    The Spiderweb.

    I. Title.
PZ4.P4676Sp   1979   [PS3566.E727] 813'.5'4   79-14102 ·
ISBN 0-517-53925-X

To my staff, Vanya and Andrea

The
Spiderweb

1

LIPSCHUTZ WAS HANDLING THE INTERROGATION badly. He knew it. The prisoner continued to regard him with cool amusement, a half smirk never leaving his face.

"We will conduct the questioning in German, I told you!" Lipschutz realized he was shouting.

"As you wish, Lieutenant." The German responded calmly, again in English. He sat with black-booted legs casually crossed, his hands jammed into the pockets of a wrinkled but well-cut gray tunic. Several days' stubble spiked a jutting chin. His long black hair was slicked back neatly, but badly needed cutting. His collar tabs bore the three square rosettes of an Obersturmführer. On his left sleeve was a small patch with the letters *SD*. The man was Manfred Dorn.

Lipschutz glared at the prisoner through watery eyes, magnified by the thickness of his glasses. He was a small man, with a soft, damp look about him. His skin was puffed and pale, and his lower lip protruded in a state of chronic petulance.

"Now, you tell me. What was in that convoy?" Lipschutz felt better. His voice was again under control.

"You are of course aware, Lieutenant, that I don't have to answer that sort of question."

Lipschutz reddened. He rose, his hands gripping the edge of his desk. He tried to stop his lower lip from quivering, then abandoned himself to his rage.

"Forget that Geneva Convention nonsense, Dorn! You're no ordinary prisoner of war. You're SS, automatic arrest category." He sank back into his chair. His breath came in heavy inhalations. The German gazed serenely out the window.

Lipschutz now spoke with mechanical precision. "You . . . cocky . . . bastard! You are going to tell me what I want to know . . . or, I am going to start dealing with you as a potential war criminal."

Dorn's eyes betrayed a fleeting terror. Still, he said nothing.

"Were there arms in the convoy?" Division G-2 had been alerted to look for any evidence that die-hard Nazis had cached weapons in the nearby Kitzbüheler Alps to carry on guerrilla resistance. "Were you part of this Werewolf business?"

Dorn eyed Lipschutz coldly. "The Werewolf is nonsense. The war is over."

The American sat back and folded his hands across a

small belly, a petty smile on his face. "Now, that's being sensible. So talk, Obersturmführer."

"I have told you what I know."

Lipschutz drew a pen from the breast pocket of his khaki shirt. "Suppose we begin again with the convoy leaving the camp."

Dorn began wearily, as though instructing a half-wit. "Ten trucks left Oranienburg . . ."

"A concentration camp?"

"I suppose. But not the kind you are thinking. We left in three groups. I commanded the first three vehicles to leave."

"And you were carrying?"

"I was not told."

"Damn you, Dorn! You weren't told, or you don't know?"

"Money, perhaps? The camp finances? I can only guess."

"Ten trucks?"

"On my three vehicles. I have no idea what the others held."

"Was it jewelry, Dorn?" Liberated prisoners at Dachau had told Lipschutz what the Nazis did with their valuables, even gold dental fillings.

"The trucks were already sealed when I arrived."

"And then?"

"My instructions were to proceed to Königsee. It's a small resort, perhaps six kilometers beyond Berchtesgaden."

"Go on."

"I was to conceal the vehicles there, somehow, until Standartenführer Kruger arrived."

Lipschutz looked up expectantly.

"The commandant of D Wing at Oranienburg, Wolf Kruger. He was in charge of the Bernhard project. And before you ask me, that is all I know. Bernhard was a closely held secret. I was in no way involved. Now, I have indeed told you everything."

"Maybe you have. Maybe not." Lipschutz's voice had a querulous whine. "I don't think we're finished with you yet."

"I have already said, I was captured before reaching Königsee. And I don't know what happened to the one truck that escaped."

Lipschutz braced a stenographer's pad against his knee and made some notes. He ripped out the sheets along the spiralled edge and turned toward a somnolent MP posted at the entrance to his interrogation booth. "Dealy!"

The soldier stirred to attention.

"Take the prisoner back to the cage. How many more have I got out there?"

"At least thirty, sir."

Lipschutz glanced at his watch and sighed.

The corporal took Dorn by the arm. The German drew back as from a leper's touch.

Lipschutz stuffed his notes into a folder bearing Dorn's name on the tab. He went to a far corner of the interrogation shed that had been set apart by a partition. Inside, a pot of coffee and a kettle of water bubbled on a double hot plate. Lipschutz rummaged in the cabinet below where he had hidden his cup and tea bags. He poured the hot water over the bag with a trembling hand.

They still got to him. The smug son of a bitch had reached him. He shook his head in annoyed disbelief. From the moment the Nazi strode unapologetically into the shed, Lipschutz had felt off balance. The last seven years disappeared. The fear, the pain in the faces of his parents in those last months before the family had fled Dresden flooded his memory. The bullying, the taunts of the American boys who mocked his speech, his hopelessness at their games, the slow, painful rebirth, it was as though he had never survived it, had never learned to value himself again. The cold gray eyes of the German had looked through him and had seen the frightened sixteen-year-old refugee kid behind the officer's uniform. He hated them most for making him feel that.

*

The U.S. Army six-by-six stirred a small dust storm as it passed by him. Julius Goldhammer sat unmoving on the ground, his arms looped over his knees. He made no effort to avoid the gritty wake settling over him. The men in the departing truck clutched small, worn valises between their legs. They sat silent, faces vacant. None looked back as the truck rolled out of the gate and departed Buchenwald.

Goldhammer had sat in the dusty courtyard of the camp for the last two days. He rose only at the shouts of American soldiers signalling mealtimes. They seemed strange to him after his previous jailers. The day after the camp had been liberated, he had seen black-uniformed SS guards forced by the Americans to dig graves for stacks of fetid corpses. The fall of these devil-gods had been too sudden. Goldhammer had watched, but could not accept what his eyes saw.

Now he idly followed the Americans. They moved with a loose, casual gait that suggested a uniformed crowd more than an army. Yet they exuded a rough, uncontained energy that shimmered amid the living skeletons they had freed.

When the Americans first arrived, they had brought huge cauldrons of a marvelous-smelling soup. The prisoners had gone at it ravenously. Most were unable to finish a bowl before they became nauseous. But now, three weeks later, his stomach rumbled with a clocklike regularity before every mealtime. Goldhammer could see his wrists and ankles beginning to thicken.

In those first days after the American tanks had rolled up to the Buchenwald gate, a maniacal joy had swept the camp. They had taken their revenge against the crudest of the kapos and guards, impaling them live on the pointed fence posts supporting the barbed wire. They had ransacked the clothing storage and flung off the prison stripes that had made wretched clowns of them. Their haunted faces, shaven skulls, and fleshless bodies looked equally ludicrous in the finery they had found. After the first crazed outburst, the survivors spent days luxuriating in the narrow wooden bunks, one body resting where three had been jammed days before.

Then depression settled over them like a killing frost. They became weak because they no longer had to be strong. Many died. The American doctors gave the survivors vitamins, gradually increasing their diet to include solid food. Their bodies responded, but their spirits remained locked in apathy. It had slowly dawned on them. Families, homes, even the homelands of many of them were gone. Their lives had been spared. But for what?

Julius Goldhammer felt emotionally eviscerated. He was alive only in one corner of his mind. The resolve had grown from the moment he realized that he would not die at Buchenwald. Goldhammer wanted justice. Not revenge. Justice was what they had perverted, and its return would finally mark their defeat.

"Frankfurt, Weez-bayden! Any you people want a ride to Frankfurt or Weez-bayden?" The American spoke, it seemed to Goldhammer, entirely through his nose.

"He's saying Wiesbaden." Someone nudged Goldhammer. He rose and moved to the lowered tailgate. He could not pull himself aboard. The sergeant with the nasal voice lifted him like a child and deposited Goldhammer on the bed of the truck. The man then passed a scarred leather satchel up to him. He held it between his legs as other passengers stumbled over him. The soldier jerked the tailgate up in a practiced motion and locked it in place with a bolt and chain. The truck drove out through the gate. Julius Goldhammer did not look back.

*

The sanitorium was the last place they had to search that day. Sergeant Moultrie sat next to the jeep driver. Private Zeiss was in the rear. Moultrie, from the flat world of east Texas, gazed at the sharp, sugared peaks of the Algäu. He leaned back toward Zeiss. "I guess it's true. The Russians got the krauts' farmland. The Limeys got the industry. And we got their scenery."

The jeep wound out of the village of Obersdorf to a promontory near the base of the towering Nebelhorn, where the sanitorium stood. A wooden deck extended around its four sides, wide enough to accommodate the cots of tuberculosis patients healing their lungs in the alpine sun.

Moultrie's combat boots thudded up the wooden stairway. He was met by a florid man in a white coat who introduced himself in German as Dr. Eich, "Director of the Bavarian State Hospital for the Tubercular at Obersdorf." Moultrie motioned with his thumb toward Private Zeiss, who had followed him. "Herr Doktor, we are going to have to search this facility." The private spoke a Schwabisch-accented German.

The doctor stammered an objection. Moultrie did not bother to wait for Zeiss to translate. He marched down a center corridor with a half dozen rooms on either side. At the end of the hallway, Moultrie stopped. He took off his cap and scratched his head. "Did you notice anything, Zeiss?"

"No, Sarge, just the patients."

"Why do you suppose there's only women stretched out there in the sun. But there's only men inside here?"

The private shrugged.

"Tell that doctor I want every man inside this place stripped to the waist."

Zeiss conveyed the instruction to Dr. Eich.

"But ... sick people. This is barbarous." A fine sweat glistened on his brow.

Moultrie found twelve men with their blood type tattooed on the underside of their arms, an SS practice. One was a pink-faced man in glowing health with a thick head of white, waving hair. He smiled with small, even teeth and complimented the sergeant in confident English on his thoroughness. He identified himself as "Standartenführer Wolf Kruger," a colonel in the SD. "Our intelligence service, mind you, Sergeant."

An olive drab bus had followed Moultrie and his search team to the sanitorium. In it sat glumly silent men guarded by two MPs cradling submachine guns. The new prisoners, still in white hospital gowns, filed aboard the bus.

*

The Central Suspect and Witness Enclosure had been set up on the grounds of the former concentration camp at Dachau. Next door was the POW compound for Wehrmacht officers. The prisoners of war clustered by old associations; infantry, Luftwaffe, and panzer veterans huddled together. The mood in the camp was compounded of relief and uncertainty. They had fought honorably the last two years in a lost cause. It was over. Now they waited only to return home.

An eight-foot barbed wire fence separated them from prisoners being screened as potential war criminals. Here, too, cliques had formed. Officers of the Waffen SS, the elite military units, clung together. The SD prisoners behaved with the cool disdain of clubmen temporarily stranded in a workingmen's café. The Death's Head Detachments, Nazis who had operated the concentration camps—almost all candidates for criminal prosecution—were shunned by the others. The currents in this enclosure were resentment and fear. These men had lost their religion, along with the war, and for them the worst still lay ahead.

The MP delivered Manfred Dorn to the guard detail at the entrance of the compound. As he approached Barracks A 21, the other prisoners greeted his return with a curious expectancy. From their midst, a white-haired figure in an improbable hospital gown emerged and seized his hand warmly.

"Dorn, Dorn, my dear fellow! What a pleasure it is to see you again."

Dorn searched the pink, smiling face vainly.

"Standartenführer Kruger! Don't you remember? You see, Dorn, our American friends have offered me their hospitality as well." His smile formed a pursed valentine.

Dorn smiled weakly.

"We did not meet at Königsee. But we meet now. I cannot tell you how delighted I was when the other gentlemen told me I would find you here."

Kruger took Dorn's arm and steered him aside. He dropped his voice to a near whisper. "You see, young man, this is the dawn of a new day for the faithful. Believe me. Your role is terribly important for us."

A siren shrieked and a voice blared over the loudspeaker. "All prisoners return to your barracks. Form up for the

evening meal." Kruger released Dorn's arm and gave him a
conspiratorial smile. "We will talk later tonight."

*

Manfred Dorn lay on his cot, his eyes fixed on the
ceiling. The men in A 21 had just been marched back from the
mess hall where the Americans had served some sort of pink
pressed meat, not at all bad tasting, and a gelatinous red blob
which they were told was dessert.

He remembered meeting this man Kruger briefly, after
he had been reassigned from the collapsing western front late
in the spring. He recalled his bemused reaction on arriving at
Oranienburg. The war was lost. Yet this old officer remained
fiercely earnest. He had summoned Dorn to a small office
dominated by an absurdly large photograph of Hitler
wreathed in flags, a martial altar. Kruger had explained the
operation with a zeal suggesting that Dorn was a Teutonic
knight about to embark on the Crusades rather than a pawn at
the end of the game.

Perhaps Kruger had glimpsed the incredulity in Dorn's
eyes. "Believe me, young man, this is realistic. We old-timers
remember best what used to be ..." his jaw had set grimly,
accentuating the pointedness of his chin, "... and what will
happen again, if we yield so easily."

Dorn had stood awkwardly, uncomfortably, as Kruger
went on. He seemed to be musing aloud rather than address-
ing the lieutenant. "You would have been a child in those
days. But I can never forget. Five years after my brother and I
came home from the last war, we at last had our own shop, a
pharmacy. My modest hope then was only to succeed in
business. I dismissed the movement at first. Visionary fanatics.
I say that with deep shame today. But what was happening all
around us?" The face tightened. His voice suggested old,

smoldering angers. "Millions out of work. Riots over a crust of bread. Communist thugs ruling the streets. Money so worthless that we had to barter. A sausage for a tin of aspirin!" He shook his head in lingering disbelief. "And that Weimar government. Weak, cringing asses for a nation's leaders. Democracy? It was chaos! Dieter and I tried. God knows how hard. But of course our business failed. My brother became a broken man. And I was too. Until a true leader and his ideal lifted me up. He gave us back our nation. Our pride. Our strength. In return, I have given the cause my life. Do you think we can now fall back so spinelessly? Imagine our Germany under the heel of corrupt democracies? Bolshevik hordes? No, my dear Lieutenant Dorn. Never. And that is why Germany's future might well depend on the execution of your mission."

Dorn had suppressed a tired laugh. Still, there had been something compelling in the man's pure heart. They had all felt it once. In the end, he had taken those damn trucks—not even knowing what was in them—as far as he could, losing four men, believing to the end in the sacredness of an order.

Dorn was dozing off when someone shook his arm. He looked reflexively at the wrist where he usually wore his watch before an American private had relieved him of it. A huge, brutal-looking SS prisoner, whom he knew only as Gerbach, gripped his shoulder. "Standartenführer Kruger will see you now. Come with me." He followed Gerbach among the rows of sleeping men to a latrine in the center of the dim oblong barracks.

Dorn looked anxiously over his shoulder to the entrance of the building. The slack silhouettes of two guards were framed in the doorway. Gerbach posted himself as a lookout outside the latrine and motioned Dorn in.

"Over here, Dorn." The voice was spirited. "It's dark, isn't it?"

As Dorn's eyes became accustomed to the room, he could make out the figure of Kruger illuminated by moonlight angling through a high barred window.

"Imagine how dark it must have seemed in '23. The party ranks broken. The Führer in Landsberg prison." Kruger shook his head. "He never wavered. We cannot now."

Dorn felt nauseous in the close, unlit room. Kruger had moved toward him and was staring into his eyes. "The cathedral has been destroyed. The faithful have scattered." His voice took on a hard edge. "But not all of them, Dorn. Not all."

The messianic tone suddenly evaporated. He became quite matter-of-fact. "Look, Dorn. The plans were already in motion even before the war ended. The Spiderweb is already operating. Don't you see? Our being here means only that some of us will be working from within, while others work from without." He held Dorn's arm and smiled benignly. "We still have one last weapon. Time. For now, it is all we need. If we can buy time, we can return. Believe me."

Dorn eyed the latrine door and saw the large head and folded arms of Gerbach.

Kruger released Dorn's arm and went on speaking. "The links are already being forged. To Italy, then to Spain. South America will give us safe harbor, particularly Argentina. All that is necessary is for enough of the leadership to survive, outside Germany until the time is right. Ah, Dorn, it need not be long. Believe me. In a matter of months our enemies will be at each other's throats."

Dorn's head throbbed. Kruger was no longer looking at him. The older man gestured toward some unseen audience.

"The British have been fools, blind, stubborn. The Americans are no more than children. But they will discover what Adolf Hitler was doing, not just for Germany, but for Western civilization!" His voice had risen to a fevered hoarseness. Then, just as suddenly, he spoke plainly again. "Where is the money?"

Dorn looked at him stupidly. Kruger seized his arm. "The money, man. Where is it? Your cargo!"

"Money? I don't understand."

Kruger's mouth curled in disbelief.

"I got as far as Ebensee. We were on our way to Bad Ischl when American aircraft struck us. Two of the trucks were put out of action. I lost two men in the attack. I gathered the others and obeyed your instructions."

Kruger eyed him apprehensively.

"We did not allow the trucks to fall into enemy hands. We pushed them into a deep part of the Traun River."

Kruger nodded. "Yes, that is good. And the other truck?"

"An American infantry patrol discovered us just as their planes left. I shouted to the driver of the remaining vehicle to get away, while we held off the Americans. The other two men were killed. I was overpowered."

"You are absolutely sure it was the lead van that escaped?"

"Yes, I had been riding in it myself."

Kruger smiled contentedly and nodded his head. "Then there is hope."

"I'm still not sure I understand."

"You did tell that driver to proceed to Königsee?" Kruger moved his face close to Dorn's.

Dorn nodded.

Kruger looked about the room. "We cannot talk any

longer, Dorn. They will check soon. But you see how impor-
tant you have been." His eyes suddenly narrowed. "You were interrogated today, I have been told."

"Yes, that's true."

"You said nothing, of course?"

Dorn hesitated. "I did not tell them everything."

"What do you mean?"

"They know only that one of the vehicles may have gotten away."

"But why did you have to tell them. anything?" Kruger sounded almost hurt.

Dorn looked squarely at the older man. He felt exhausted beyond caring. "Because the war is over."

Kruger recoiled as from a blow.

"The war is ended. There will be no war between the Allies. The Reich is finished. Dead. As dead as Adolf Hitler is dead." Dorn spoke with unaccustomed passion. Kruger's body began to tremble. Dorn hurried out of the dark room, past the giant Gerbach, picking his way among the cots toward his own. He collapsed onto the taut canvas and fell into his first deep sleep since his capture.

At 2 A.M. the guard detail made its bed check. Ten minutes after the guards resumed their post, Gerbach gathered another group in the latrine. Kruger spoke to them in a heavy whisper. "The lieutenant, Dorn, he is not Führer true. He is a menace to our plans."

Gerbach nodded his huge head eagerly.

2

THE SIX-BY-SIX THREADED ITS WAY AMONG THE
bomb craters pockmarking the Erfurt–Frankfurt Autobahn,
sometimes leaving the roadbed entirely, then regaining the
hard surface for long, comfortable stretches. It was a well-built
road. The hillsides had exploded in the gold of wild Butterblumen. Goldhammer stared ahead, unseeing.

The hands resting on his knees were unexpectedly strong
looking for a man who, before his imprisonment, had been a
plump figure with full cheeks and a bald pate giving a
repeating roundness to his appearance.

Six years before, Julius Goldhammer had been, by his

own reckoning, the best engraver in Leipzig. And to be the
best in that capital of graphic art was to be the finest in
Germany. He was also, he later concluded, the greatest fool. A
Jew living well in Germany that late in the day could only
have occupied a fool's paradise.

Their friends, their families had all gone into exile or had
disappeared into the camps. Still, his Hannah, a plain, affable
creature fifteen years his junior, had placed her trust in Julius.
The marriage had been arranged, but it had been a happy
pairing. Hannah was hardly beautiful. Her prospects had been
unpromising. Her girl friends found the bald, older Goldhammer laughable, though none said so to Hannah. She had
heeded the wish of her father, a perpetually impoverished
schoolmaster at the yeshiva to marry the printer, yielding to
his will just as she would later unquestioningly obey Julius.

Goldhammer had proved a loving, devoted husband and,
as her father had predicted, more than a good provider. They
occupied a handsome second-floor apartment on Zeitzerstrasse
until the fifth year of their marriage, when Goldhammer's
modest passions had been rewarded by the birth of their only
child, Neda. They had then taken an even larger, more
fashionable apartment on Hartelstrasse.

Hannah was incapable of complaining. But after her
mother and father fled Germany with her younger brother,
Goldhammer often found her weeping softly. Later, when her
two older brothers were arrested, he had read the muted terror
in her eyes. But the deeply religious Goldhammer placed his
faith in God and Verlag Kunstwerk, A.G.

Kunstwerk was the preeminent art publisher in Germany. Goldhammer had begun his apprenticeship there as a
boy of fifteen and had risen to become chief engraver, with
twelve craftsmen under him. When Dr. Dietrich made his

monthly tour of the plant, the director, a brash, self-important man, never failed to address Goldhammer personally. "All for art, eh Goldhammer?" The tired jest never failed to flatter his Jewish werkmeister.

"Can one have the finest pastry shop without the finest pastry chef?" It was Goldhammer's effort to cheer Hannah, always accompanied by an affectionate pinch on the cheek, whenever he saw her frightened. They were safe at Verlag Kunstwerk while his talent lasted, of that he was sure.

*

Julius Goldhammer was arrested during the small party Hannah had arranged with a handful of remaining friends and children for Neda's sixth birthday. At the Gestapo headquarters, he pleaded for a chance to call Dr. Dietrich. It was not necessary, he was told. The secret police had already talked to Verlag Kunstwerk. Dietrich had not raised a finger.

Goldhammer was sent to the concentration camp at Bergen-Belsen, northeast of Hanover. He had no idea what had become of his Hannah and Neda. For days he cried, inconsolably and without shame. Then he began to pray. The crying and praying seemed to inflame his jailors. Goldhammer became a favored target for random blows and kicks. His soft body was forever marbled with bruises.

Eventually, his prayers were answered. Dr. Dietrich had not failed him. In January of 1940, after six months at hard labor, Goldhammer was transferred to Oranienburg, a camp just north of Berlin. He had been transported with twenty other men, huddled against each other in the back of an open truck during a driving snowfall.

As they entered the Oranienburg gate, Goldhammer felt his spirits lift. The camp was unremittingly grim. But the prisoners walking the yard appeared reasonably well fed and clothed. They moved with traces of surviving dignity. The palpable terror of Bergen-Belsen was absent here.

The new arrivals were assigned to Block 16, where they found other prisoners recently transferred from camps all over Germany. For two days they were left alone and spent the unaccustomed idleness speculating on the meaning of their transfer, since they discovered that all of them had been previously engaged in printing.

On the third day, a squat SS man entered the block shouting Goldhammer's name. Goldhammer had not risen quickly enough from his wooden bunk and the guard delivered him a backhanded blow that drove a tooth through his lower lip. He held a sleeve to his mouth to stanch the bleeding as the man prodded him out of the block with a nightstick.

They crossed the courtyard of the compound and went up the stairway of the gray concrete administrative block, where Goldhammer was taken into the office of a ridiculously boyish-looking SD officer. The guard saluted and announced: "Captain Frommer, the Jew, Goldhammer!"

Goldhammer stood with cap in hand, arms pressed to his sides, head bent. His lip had swollen but no longer bled.

The officer thumbed through a thick sheaf of papers on his desk without acknowledging the prisoner's presence. The guard posted himself at the doorway. "Yes, yes. Here you are." The captain pulled several sheets from the pile and scanned them quickly. He looked up. "Well now, Herr Julius Goldhammer, we are honored indeed. A true artist, aren't you?" He smiled without baring his teeth. "Do you know why you are here?"

Goldhammer's bruised mouth hung slack. He shook his head.

"You are going to practice your profession, my good man. You are going to practice it at the very zenith of your art." Frommer smiled again.

"I am going home?" Goldhammer's voice was barely audible. He dared not look up.

"No, not home." Frommer shook his head in mock disappointment. "You will work here, at Oranienburg." He reached into his desk and withdrew a shining black leather case. "Look, nice little Jew man. Look at this." He drew a bank note from it and handed it to the prisoner. "What is it, Goldhammer?"

Goldhammer took it with a shaking hand. "Money. English money."

"Yes, of course. It's an English five-pound note. The question is this. Can you make it?" Frommer enjoyed the confusion in the man's face. "Well, can you make it, master printer? Don't you see? This is what you are going to do. That is why we have brought you here." He was smiling his little boy's smile. "That bank note is going to save you from the mercies of my Gestapo colleagues. Now, tell me. Do you think it can be done?"

Goldhammer rubbed the note between his thumb and fingers. It had a dry, thin feel like the parchment that separates the layers in a box of chocolates. He studied the face of the note up close for a long time, then handed it back.

"I don't know." His voice was feeble. "I suppose . . . it could be done."

"Good, good. Now, you will return to the block. You can start organizing your crew from the best people there. In a few days I will have further instructions for you."

Goldhammer's heart was pounding furiously. His throat ached. The words croaked from his mouth. "I cannot do it."

Frommer eyed him uncertainly. "What did you say?"

Goldhammer swayed dizzily as he spoke. "I have a wife
... a child ... I have no idea where they are."

"So?"

He lowered his head and spoke in a bare whisper. "I will do nothing for the Nazis."

The officer was instantly up from his desk and before Goldhammer. The blow caught him full in the face. He sank to his knees. He looked up at Frommer. "I will do nothing for you while they are in danger." Blood again ran from his lip.

The kick to his ribs sent Goldhammer sprawling. He held his side and gasped convulsively. Frommer screamed at the guard. "Take him back!"

As the guard dragged the limp, groaning figure, Frommer spoke with icy precision. "Do you know where you are going, you scum? You are going to your death!"

*

But he did not go back to Bergen-Belsen. Goldhammer was left alone in Block 16. Two days later he was taken again before Captain Frommer. The young officer's earlier arch geniality had vanished. He spoke without looking at the prisoner.

"We have some women prisoners assigned here. They work in the kitchens, collect garbage, run the laundry. Your wife and child are here now. They will work in the officer's scullery."

Goldhammer stared into Frommer's spoiled child's face. Tears streamed from his eyes. He swallowed the sobs that rose in his throat.

*

Life at Oranienburg took on a perverse contentment for Julius Goldhammer. For one hour each Sunday evening, he was allowed to visit Hannah and Neda in the block where they were quartered with two hundred other women. He found them thin, perpetually exhausted. Hannah's hands were raw and cracked. The child's frail arms were blistered with burns from hauling boiling kettles. The three of them spent the hour holding hands, speaking little, their eyes glistening with an inexplicable joy.

The rest of the time Goldhammer steeped himself in Project Bernhard. Frommer had been right. It was the ultimate challenge. For a master engraver to attempt a perfect reproduction of the most powerful currency on earth began to seem to him a self-justifying end.

Goldhammer became werkmeister of the most skilled men he had ever directed. The finest presses, cameras, lights and engraving tools were available to him. Goldhammer surveyed the shining print shop and felt a perverse pride in the superiority of German technology.

Bernhard had been born in the febrile mind of Alfred Vogel, a thirty-year-old SD major known in his youth as a formidable Communist head cracker in the street battles between the Reds and Nazis. In 1939, Vogel had become an instant legend in intelligence circles by engineering the brilliant kidnapping of Britain's top two spy masters on the European continent. Thus, months later when Vogel first introduced the Bernhard proposal to his superiors, he earned a respectful hearing.

The plan was simplicity itself. They would gather the finest printing talent in the Reich and put these craftsmen to work counterfeiting English money. They would then try to undermine the enemy's economy by flooding the world market with billions of bogus British bank notes.

SD operatives went to work canvassing the leading

publishing and printing houses, like Verlag Kuntswerk, which yielded the name of Julius Goldhammer. Most master craftsmen also turned out to be imprisoned Jews.

"He is easily the best engraver," Dr. Dietrich had assured the pleasant young Captain Frommer, whom Vogel had made his chief recruiter. "He also knows every other phase of printing, and he has something that can't be taught."

Frommer looked at him, waiting.

"He has a passion for his craft bordering on an obsession. Of course, I don't question the racial policies of the government. But Julius Goldhammer was not easily replaced at Verlag Kunstwerk."

*

Goldhammer studied the British bank note as a general scouts his enemy. He probed its strengths and weaknesses through a twenty-power loupe. The British money was printed from a steel engraving. The process was the reverse of producing a book or newspaper. Instead of paper being passed over raised letters, as in most printing, the paper in engraving passed over a flat plate into which the image had been carved, deep cuts for solid areas and shallow, hairlike cuts for fine lines. The ink in these recesses was transferred to the paper during the printing process. The paper, when pressed against the recesses in the plate, was raised up slightly, giving engraved currency its distinctive texture. Goldhammer could tell merely by touching a piece of printing whether it had been engraved or printed on an ordinary press.

Goldhammer examined the English notes with professional admiration. Framing the outer border was a filagree of fine lines produced by a geometric lathe, a machine using the same principle as a child's spirograph. The complex pattern was virtually impossible to duplicate, even with another geometric lathe, since the number of settings for the engraving needles was infinite.

The watermark presented another towering obstacle. It covered 80 percent of the note. The lettering, numbers, and figures were superimposed over the watermark.

Most intimidating, Goldhammer found, was the work in the upper left-hand corner, a medallion of the seated figure of Britannia, with a scepter in her left hand. Goldhammer paid a silent tribute to the English guild brother who had engraved this complex lady.

He guessed that the parched, rustling paper on which the notes were printed was made from an exotic fiber, probably grown somewhere in the British Empire.

Yet other elements of the bank notes were so simple that he marveled at British innocence. They were printed only on one side of the paper and in a single color, black. The design, he learned, had not been changed for years. He developed a fondness for the man whose signature was becoming so familiar. "K. O." or "K. V. Peppialt," or was it "Peppiatt"? the Chief Cashier of the Bank of England. He was not sure. The signature was semilegible. It would be an easy forgery.

Goldhammer ran a crew of twenty printers, pressmen, artists, engravers, photographers, retouchers, and layout men who lived and worked in a section of Oranienburg designated D Wing. They slept in a plain but not particularly crowded barracks and were allotted extra food rations. Goldhammer's body began to recover some of the fleshiness that he had lost at Bergen-Belsen. He saved a share of his ration for his Sunday evening visits to his wife and child. The crew worked a twelve-hour day, seven days a week. On Friday nights Goldhammer led them in prayer. The D Wing prisoners were hated and envied by the other Oranienburg inmates.

The Nazis had given Goldhammer and his men a powerful incentive. Succeed, or return to the death camps. There were hundreds of skilled men rotting in other camps eager to take their places.

Goldhammer relied most on another master engraver, Avram Rosenthal, a sixty-two-year-old Berliner of melancholy outlook, a gaunt, stooped figure who stared out at the world from deeply socketed, brooding eyes. Rosenthal spoke little. When he did, it was with the rumbling voice of an Old Testament prophet.

What had first impressed Goldhammer was that Rosenthal wet his tools with his own saliva. He knew immediately that he had a seasoned engraver. Rosenthal had been assigned by the werkmeister to engrave the formidable medallion of Britannia, whom Rosenthal railed at as "The English bitch."

The other men made an unconscious division of leadership. They looked to Goldhammer for direction in their work. They came to Rosenthal in their sadness. Only one of them failed to respect the old man. The photographer, Fischl, was a blond, blue-eyed, twenty-year-old Jew who sucked up shamelessly to the guards and despised the cowed, older inmates. He mocked Rosenthal, as "Father Moses." Fischl was, nevertheless, a skilled craftsman, and it was he who blew up the tenfold enlargements of Britannia from which Rosenthal worked.

They had returned on a March evening after repeated unsuccessful efforts to duplicate the stylized leafwork bordering the figure of Britannia. The old engraver lay in the bunk above Goldhammer. He heard the nasal drone beneath him and leaned over the edge.

"You pray, Julius." He laughed hollowly. "Every night you pray."

"You don't?"

Rosenthal laughed again. "The Nazis have done what

the most thick-headed rabbi could never do. They have made me a skeptic."

"That saddens me, Avram. Here, we have reason to pray." Goldhammer looked up into the deep-set, piercing eyes.

Rosenthal made his deep, unhappy laugh again. "Shall we play a little game, Julius? You will ask, 'How is your dear wife, Herr Rosenthal?' Then I will ask, 'How is your dear wife, Herr Goldhammer?' 'Your son, Rosenthal?' 'And your daughter, Goldhammer?' "

Goldhammer was silent for a time. At last, he spoke. "I am sorry, Avram. It was selfish." Rosenthal, he knew, had seen his son beaten to death by Nazi street toughs. Shortly afterward his wife had taken her own life. He had a daughter married to a gentile. He had heard nothing from her for years.

*

During the first fruitless six months, they were saved only by Major Vogel. The man appeared to have no particular compassion, but Goldhammer appreciated a quick, practical intelligence in the Nazi. He had only to explain the mechanics of printing once to Vogel, and the man immediately understood their problems. He knew the questions to ask, peeling away layers of complexity like a clever prosecutor, until he had exposed the core issue. Then he would order a practical solution.

After shredding hundreds of English bank notes, they found that the money was not printed on some rare fiber, but on ordinary linen rags. Yet, after weeks of attempting to reproduce the off-white color and distinctive dry texture, success had eluded them.

Vogel brought to Oranienburg an expert from Spechthausen bei Eberswald, a Berlin plant that conducted the

Bernhard project's paper tests. Vogel sat on the edge of
Goldhammer's small desk in the print shop, frowning in
thought.

"The British paper is made of ordinary linen rag. Is that
not right?"

The paper expert and Goldhammer nodded.

"We are using linen rag. Is that not also right?"

"Yes, the same Turkish linen as the British," the papermaker answered.

"Yet, using the identical ingredient, we have failed to
match the British paper. Is that not also true?"

Goldhammer's eyes were riveted to the floor.

"Logic tells us there is something in their linen that is
not in ours." Vogel paused. "A secret ingredient? No.
Nothing so mysterious." He rose from the desk and paced the
floor. He stopped abruptly and turned. His face beamed in
triumph. "Dirt!"

"Dirt?" Goldhammer looked up. The paper expert
blinked.

Vogel continued to pace. "They don't use some fancy
fiber to produce the paper, as we first thought. They use
ordinary linen rag. Well? Who says they are clean, unused
rags?"

Thereafter, Vogel ordered that the virgin Turkish linen
be distributed throughout the camp as cleaning rags. They
were then picked up, laundered, and the process repeated. The
next run of paper was produced with used rags. The result was
a paper indistinguishable from the British stock. On that day
Vogel released the printing crew at six in the evening and
ordered sausage served with their meal.

Vogel invariably entered the shop with the same flourish.
The print shop was on two levels, with most of the machinery

on the lower level, and most of the supplies on a steel-grated balcony. The entrance was on the balcony level. The door would burst open, revealing an SS guard in the lead bearing a submachine gun. Then came Vogel followed by the faithful, baby-faced Frommer, note pad ever in hand, and finally another guard with a submachine gun. Their hob-nailed boots clanged along the steel flooring, then down a rattling steel stairway from the balcony to the main floor.

The entourage arrived on a stifling July day with the customary clangor, although Vogel's usual gruff heartiness was missing. He went directly to Goldhammer.

"When will the old man finish?" His tone was ominous.

Goldhammer wiped the sweat from his neck. "Soon, Herr Major. I have told him he must finish soon. He will."

"Eight months, Goldhammer! How much longer do you expect me to wait? Are you sure he is capable?"

"Capable? Oh no, Herr Major, Rosenthal is not merely capable. He is an artist. I promise you. Just a few more days."

The assistant, Frommer, scribbled a date in his note pad.

"Let me see what we have today." Vogel snapped his fingers.

Goldhammer went to the table where Rosenthal, head bowed resolutely, was working. The man did not move, even as Goldhammer slipped the thin steel sheet from his hands.

"You see, Herr Major. This plate is almost complete."

Goldhammer went to a proof press, set the plate, made some adjustments, spun a wheel, and handed Vogel a sheet of paper imprinted with the medallion of Britannia.

Vogel studied the image and shook his head. "What do I know? It looks fine to me."

"Yes, it is good, Herr Major, but not yet undetectable."

"It had damned well better be perfect." Vogel laughed grimly. "Or Heydrich will have all our asses."

Young Captain Frommer laughed too. Goldhammer smiled feebly. The armed guards remained stone faced.

*

A week had passed. Goldhammer was at his desk, studying some unsatisfying attempts at the British watermark. The door to the upper-level balcony burst open and five SS guards marched in. Neither Vogel nor Frommer was among them. They clattered down the steel-grated stairway and marched directly to Rosenthal. He remained motionless, head bowed, at his table.

The sergeant in charge seized the old man by the collar and shoved him backward. His stool clattered across the floor. The other workers stared silently from their machines. Goldhammer came over and began to speak. The sergeant shoved him aside, as his men pinned Rosenthal to the floor, one on each limb. The sergeant stood, hands on hips, scowling at the struggling figure. The rhythmic thumping of the presses and the old man's gasps were the only sounds in the room.

In the center of the shop stood a linotype machine occasionally used for routine printing. The sergeant went to it and plunged a dipper into the leadpot. He came back and straddled Rosenthal, holding the dipper a foot above the man's thin, heaving chest. Rosenthal's lips moved wordlessly. As the lead poured over the place where his heart was, he gave out a long, piercing wail. His body went rigid, and his eyes bulged from his head. The smell of burning cloth and flesh seared the air. A terrible silence reigned. Then a man vomited. The sergeant ordered two workers to drag the body outside.

Goldhammer's arms shook. He struggled for words. "But ... he finished it ... we sent the medallion to Major Vogel ... two days ago."

"You Jew worm." The sergeant glared at him. "Did you think you could deceive us?"

Tears filled Goldhammer's eyes. "I ... I don't understand. What is happening?"

The sergeant looked out at the men standing mute at their machines. "The Jew Rosenthal attempted to sabotage Project Bernhard. If any of you have similar plans, you have just witnessed your fate." His eyes settled on a figure crouched in the corner of the shop. He smiled enigmatically, then marched the guard detachment out of the shop.

Goldhammer looked at the huddled form in the corner. Fischl, the young photographer, clutched his stomach and retched convulsively.

"I didn't know they would do this." He sobbed between gasps. "Believe me, Goldhammer. I didn't know."

Goldhammer knelt beside him. "What do you mean? Tell me."

"I told them ... about the hand."

Goldhammer gaped at him, mouth open, uncomprehending.

"The hand. Don't you know?"

"What are you talking about?"

"Oh God! Rosenthal left two lines off Britannia's right hand. I know he did. I spotted it in the blowups. He admitted it."

"Why did he do this? Why?"

"To alert the British."

Goldhammer's voice was a disbelieving whisper. "You told the guards?"

Fischl held his trembling hands outstretched. "He was an old fool. He was going to get us all killed. Don't you understand?"

Goldhammer let out a mournful cry. He raised his clenched fist over Fischl's tear-streaked face, poised to strike. Then his arms dropped to his side. He rose and moved lifelessly to his desk. He sank into the chair, buried his face in his arms, and cried softly.

*

Goldhammer personally completed the Britannia medallion begun by Rosenthal. But the scrollwork done with the geometric lathe still eluded him. Its intricacy was beyond anything reproducible by hand. They also wasted thousands of sheets of paper unsuccessfully attempting to match the watermark. Their efforts had been good but never beyond detection. After a year's effort, Project Bernhard had stalled hopelessly.

Goldhammer went to visit Hannah and Neda on a Sunday evening. It was January of 1941. The women's barracks was unheated. The child was sick. Vogel had been threatening Goldhammer all that week, passing along the pressure that he was taking from his superiors to complete the project or end it.

After the visit, Goldhammer wandered across the courtyard back to the shop, lost in melancholy as he contemplated what the failure of Bernhard meant. Inside, he heard the sounds of an offset press, whirring, clanging and monotonously spewing out sheets which skidded down the rollers and floated into the delivery bin.

Vogel had been asked by the camp commandant to have his Jews do some odd job printing. He resented the intrusion into Bernhard, but was anxious to buy time and goodwill for his endangered scheme.

The hiss and clatter of the press comforted Goldhammer. They formed a lovely and reassuring metronome in his life. He nodded to the printer, absently fished a sheet from the delivery bin, and took it to his desk. It was marvelous work, a poster intended to lift the spirits of the Oranienburg SS detachment. It presented a black-uniformed SS guard next to an infantry-man in field gray. The caption read: "For Führer and Father-land—Both Serve Equally."

The poster had been drawn by another Oranienburg inmate, a Jew named Faust, formerly a popular cartoonist on the Berlin Morgenpost. Goldhammer noted wryly that Faust's customary signature was missing from the right-hand corner. But the style was unmistakable. The fine-lined detail gave the work a rich texture. Fischl had done a good job of pho-tographing the original and had caught the detail sharply. The poster, Goldhammer thought, looked almost engraved.

He jumped from his desk. "Where is Fischl? I want him right away!" The pressman pointed up to the balcony where the photographer lay sleeping on a pile of linen rags.

Goldhammer ran up the stairway and shook him.

"God, man. What do you want now?" The photogra-pher rolled his head dazedly.

"Shoot the five-pound note!"

"Are you crazy? I've shot it a hundred times."

"Do as I say. Shoot the five-pound note right away."

Fischl put on his striped jacket, which he had wadded into a pillow. "What size enlargement?" he grumbled.

"No enlargement. Print it actual size."

Goldhammer had a printing plate made from the photo-graph and spent much of the night running proofs from it. The trials were unsatisfactory, but promising. In the morning, Goldhammer asked to see Major Vogel.

Vogel's office was walled with signed photographs: Vogel with the Führer, after kidnapping the two top British intelligence agents at Venlo; Vogel receiving a medal from Reinhard Heydrich, chief of all Nazi security forces; Vogel chatting with Goering when that sybarite was founding the Gestapo.

"I don't understand what you're talking about, Goldhammer. Keep it simple."

"You see, so far we have been engraving, that is, printing directly from a plate of engraved steel. I would like your permission to try something entirely different."

"God man! After a year. You tell me we have to start over?"

"Herr Major, most routine printing is increasingly done on an offset press. Its potential has not been fully tested for fine printing such as this subject."

Vogel fixed him with his hard, unrelenting gaze, "Go on."

"In the offset process, we take a photograph of what we want to print. From the negative of the photograph, we make an aluminum plate. Then we print from that plate. The system is called offset because the paper does not come in direct contact with . . ."

"Please. Spare me the details. What are the advantages of this system over what we have been doing? And, since you have taken a year to tell me about it, what are the problems?"

"You are right, Herr Major. There are obstacles. Serious obstacles. But our main advantage is that the camera cannot lie."

Vogel eyed him dubiously.

"We have not been able to duplicate the engraving on the English bank notes by hand. But a camera can pick up every detail perfectly."

"And the obstacles?"

"The texture. That will be serious. Something printed on an offset press does not have the feel of engraved work. And the watermark. That is ticklish, too. But I have some ideas."

"What do you need?"

"The highest resolution film and a better copy camera."

"What else?"

"Three months."

Vogel was silent, his face buried in his hand. He then looked up at the dumpy, unimpressive figure before him. "We are odd allies in this venture. Yet I think you understand, Goldhammer, that my failure ends rather differently from yours."

Goldhammer's head was bobbing slowly. "Yes, of course, Herr Major."

"Good. You will have what you need."

*

"Five-hundredths of a centimeter? This new film is fantastic. But ..." Fischl frowned. "I don't know."

"You will do it." Goldhammer's eyes had a wild sheen. "Then after you make the first negative you will shoot another, also shrunken by five-hundredths of a centimeter. You get started. I am going to begin work on the water-mark."

Goldhammer had taped an enlargement of a five-pound note to a light table. He went to work with a tiny brush. He dipped its point into a solution of ferricyanide and pain-stakingly blanked out every letter, figure, and design on the bill until all that remained were the photographed shadows of the watermark. He had the result photographed again, this time normal size. He made an aluminum plate from the negative, then had a press loaded with an opaque white ink.

The paper was then run through the press. Instead of attempting an actual watermark, Goldhammer had, in effect, printed its rippling design on the paper.

Fischl came to him nervously. "I wasted so much film. But I think I've got it." He showed Goldhammer three negatives of a five-pound note that looked identical to the naked eye, though each was progressively five-hundredths of a centimeter smaller than the other.

"Good." Goldhammer nodded without stopping. He was moving with fevered intensity. "Schwartz? Where is Schwartz? I want Fischl's negatives burned into plates right away!"

The inmate Schwartz placed a negative over an aluminum plate coated with a solution of albumin. He pressed a button and a light of blinding whiteness shot through the negative and seared the image of the bank note into the plate. He repeated the process with each of the different-sized negatives.

"Set press number two." Goldhammer's tone had a brittle, impatient authority. The men leaped at his orders.

The press was loaded with the paper that had already been printed with the simulated watermark.

"Lock in the first plate."

A pressman snapped the thin aluminum sheet into place.

Goldhammer's thumb pressed the starter. Cylinders began to turn and air hissed. Rubber suction feet gently urged the sheets toward the press, where a row of grippers seized and fed them between rollers. The image passed from the aluminum plate onto a rubber cylinder, then onto the sheets of paper. The sheets fled down a skid, passing under an infrared lamp that dried the ink almost instantly. Then they fluttered into the delivery bin.

With the run complete, Goldhammer turned off the

press. "Lock in the second plate."

The pressman snapped the plate into place as another man lifted the finished sheets from the delivery bin and placed them again in the loading tray.

Fischl studied Goldhammer's actions, puzzled.

"Is that the plate with the first five-hundredths shrinkage?"

"It is," Fischl assured him.

Goldhammer snatched one of the printed sheets. He studied it under a bright light, went to the ink fountain, and added more drying solution. He stirred the fountain with a knife to keep the ink supply uniform, then started the press rolling again. When the run was completed, the entire process was repeated, this time with the last plate Fischl had photographed.

Goldhammer stood at the delivery bin, staring between the rollers from which the freshly printed sheets leaped, all the while shouting orders to the crew.

Fischl leaned into Goldhammer's ear and was now grinning widely. "I see what you're doing. You little bastard. Now I see."

"Of course you do." Goldhammer smiled tightly without turning his head, all the while watching the sheets flip, flip, flipping into the delivery bin.

He then moved to the paper cutter. "Come. Come quickly." Fischl took the sheets and dropped them on the flat metal surface of the cutter. Goldhammer seized the paper and blocked the corners until the forward edge became a smooth, solid plane. The knife dropped with a remorseless stroke.

Goldhammer grabbed the stack, turned it at a right angle, and began to shape the edges again. He noticed the man who ordinarily ran the knife standing close to him. He smiled and backed off. "I am sorry, Feldmann. Of course, you cut it and trim it." Goldhammer collapsed into his chair and wiped his bald head with a linen rag. He could hear the last strokes of the knife, then heard Fischl screaming.

"We've done it! We made it!"

The young photographer hurried to him with a stack of bank notes. Goldhammer took an authentic five-pound note from his breast pocket. He held it and a fresh counterfeit behind his back and ran them between his fingers. His face assumed a beatific serenity. "I cannot tell the difference."

"I couldn't imagine why you wanted those slightly smaller pictures," Fischl said.

"Of course." Goldhammer continued to stare at the freshly printed notes. "The buildup of ink after the three passes has given them the feeling of an engraving. By shrinking the image a bit, we avoided having any print overlap the edges on the second and third runs."

He placed a fabricated bank note over the light table and laughed. "It does look like a watermark." He collapsed again into his chair. Faint rays shone through the iron-grated windows. They had worked through the night.

"Tell the guards to ask Major Vogel to come."

The rest had been mechanical. Blank spaces had been left on the bank notes in which a numbering machine printed different numerals for each series of bills. A variety of dates were added in the same way.

After several failed efforts, Major Vogel hit on a way to age the money convincingly. He had the notes scattered over the floor of the Oranienburg records office. The door was kept locked throughout the working day. At night, the clerk-inmates had to strip and be searched before they returned to their barracks. The notes, trampled underfoot all day long, quickly acquired an authentic appearance of age.

*

On March 1, 1941, Martin Wenck was warmly received on his arrival at the Bank Prokredit Zurich. A.G. Prokredit served numerous German clients and Wenck represented one of the most consequential. Ever since France and the Low Countries had fallen, the Swiss bankers, he noticed, had treated him with even greater deference.

He was quickly ushered into the vaulted oak office of Dr. Nebel, Assistant Director for Foreign Deposits, a dessicated figure whose corded neck rose like a dried stalk from a wing-tipped collar.

Nebel read, with obvious pride, the letter Wenck handed him. The Germans had a problem. Their banking officials had been unable to agree as to whether a supply of English currency which they had confiscated was counterfeit or legitimate. They were asking the more expert Swiss for an authoritative decision. The letter was supposedly signed by the director of the Reichsbank. It had been forged in the D Wing at Oranienburg.

"Herr Wenck, I will do more than verify them. I am going to cable the Bank of England to find out if they did in fact issue notes in these denominations with these serial numbers on the dates shown."

"That is most kind of you, Dr. Nebel. A proof of friendship between our countries."

*

Martin Wenck gazed out contentedly as the train rolled past the flatness girding Lake Constance. In his hands he held the *Neue Züricher Zeitung* and on his lap was a leather briefcase carrying the bank notes Dr. Nebel had pronounced absolutely authentic. As good as his word, the old fool had also cabled England and found out that the Bank of England had issued

notes in these series. An audacious man, that Vogel, Wenck
thought. It had indeed been an ingenious test.

*

The print shop door flew open and Major Vogel appeared with his retinue. He remained on the balcony where he gripped the iron rail and looked out over the prisoners below. Frommer, his assistant, nodded to a guard who threw a switch cutting power to the machinery. As the presses wound down into silence, Vogel spoke.

"Last month, the future of this project, and your fate, hung in doubt. Today, I can tell you that Bernhard goes on. Indeed, we now shift from experimentation to production. Those of you who work and obey will continue to be safe here. Those of you who do not can have little doubt of your end. Very good. You are now at liberty for the rest of this day. Also," he waved grandly, "we have provided a token of appreciation for your efforts."

On cue, Frommer nodded to another guard, who marched down the steel steps and placed a case of a rather respectable Sekt on Goldhammer's desk.

Vogel turned to lead his party out of the print shop. Goldhammer hurried to his side, asking for a word.

A guardedness fell over Vogel's face. "What do you want?"

"You have said we will be safe here, Herr Major." Goldhammer spoke in a hurried whisper. "Does that mean my family too?"

"While I am here. Yes."

*

The period that Vogel described as the "production phase" troubled Goldhammer. With the technical puzzles solved, he fell heir to an unwanted gift, time to think of what he had done. The religious Jew agonized over his complicity with the devil.

Through the guards' gossip, he knew of Bernhard's stunning success. The forged bank notes had passed in Turkey, Sweden, Switzerland and Portugal, where they were used to finance the Nazi spy network among these neutrals. Goldhammer's handiwork had traveled from these channels directly into England, where the bogus currency was accepted without question.

Either through a bureaucratic blunder or someone's delicious sense of irony, Goldhammer and two other Jews in the crew received elaborate citations for the success of the Bernhard project. Goldhammer guarded his award jealously as another claim on the Nazis for the protection of his family.

Thus three years of Project Bernhard passed.

The routinized operation no longer demanded the talents of a Vogel. That gifted officer was transferred in 1944 and replaced by an older man, Standartenführer Wolf Kruger.

Goldhammer saw the new commandant rarely. The first occasion had been several days after Kruger relieved Vogel, when Captain Frommer escorted his new superior on an inspection of D Wing. Goldhammer saw a man in his mid-fifties, whose appearance contradicted the deathly elegance of the SS black he wore. The man's mouth seemed permanently set in a small smile. He had white, flowing hair and glowing skin. His chin tapered to a point, giving his face a triangular shape. All that detracted from an aura of affable good nature were cold, blue eyes, which seemed removed from anything the face expressed.

Kruger had listened to Frommer describe the Bernhard operation without a question, nodding and smiling, and, it seemed to Goldhammer, without a glimmer of comprehension or interest.

At the end of the tour, the inspection party remounted the stairs to the balcony hanging over the print shop. Frommer spoke.

"The new Commandant of D Wing has one message that I am asked to convey to you. Continue your work, and you will continue to be safe." Kruger stood by his side, the small, fixed smile never leaving his face, the eyes glacial.

*

The beginning of 1945 brought mixed fortune to Julius Goldhammer. The Reich was sinking, as Allied armies liberated France and penetrated Germany. Goldhammer cared only that Bernhard, which had provided a safe harbor for him and his family, was now threatened.

The prisoners noticed the shifting demeanor of their SS jailers, heard the graveyard humor, saw a trace less arrogance in their bearing, except for Standartenführer Kruger, who went about his duties serenely, even as Allied bombers pounded nearby Berlin day and night.

Goldhammer sat at his battered desk opening a cardboard box stamped in bold, gothic lettering, "Reichsbank." He had been summoned earlier that day to Captain Frommer's office, the first time he had been there since his recruitment into Bernhard. Frommer now treated the prisoner with the familiar yet respectful manner of a gentleman toward a valued wine steward.

"Look these over, old fellow. We managed to pry them from the bank people. I'm sure there's something there to intrigue you. Let me know what you think."

"Yes. Of course." Goldhammer found his head bobbing,

as it always did before this preening young ass.

"And don't you get lost with it on your way back." Frommer gave an avuncular smile, ridiculous on his little boy's face.

Goldhammer attempted a feeble grin.

*

The contents of the box had the prettiness of Victorian wallpaper, pale greens, golds, pinks, reds, and silver grays. He examined Swedish kronor, Portuguese escudos, Swiss francs, and Australian pounds through his loupe. He withdrew a thin packet from the bottom of the box. The wrapping band was stiff with age. It read, "U.S. Emb. Berlin, 6/19/34." Confiscated funds, he concluded. Goldhammer slipped some of the bills from their wrapper. They too were stiff and faintly yellow. He snapped them between his fingers and smiled appreciatively. Marvelously strong paper, he thought.

He put the currencies back into the box. A contentment overcame him as his mind began to explore the possibilities. His talent was again engaged and could crowd out unwanted thoughts.

"How much longer do you think we can last?" Fischl came over and spoke to Goldhammer. The photographer had noticed that men from the printing crew who became sick were not returned to the shop. Two who had died in the last year had not been replaced.

The once callow Fischl now seemed as old and spiritless as the others. Goldhammer would occasionally converse with him, the bitter memories of Rosenthal and other early betrayals having long since been blunted by their common plight.

"We should be all right. We will be working on some important new matters now, you know."

The end came swiftly. On a day early in April, ten trucks were lined up before the loading dock. The first vehicle, a small paneled van, was loaded with the master plates, packed in a trunk with five-pound notes. The next two larger trucks also carried currency. The rest were loaded with presses, lamps, cameras, other equipment and the paper supply, until the print shop was stripped bare.

With the loading nearly complete, Goldhammer spoke to Moser, a strutting loudmouth, but one of the less brutal guards. "Where are we going?"

"*We* are going into cold storage." The man laughed coarsely. "And all of you are going to Buchenwald."

Goldhammer's face became a mask. When he spoke, the words caught in his throat. "And . . . the women?"

"Already gone. Kruger had them cleared out of their barracks early this morning."

*

Buchenwald in early April of 1945 was an orgy of slaughter, as gas chambers and ovens functioned around the clock. Still, struggling, exhausted SS detachments found themselves unequal to the workload. When the Americans liberated the camp on April 12, thousands of inmates, including Julius Goldhammer, still lived.

While others had cavorted with a maniacal glee in ill-fitting finery they had seized, while the hardiest vented long-suppressed rage by skewering the guards on fence posts, Goldhammer searched. His eyes blazed as he moved with flat-footed, awkward energy through the chaos of the camp, tugging at the arms of uncomprehending GIs, badgering inmates. "The women from Oranienburg? Do you know them? Where did they send the women from Oranienburg?"

His quest brought him to the northern edge of the compound, past decomposing heaps of the dead being shouldered into mass graves by bulldozers. His Hannah and Neda could not be part of this human refuse.

He found the block with the stencilled *IV2* over the open doorway. Outside the air was rent by the shouts of freed prisoners riding by on U.S. Army trucks, the shrieks of former guards tasting the tortures they had once taught and soldiers yelling as they tried to stop the drumhead justice.

As soon as Goldhammer stepped into the grim structure, all sound faded behind him. The stench of feces and urine had steeped into its scarred, smooth-worn wooden bunks and walls. A few heads turned listlessly from the bunks, following the steps of the new arrival. They were all women.

Another knot of them sat on the floor in the center of the barracks munching American C rations. They looked with dead eyes at the trembling figure hovering over them.

"The women from Oranienburg? They are in this barracks?" He spoke with a desperate certainty.

"Were." The one who answered him had probably been a large woman once. The shoulders were still broad, but they now stretched her prison stripes like a wire coat hanger. The open, sagging shirtfront revealed shriveled breasts. "They were taken the day before the Americans came."

"All?" The voice was tortured. "Was there a little girl, too?"

The woman nodded. "Children, too. They all went. All from Oranienburg." She added the last thought with a curious tone, as though struck by the coincidence.

Goldhammer's sloping, defeated shoulders shook. The woman gazed at him, her lean, flat features softening slightly. "Your wife? Child?"

A shuddering moan rose from deep within him. He turned away and reentered the gray afternoon.

Now, three weeks after liberation, Julius Goldhammer found himself in the back of a U.S. Army truck bound for Wiesbaden. He had heard that the Americans had established their headquarters there for tracking down war criminals.

3

SECOND LIEUTENANT LEOPOLD LIPSCHUTZ STOOD
before the clerk-typist's desk waiting to have his existence
acknowledged. "I need to see the Colonel, O'Day." His accent
always seemed most pronounced to him when he wanted to
sound most American.

"Colonel's busy, Lieutenant Lipschutz." The enlisted
man's sibilant voice lingered over the last name. He kept on
typing.

Lipschutz strode angrily around the desk and rapped on
the door.

"Can't you hear?" O'Day made as if to block the way.

Neither man was physically capable of cowing the other.

"Who is it?" The voice behind the door had a foghorn's resonance.

"Lieutenant Lipschutz insists on barging in," O'Day whined.

"He's a citizen. At least the Army says so. Let him in." The laugh from the other side of the door was forced and harsh.

The clerk-typist stalked off, as Lipschutz eased the door open.

"I'm sorry to bother you, Colonel. I think it's important."

"Make it quick, Lipschutz. I'm kind of busy."

Lipschutz looked into Lieutenant Colonel Daniel Houlihan's broad, flat face. The man's color was wine red at 11:30 in the morning, although Lipschutz did not think it was yet from drink.

"I'm waiting, Lipschutz." He yawned and belched softly.

"I interrogated an SD lieutenant early this morning."

Houlihan nodded absently with eyes half-closed.

"This prisoner is hiding something that I suspect could be serious."

"The plan for invading Boston?" The Colonel looked disappointed when Lipschutz did not join in his rolling laughter. "Come on, Lipschutz We've got to screen eighty-two thousand krauts out there in automatic arrest. What's special about this one?"

Lipschutz repeated Dorn's account of the truck convoy. Houlihan heard it with ill-concealed boredom.

"What do you want me to do?"

"There is something unusual about that convoy. I am suggesting that you authorize a full team interrogation of this man, Dorn. I can't handle it alone."

"Be a nice boy, Lipschutz. Write it up and send the report to me. Okay? Anything else?"

"Yes. There is. The convoy was involved with an SD operation called Bernhard."

Houlihan concealed a flicker of recognition. "Sure. Fine. You write it up. I'll take a look at it."

Lipschutz saluted and was through the doorway when Houlihan called him back.

"Have you mentioned this one to anybody else yet?"

"No, sir."

"Good. Keep it to yourself, at least until I decide what to do. You know, 'need-to-know' basis."

"Of course." Lipschutz nodded his head, although he did not understand. But then, he rarely understood Colonel Houlihan.

This is what I love about the business, Daniel Houlihan mused, after the lieutenant had left. A scrap here, a fact there, throw in a rumor. Soon two and two make five. He imagined himself at the end of a funnel, fed by his men, none of whom knew quite what the others put in, the whole of their knowledge possessed solely by him.

With the war over and everyone scrambling to get home, they were desperately short of personnel. As the 87th Division's intelligence officer, Houlihan was now responsible for conventional intelligence and collecting evidence of war crimes. The combination had produced curious possibilities, and opportunities, he concluded.

Last week, he remembered, that Princeton smartass had submitted an interesting report. Westcott had interrogated an SD courier who had taken bags of English currency to neutral countries via the German diplomatic pouch. The courier had been assigned to "Bernhard." Two weeks before, GIs from the Third Army had found some English bank notes floating on the Traun River. Now Lipschutz was telling him that he had a guy connected with Bernhard who had lost a convoy along the Traun.

"O'Day!" Houlihan's bulk filled the doorway. "Bring me Westcott's memo and that transfer request from COMINTSERV."

O'Day scurried to the makeshift cardboard files. He loved working for the Colonel. It was as though he had never left home. Houlihan was so like Father Patrick, whom he had served at the altar right up to the week he had been inducted, the same familiar South Boston speech, the firmness when required, the occasional trace of whiskey on the breath.

Houlihan closed the door and went back to his desk. He reached into the bottom drawer and drew out a bottle. He poured the liquor directly into the brown residue of his coffee cup and drank. He swallowed hard. Opportunity. He smacked his lips. That was the word.

*

It had been the Hahn elementary school just weeks before. Now the cream-painted concrete building was part of a constellation of camps for displaced persons outside of Wiesbaden. Julius Goldhammer had been in the camp two weeks. He kept to himself, playing no part in the endless speculations of his fellow DPs, as waves of rumor washed over the camp daily.

One day the word was that Brazil, Venezuela, and Peru would take any Jew with a trade. On another afternoon, an old man from Warsaw had hobbled down the littered corridor intoning, "God bless them. Bless them. America throws open her arms to us." They were all going to receive visas to the United States, he had been assured. Then there was absolute confirmation that the British were going to open up Israel to all survivors of the camps.

Goldhammer listened unmoved. He spoke to almost no one. The DPs from eastern Europe saw his reticence as the customary arrogance of a German Jew. It was easier not to try to explain.

Goldhammer heard them, disbelieving, as the DPs railed at conditions in the camp, shortages of water, lack of privacy, fetid toilets and broken showers; people who, two months before, had submitted to death as unresisting as stray dogs.

On his arrival at Wiesbaden, Goldhammer had nearly collapsed from fatigue. His recovery had taken longer than expected. He spent two weeks building his strength from the fairly generous rations the Americans supplied, 2,000 calories a day for DPs, less than the 3,600 provided to American soldiers, but well above the 1,100 calories allotted to German civilians.

Goldhammer's information on Wiesbaden had proved correct. It had become the involuntary host to the U.S. Army's War Crimes Investigation Center. From this city, the Americans directed an apparatus for tracking down potential war criminals from among seventeen million Germans in their zone of occupation. All SS, Gestapo, and significant Nazi party members were automatically arrested. Ordinary prisoners of war had to be screened for possible involvement in war crimes. In the weeks immediately following the surrender, almost every able-bodied German male was caged somewhere.

Goldhammer cultivated only one man at the Hahn camp, Jacob Edelmann, an irrepressibly cheerful German Jew who had been hired by the Americans as a camp administrator. Edelmann had survived Dachau and had returned home to Wiesbaden to look after aged parents. The old people had been hidden throughout the war in the home of Otto Blauvelt, a retired postman who had served under the Kaiser with Edelmann's father. Blauvelt's wife had lived in terror during the five years that the old Jews occupied her attic. She considered her husband a complete fool.

"I want to work with the Americans, too." Goldhammer was again badgering Edelmann. The man had promised he would try to help, though he found the morose printer a tiresome ass.

"You want to stay here? I would leave like a shot if it weren't for the old ones. As soon as they are gone, I will leave. Count on it. And don't tell me again about 'justice,' please." He rolled his eyes wearily. "You want to wash the stink from the slaughterhouse. I would rather leave the slaughterhouse."

He saw the pain in Goldhammer's eyes. "I'm sorry. Believe me. I understand what you feel. How could I not? I'll see what I can do."

Goldhammer spoke poor but serviceable English, so Edelmann arranged for him to be interviewed for a job by a lieutenant assigned to interrogations. The young officer, recently a Texas Aggie, looked into a pair of eyes that often seemed unmoored, and listened to a man who shifted from autistic silences to tumbling bursts of speech. Goldhammer's frenzied account of Bernhard left the lieutenant mystified. He did not want this crazy little Jew around him.

Still, the occupation forces were under orders to employ camp survivors wherever possible. Goldhammer's printing background led to a job as mimeograph operator at the Wiesbaden motor pool.

Edelmann also arranged for Goldhammer to room with him and his parents at the Blauvelts' home. The small house was badly crowded, but Herr Blauvelt and his wife needed the food that two U.S. Army employees could siphon from the PX.

Edelmann also had contacts working in an office known as "Crowcass," the Central Registry of War Criminals and Security Suspects. What Goldhammer sought could best be found there.

He told Goldhammer to meet him outside the Crowcass office one day after work. The printer waited before the building, his eyes darting furiously among the figures hurrying into the darkening afternoon. His gaze automatically screened the uniformed, ambling young Americans and searched out the familiar figure of Edelmann.

Goldhammer noticed the young man first. He looked no more than seventeen. His head was closely shaven, revealing raw patches of a hideous scalp disease. The large lips were twisted into a cynical curl. Edelmann walked beside him.

"This is Schrecker. He's Buchenwald, too." Edelmann jerked a thumb toward the youth, who eyed Goldhammer with a casual contempt. "He can help you."

"Sure. Just say it." Schrecker broke into a full grin, exposing a file of rotted teeth.

Goldhammer knew Schrecker, not the boy, but the breed. He had obviously been a commando, Jewish youths who survived by loading and unloading the crematoria for the Nazis. Pariahs among their own, but pariahs who had lived.

Goldhammer looked into the pitiless, grinning face and explained what he wanted.

Schrecker spoke. "Your cigarette ration?"

Goldhammer looked confused.

Edelmann eyed him hopelessly. "He wants your cigarette coupons to do this thing for you."

Schrecker's shrug said, what else?

"Cigarettes? Yes. Yes." Goldhammer slapped at the pockets of his jacket and burrowed into his pants. He finally

came up with wrinkled coupons, holding them beamingly
before the boy as a small child does, seeking an adult's
approval.

Schrecker snatched the coupons and stuffed them into
his jacket with a patronizing wink. Then he was off.

"Can he really do something?"

"Don't worry." Edelmann put his hand around Goldhammer's shoulder and steered him toward the buses that
returned the workers to Wiesbaden. "Crowcass gets the daily
reports of all new arrestees in the Zone. You can trust him."

The weight of Edelmann's arm on his shoulder felt good.
Goldhammer looked at the other man contentedly.

*

Goldhammer emerged from the motor pool, walking
slowly, eyes downcast, past the sentry. A voice called out.
"Hey! Old man! Why so glum? I have good news for you."

Goldhammer turned to see Schrecker's hardened grin.
The boy was sitting on a stone wall, his legs drawn up under
him, dragging deeply on a cigarette. As Goldhammer approached, Schrecker reached into his pocket and withdrew a
flimsy sheet of paper. He unfolded it deliberately, the cigarette
dangling from tightly curled lips. He waved the open sheet
before Goldhammer. Goldhammer raised his hand. The boy
lifted it beyond his reach.

"One-quarter of your June rations." Schrecker dangled
the sheet close to his cigarette.

Goldhammer searched agitatedly through his pockets
and shoved all his papers at Schrecker. The boy flipped
through them. He carefully tore a block of stamps along a
perforated edge and returned the rest to Goldhammer. Then
he held out the sheet between thumb and finger before letting

it flutter to the ground. Goldhammer dove for it. When he looked up, Schrecker was gone.

Goldhammer held the page in trembling hands, a smudged carbon, difficult to read. His eye trailed the left hand edge, *Fs, Gs, Is, Js, Ks*. There it was, "Kruger, Wolfgang, Ohrdruf, 6/3/45." He felt a tightness in his throat. He refolded the page along the original creases and inserted it into a battered wallet he had recently fished from a GI trash barrel.

Goldhammer plodded after a six-by-six coming out of the gate. He began banging crazily on the door. "Ohrdruf? Ohrdruf?" The driver shook his head. Goldhammer was already starting for another vehicle, waving furiously.

*

Julius Goldhammer sat fitfully on a folding chair in the damp, cavernous room at the Prisoner Processing Station. A conspicuously bored officer with brown wavy hair and a dandy's slick looks sat next to him, languidly flipping through *Stars and Stripes*. Lieutenant Devane had drawn the duty of escorting the strange Jew who had shown up at Ohrdruf claiming the camp held a major war criminal. Devane had taken Goldhammer into the barnlike room where they waited for the guards to extract the suspect from the sixteen thousand prisoners there.

From the corner of his eye, Devane watched Goldhammer clasp and unclasp his hands endlessly. The officer exhaled in irritation. Goldhammer continued to gaze ahead, clasping and unclasping, his eyes occasionally rolling out of sight.

They heard the approach of tramping feet. Goldhammer stiffened. His heart pumped rapidly. He felt faint as the door flew open. The soldier gave Lieutenant Devane a muscular salute. "This here's the prisoner Kruger, sir." Two other GIs who had entered with him stood to one side, leaving the man standing alone.

Goldhammer gaped, a stupid, disbelieving expression overtaking his face. Lieutenant Devane glared at him. The prisoner was young, in his early twenties, though his blond hairline had already begun a rapid retreat. His body swelled from his shoulders, reaching its apogee at a generous waist, then tapered off again to ridiculously small feet.

Devane spoke an Americanized but adequate German. "Are you Wolfgang Kruger?"

The young soldier nodded his head, smiling as though eager to please.

Devane turned to Goldhammer. "Is this the war criminal?"

Goldhammer's voice was tenuous, embarrassed. "You have a father?"

The soldier spoke with condescension. "Of course I have a father."

"He is an SD colonel?" Goldhammer's voice rose hopefully.

The private gave a short, ugly laugh. "My father is in the nuthouse in Stuttgart. Ten years now."

*

"You fool! You don't walk off a job in these times. A job with the Americans! Then you expect to waltz back?" Edelmann shook his head at the man he had hoped never to see again.

"I am sorry." Goldhammer was miserably contrite. "But the work is nothing to me. You know that. Being here, where one day I will find him, that is everything."

Edelmann moaned. "This may be the only time when it

will ever be an advantage to be a Jew from the camps. They may take you back for that reason. I don't know."

"The job is not important," Goldhammer mumbled again.

"Then what will you use to bribe Schrecker?"

Goldhammer nodded in abject agreement.

*

In the following weeks, Goldhammer tracked down a Wolfe Kruger at Darmstaat, a former baker with an SS infantry division, and after that, a bona fide SD colonel Wolfgang Krueger at Mannheim. After his third unannounced disappearance, the Americans fired him. He now spent his entire day in the Blauvelts' house waiting for Edelmann to return from work so that he could badger him with questions.

*

Edelmann grabbed the sneering Schrecker with unexpected strength and shoved him against the stone wall. "I don't give a damn if he can't give you any more coupons. Do you hear me?" He reached furiously into his own pocket and pulled out some stamps. "Here. Take my cigarettes. Curse you! But find me another Kruger. Any Kruger! I have got to get that lunatic out of my life. Do you understand?"

Schrecker shrugged and nodded obligingly. "I'll see."

*

"Julius." There was a tenderness in Edelmann's voice. He had returned to find Goldhammer sitting in the dark of their room. He did not stir when Edelmann entered.

Edelmann took a slip of paper from his jacket. He blew

some tobacco shreds from it and spread the page on the bed.
"I must speak to you frankly. I am going to give this to you.
This time, you must not come back. I am sorry. We cannot
carry you any longer. Frau Blauvelt insists. You must leave."

Goldhammer nodded numbly. He held out his hand
without looking at Edelmann, as a blind man does. Edelmann
put the sheet in it. Goldhammer rose with painful slowness.
He went to the window where the last rays of afternoon sun
were still seeping in. His eye ran down the list. He felt no
pumping heart or shortened breath this time. Still, it was
there. Kruger, Wolf, CSWE, Dachau 6/27/45.

"I will go in the morning."

Edelmann felt relieved.

*

"He's dead!"

"You don't have to sound so happy, Lipschutz."

"I knew there was something odd, Colonel." The Lieutenant was staring into the soles of Houlihan's shoes, propped
on the desk, the heels run down, his officer's pinks soiled at
the cuff line.

Houlihan gave a superior smile. "The MPs already called
me this morning. They found Dorn after the four A.M. bed
check. They said he must have stood on the toilet bowl, tied
himself to the pipe and stepped off. Why do you suppose he
did it?"

"He didn't."

Houlihan's eyes narrowed.

"I just don't believe it, sir. He was depressed by the loss
of the war? I talked to that man the day before. He wasn't that
kind. And there is something that cannot be explained by
coincidence." Lipschutz made a tight-lipped smile and paused
for Houlihan's reaction.

"Never mind the 'My-Dear-Holmes' bullshit. What's this coincidence?"

Lipschutz flushed red and doggedly went on. "Dorn's former commander, SD Colonel Kruger, the one he was supposed to deliver the convoy to in Königsee, he was arrested and placed in the same barracks yesterday afternoon."

"So far, Lipschutz, you've got two and two adding up to three."

"I'm sorry, Colonel. Unlike yourself, I'm not a detective."

"Police sergeant. I was a police sergeant. Not a detective. While I was going to law school nights."

Lipschutz had heard the story often, the first time the day he had reported to the 87th Division's G-2 staff. Daniel Edward Houlihan, policeman son of a policeman father, elevated in fifteen years to desk sergeant. Attended law classes at night at St. Ignatius College.

Houlihan also enjoyed regaling his subordinates who made him less uncomfortable than Lipschutz with stories of how he had shaken down Italian grocers, shoemakers and restaurateurs on his early beat in Boston's North End.

"Let me tell you, Lipschutz, you people think you got all the grief? The Houlihans have been in the U.S. of A. three generations, and none of those Beacon Street firms were breaking their asses to hire old Dan Houlihan out of St. Ignatius. Busted my balls chasing ambulances two years. Finally had some nice divorce action going when they drafted me. But I'm not complaining. And if you've got any sense, you won't. Occupying army in a defeated country! We've got our asses in butter here, little man. You better know it."

That had been Lipschutz's welcome and indoctrination to 87th Division G-2 four months before.

"What I suggest now, Colonel, is that we combine the

Criminal Division's investigation of Dorn's death with the intelligence interrogation of this man Kruger. I'm convinced they are linked. I would be happy to organize the investigation . . ."

"Yeh, sure, kid. Look, sit down." Houlihan took a cigar from a box. He bit off the end, spat it on the floor, and disappeared briefly behind a blue haze as he lit the cigar. "Oh, sorry." He made a perfunctory pass of the box toward Lipschutz. The lieutenant did not move.

He puffed meditatively, his gaze angled toward the ceiling. "You're going home, Lipschutz."

The lieutenant's pale blue eyes widened and searched Houlihan's face, uncomprehending.

"Did you hear what I said? You're going home. I mean back to the States. I guess you're already home here."

Lipschutz felt a hot anger.

"Sorry. Just kidding. But I'm serious about this. You're really going home."

"I don't understand. Is something wrong? My father?"

"No. Nothing like that. You've been transferred to Washington, to COMINTSERV staff. They're putting together a group of German-speaking intelligence types to review some hot documents that the SD kept on the Russians."

"There must be half a dozen men in the unit with more discharge points than me."

Houlihan suddenly swept his thick legs from the desk and leaned forward. "Don't you want to go home, soldier?" The voice was menacing.

"Yes . . . of course . . . I was only curious." Lipschutz daubed at his damp brow with a handkerchief. "When will I be going?"

"COMINTSERV asked for you right away. You can

start packing tonight. O'Day will cut your orders first thing in the morning."

Lipschutz rose dazedly and moved toward the door. He turned back. "This Dorn business?"

"Yeh, sure. Pull your file on him and bring it over here before you leave. I'll handle it personally."

Lipschutz saluted and left.

Corporal O'Day was immediately through the door clutching a sheaf of files to his chest. "It upsets me so much that he's the one you chose to transfer home, Colonel. I just have to say that. But still I'm glad he's leaving."

"Imagine the Army commissioning a creep like that." Houlihan shook his head and puffed serenely on his cigar.

*

Königsee lay wedged between two near vertical peaks at the northern tip of a long blue lake. The village was seven miles from the Eagle's Nest, Hitler's retreat in the Berchtesgadener Land, where Allied leaders had thought the Führer would stage his *Gotterdämmerung*. Hitler had chosen Berlin instead. In the meantime, tens of thousands of American troops had penetrated this mountain fastness on the German-Austrian border.

Though cheated of the Führer, the Americans had inherited a land of staggering beauty. The views were easily the most awesome in the Alps, and the Hotel Bonalpina in Königsee had immediately been requisitioned by the victors for its commanding vista of the lake and surrounding mountains. The Bonalpina looked to the Americans as a Bavarian chalet should. The proprietor, Alois Gluckhertz, looked the proper Bavarian hotelier, down to the lederhosen and feathered hat. He was tomato faced, genial, and fawning. Gluck-

hertz was also, though the Americans did not know it, a
former party official.

At first, joining the Party had been a convenience. "Fleas do not quarrel with the politics of the dog. They go along," he had explained to his late wife when he first applied. The move turned out to be not only profitable, but a social triumph. Junior officers who followed the Führer's inner circle to Berchtesgaden favored the nearby Bonalpina for their own lodging. Occasionally one of the Nazi *Bonzen,* numbed by the Führer's monologues, sought a brief retreat at the Bonalpina. Dr. Ley, Hitler's drunkard labor chief, had once spent a night there. To Gluckhertz it detracted only slightly from the honor that the man had passed out and had not been able to return to Hitler's lodge.

His friendship with the near powerful had won for Gluckhertz a respect he had not previously enjoyed in Königsee. He was named Zellenleiter, party chief for the village. When the end came, he reluctantly locked away his Party sash, his swastika armband, and a photograph taken just before Dr. Ley had collapsed.

Gluckhertz readily absorbed the preferences of his new clients and, at the suggestion of a former tavernowner from a place called Wilkes-Barre, Pennsylvania, set up an American-style bar in a corner of the Bonalpina's dining room.

On this July afternoon, the room was almost empty, except for a lone American officer seated at the bar, obsessively swirling and spilling his drink. Werner, a factotum, bustled about, setting the tables for dinner.

The officer suddenly stiffened from his crumpled slouch. A young woman strode past, oblivious of him. He rotated slowly, his glazed eyes fixed on her as she passed between the tables and out to the balcony overlooking the lake. She carried a book.

The woman was tall, almost haughtily erect. The shapeliness of her limbs gave her slender body a willowy, rather than lean, appearance. Dark brown hair, parted in the middle, fell straight and unadorned to her shoulders and framed a sculpted face with planed cheeks and an exquisitely carved mouth. Sensual, hooded eyes wandered between gray and green. She exuded an unaffected elegance and a trace of mystery.

The officer gulped down his drink. He rose unsteadily and mashed an overseas cap on the back of his head. He leaned back against the bar, supported by his elbows, a sodden hawk reconnoitering his prey. She had seated herself on the balcony, facing the vanishing afternoon sun, and had opened her book.

The officer was a gangling clutch of knobs and angles. A large hooked nose dominated a face pitted with the raw, red scars of a hard adolescence. His undisciplined hair escaped from all sides of the cap like a thatched roof. His tie was tucked between the third and fourth buttons of a stiffly starched khaki shirt and hung loose at the open collar.

He took slow, uncertain steps toward the balcony with long legs, until he stood over her, reddened eyes peering into the part in her hair. She had sunk into a deep wicker chair with her legs crossed on a footstool of the same intertwining weave. The legs were unexpectedly voluptuous in contrast to the understated fineness of the rest of her figure.

The officer sat on the edge of the footstool. She glanced up at him coldly, moved her feet a symbolic inch, and continued to read.

He reached forward and closed the book with a hugely knuckled hand. "Hey, baby. Put that thing away. Have a drink with old Cal, huh?" The voice had a whining twang. A thrusting Adam's apple bobbed with each word. He grinned at her.

She stared at the officer as though examining a specimen.

"Sprechen Sie Englisch?" The teeth his smile revealed were large and protuding.

"If you don't mind." Her English was accented but unflawed, the voice rich and throaty. She reopened the book.

The officer rose, his face now an angry crimson. He remembered that tone from slick eastern bitches. He did not have to take it here. He stuffed his thumbs into his belt. "You going to drink with me or not?"

She spoke without taking her eyes from her reading. "Perhaps some other time."

"Fucking kraut bitch." He muttered. "Who the hell won this war?" As he started toward the door, Gluckhertz appeared from the kitchen, smiling waxily. "Off to the front, Lieutenant Cal?"

The officer snarled something unintelligible.

"Don't forget tonight. *Speck mit Kartoffeln,* and an excellent chilled Niersteiner."

"Listen, Putzi." The innkeeper had encouraged the nickname. "You better can that one." He motioned toward the balcony. "She'd freeze the balls off a statue."

Gluckhertz smiled uneasily as the officer wove his way out. Then the smile vanished. He marched to the woman, his ruddy squirrel's cheeks working furiously. "You could at least be civil to them. I don't ask you to do anything more. But you could be polite." He hissed the words.

She glanced up at the puffed, apoplectic face with weary disinterest, then returned to her book. "I am not one of your peasant tarts, Father. And I don't have to bow and scrape before these people like an . . . innkeeper."

Gluckhertz flushed deeply. His clenched fists shook as he stormed back into the kitchen.

She turned toward the small man busily clinking down forks and knives on the tables. He had appeared unaware of the skirmish.

"Werner, Wernerchen. Would you be a dear and bring me a small glass of wine?" Her smile was now glowing.

The man nodded and disappeared. He returned and set the wine at a table beside her.

"I think he will kill you someday."

She threw her head back and laughed. "You foolish little man. Haven't you learned yet? My father is spineless."

"You shouldn't talk like that. Sometimes you are cruel to me. That is bad enough. But a daughter must respect her father." He shook his head sadly.

*

Werner Goren was a small, slope-shouldered man with the tapered face of a ferret. He moved with quick motions, his eyes darting about, giving a furtiveness even to setting a table. Goren had arrived at the Bonalpina shortly before the war ended, at the wheel of a gray paneled Wehrmacht van. He had been strafed by American aircraft and besieged for rides by troops trying to speed their retreat. But, in the end, he had delivered the vehicle to Königsee as ordered.

The streets were deserted and night was falling on his arrival. Goren had driven about aimlessly, finding no one. He left the van and began pounding on doorways, to no response. He glimpsed a light in a house. He drew his Mauser and banged furiously on the door with the butt. He fired through the lock and shouted for whoever was in to come out. An old man cracked open the shutters.

"*Willkommen, Amerikaner!* Please don't hurt us. We will come out."

"It's not the Americans, you old fool. It's the SS. Now, get out here." The man appeared at the door instantly, trembling so badly that Goren thought he would collapse.

"Where is the army command post in this goddamned graveyard?"

"There's no army. The soldiers left two days ago."

"Then who is the Party chief?"

"Gluckhertz. He is Zellenleiter. At the Bonalpina."

"Get in the truck, old man."

"Please. I have my wife in this house." He backed toward his doorway. "She's sick and she's frightened."

"Get in the damned truck! Take me to this Gluckhertz."

*

"What do you expect of me?" The innkeeper was abrupt.

"I must find a place to dispose of the van."

"Are you an ass? What are you carrying that's so important? What's the use now, anyway?"

"It has something to do with secret SD operations. Besides, that is not our concern. My orders were to get here, and you must help me."

Allied victory was days, at the most weeks, away, Gluckhertz knew it. Still, elite SS regiments were encamped between Berchtesgaden and Königsee. They could sweep back into the town within minutes.

"Why don't you take your stupid van to our lines?"

"My orders were to come to Königsee. This is Königsee."

"Of course, orders," Gluckhertz muttered contemptuously, shaking his head. He disappeared and returned with a huge ring of keys. He wedged his bulk into the cab and pointed toward a dirt road winding behind the Bonalpina. The roadway quickly narrowed to little more than a rutted path under an archway of overhanging branches that scraped against the side of the vehicle. They rounded a curve and came upon a small clearing where a crumbling stone storehouse stood.

"Here," Gluckhertz ordered. Goren brought the truck to a stop. The innkeeper slid from the cab and fumbled in the failing sunlight with the keys. He worked a key into a rusted lock. The lock resisted. He cursed quietly, while Goren peered about uneasily in the stillness. He could hear Gluckhertz breathing in deep, asthmatic wheezes.

The door creaked open and a rank odor rolled out. They entered and waited for their eyes to adjust to the darkness. An outline of wine cases set amid broken bales of hay began to take shape.

"I can't fit the van in here."

Gluckhertz eyed the soldier wearily. "That's not what I mean. We'll unload it."

"The van is sealed."

"God in heaven, man! We'll break the seal!" He snatched an iron bar off the wall and marched to the rear of the truck.

"Give that to me." Goren wrestled for the bar. "I'm still responsible." He shoved the pointed end of the bar between the wires that held the seal and snapped them with a quick twist. They opened the rear door, peered into the van, and saw only a gray trunk. It too was sealed. Goren leaped in and tried to push the resisting burden out. "Pull! Pull the damned thing, will you?"

Gluckhertz reached for the wooden handle of the trunk. They pushed and pulled it to the edge of the van. Gluckhertz grabbed at a tag on the handle. "What is 'Bernhard'?"

"How should I know?"

They dragged the heavy container into the storehouse. Gluckhertz sat down on a bale of hay and wiped his brow with the back of his sleeve. He was panting heavily. Goren was already clearing a space for the trunk among cases of empty wine bottles.

"Aren't we going to open it?" Gluckhertz asked.

"On whose authority? Come and help me cover it."

They shoved the crate into the space Goren had prepared and piled bales of dank-smelling hay over it.

They went out. Gluckhertz locked the door while Goren started the van's engine. He backed around in the clearing and drove to the curve bordering on a ravine. "Tell me when the front wheels are at the edge."

Gluckhertz puffed alongside the vehicle. "Another half meter." The truck ground slowly forward. "A little more." He held up his hand. "Stop."

Goren shoved the gearshift into neutral and cut the engine. He leaped out and went to the rear of the truck. "Come on. Help me."

"One!" Goren grunted as they began rocking the vehicle. "Two! Three!" The front wheels cleared the edge, and the van began crashing through the thick underbrush. They heard it rolling, but could see nothing as the dense growth closed in behind. Goren smiled, exposing his large ferret's teeth. They walked in the graying twilight the several hundred feet back to the Bonalpina.

Goren spent the following days in an upper-story room at the inn. He remained in uniform as long as any possibility existed of German troops reoccupying Königsee. Gluckhertz had sent his help, villagers and local peasant girls, home while the war sputtered to an end. The only other occupant of the Bonalpina was his daughter, Erika.

During that subdued interlude, she would call up the hallway to Goren, "Don't be afraid, Wernerchen. The SS won't get you. And the Americans aren't here yet. Come down and keep Erika company."

He would look out the window to make sure the town was still free of uniforms, then come to the balcony with its glorious view of the lake and Mount Watzman. There he would find the young woman with two glasses and a bottle of Bierenauslese.

Goren sat next to her, sipping the yellow-gold wine, his pellet eyes fastened on her as she aimlessly reminisced. Occasionally Gluckhertz would look in disapprovingly. He would say nothing and soon leave. Erika stopped speaking whenever her father appeared.

"I went to Munich in 1938, to the Ludwig-Maximilian Universität. I couldn't bear this little place after my mother died. I despised those bourgeois families from Dortmund and Essen and Düsseldorf who came here. My father falling all over them. God! That's when I met Erik. In Munich. Isn't that pretty? Erik and Erika."

Goren gave a simpering smile. "Did he make love to you?"

She ignored him. "The Falkenhausens were quite wealthy. Art dealers in Munich. Erik was studying cultural history at the university." She stretched her arms luxuriously over her head, straining the outline of her slender body against a white linen dress. Goren stared from the corners of his eyes at the small, rounded breasts.

She sipped some wine. "It was so marvelous. Of course, his family didn't give a fig for me. Well, not me so much.

What I came from. What he is." She gestured vaguely in the direction from which her father had last looked in on them. "We were married in July of 1938, and we went to live in London. Erik managed the family office there.

"Oh, I came home once before that. It was awful. Papa scraping before his elegant new son-in-law. Erik was so sweet. He told me Papa reminded him of a favorite Tyrolean gardener they had at Chiemsee when he was a child. And there was Papa, trying to impress Erik with his party office!" She laughed gaily. "The Falkenhausens despised the Nazis!"

Then she was quiet, seemingly lost in memory. Goren broke the silence.

"Where is your husband?"

"Dead. Russia." She answered without looking at him and could not see the faint trace of a smile on Goren's thin, lipless mouth.

"Captain Bauer, Erik's commanding officer, visited me two months later. They had been within sight of Moscow. Then winter came. They didn't have enough clothing. Can you imagine? That maniac sent the army to Russia without winter clothing! Captain Bauer told me that Erik had been wounded in the leg at nightfall. They couldn't look for him until morning. When they found him, he had frozen to death.

"You should have seen Bauer. He was a great bear of a man, with bushy eyebrows. When he told me about Erik, tears streamed down that strong face. It moved me deeply."

She paused. "I don't know why I'm telling you all this." Her voice became wistful, and she was staring far off. "After Captain Bauer told me about Erik, we talked all evening. Oh, we talked and talked. Behind that rough face, he was terribly sensitive. I remember he said how different we Germans might have been if we had swallowed a little more Schiller and a little less Hegel. And I said, 'and a little more Mozart than Wagner!' We both laughed so hard. It was wonderful. It was the first time I had felt anything since Erik's death." She turned directly to Goren and spoke with a quiet defiance. "And then, I went to bed with him."

Goren reddened. He could not look at her.

She turned away and settled back into the chair. Again she was gazing far off. Her voice became distant, too. "It was so important. That night. I knew then, that even without Erik, I was still alive. Bauer went back to the front. I don't know whatever became of him. Even if he survived. He was a married man. I hope he is home and I hope he has found a scrap of happiness in this burnt-out asylum."

"Then what?" Goren's head leaned forward, his darting, rodent's eyes locked on her.

"Oh. Not much. I was on my own. Before Erik died, the Falkenhausens had accepted me. Tolerated me, I suppose. Afterwards they dropped me, in a civilized way, of course. His father gave me a rather large check. But I never heard from them again."

Goren poured more wine, spilling it.

Erika drew up her knees and clutched her arms around them. She shivered slightly. "God. That last year of the war. It was terrible. Munich was hell with all the bombing. I was living with three other women in a single room. We were supposed to be working in an aircraft factory. But it had been destroyed for weeks.

"One night I had come out of the shelter in the basement of the old post office. It had been especially awful. The ground shook that night like an earthquake. People were hysterical in the shelter. Fights. Like animals. Outside, the air was filled with smoke and dust. I stumbled home through the dark. But when I got back, there was nothing." She turned to Goren, eyes wide. "Absolutely nothing. The building was gone. For the first time in all those months, I cried. With no shame. Not for the ridiculous little room, but because it was all so mad. So senseless. All the world was a ridiculous, dirty little trick."

Goren fidgeted. His mind struggled vainly to say something significant.

"And then I felt a hand on my arm. 'Don't be frightened, child.' I turned not knowing what to expect. But the voice was so soothing, the feel of the hand so reassuring." She gave a nostalgic laugh. "And there he was. A fat, utterly unimpressive officer. At least as old as my father. In fact, I learned later that he had two daughters older than me. He dried my tears gently and guided me to a command car. He said something to the driver. He spoke to the young man gently, too, not the way officers do. The soldier handed him a canteen. He opened it and passed it to me. It was cognac. And it felt quite good. That is how it began." She folded her tapering hands primly.

"What began?" The ferret was sniffing.

"His name was Fritzchen. He was the kindest, sweetest man I have ever known. He was clever, too, and could be terribly funny. He had been a jewelry wholesaler before the war."

"And he made love to you, too."

"I went to live with him."

Goren turned his head away.

"Come now, Werner." She patted his arm. "Don't be upset. I have no one else to talk to. I had literally no place to go. He was kind and he was honest. We were always honest with each other. Anyway, it doesn't matter. He's dead, too.

We had stayed in a rather nice flat on Prinzregentenstrasse. Fritzchen was a supply corps major. He had black market connections. It seemed everybody in the supply corps did. I don't remember lacking for anything. Then, in that last nonsense, in December, they rushed everybody to the western front, even my poor, fat, funny Fritzchen. He died of a stroke on the train heading for France."

"Did you learn that from his commanding officer, too?" Goren spoke with disdain.

She looked at him coolly. "I'm sorry. I don't know why I'm boring you with all this. Anyway. Here you see me." There was mock resignation in her voice. "Back where it all began."

*

The arrival of the Americans abruptly ended the afternoon idylls of Werner Goren. He put on civilian clothes and became Gluckhertz's man of all work at the Bonalpina, after the inn became a transient billet for American officers.

After that, he saw little of Erika. She kept to her room, even having the servant girls bring her meals there, until her father stopped it. Thereafter, she tried to time her arrivals at the dining room to rare, slack periods. She tried to take long walks by herself among the mountains during the day. Invariably, an American would invite himself to join her.

She hoped to avoid them most in the evenings, when they drank heavily and taught raucous, tuneless songs to obliging local girls. She felt "Pistol-packin' Momma" had seared into her brain.

They astonished her in the way they equated sociability and drunkenness, as though one were impossible without the other. They were, in that, she had to accept, no different from a certain class of German.

They had also set up a ping-pong table on the balcony, which was used interminably, until Erika's evenings seemed composed of "Lay that pistol down, babe," punctuated by the *thwack* of paddles against little hollow balls.

Werner Goren was now endlessly busy serving the stern taskmaster who hid behind Gluckhertz's innkeeper smile. At the end of the day, with the bar finally closed, the last glass washed and final drunk carried to bed, he dragged himself to the top floor and paused reverently before Erika's door before entering his own room. She had barely noticed him now for weeks. Still, he had hope. He knew one truth about this woman who obsessed him. She prized life's comforts. It was quite possible that Werner Goren could provide them for her.

4

"IT'S A JOKE." HOULIHAN GRINNED AND TOSSED the report on his desk. "I'm a cop, Kruger, and a lawyer. I was into this stuff when these kids on my staff were still playing with themselves."

The German struggled to understand. His eye was caught by Houlihan's shirt, which was open at the waist, spilling a small triangle of belly over his belt.

"When everybody's story fits perfectly, you know you're not getting the story."

It was true, Kruger recognized. This rude fellow and he were unlikely brothers in the same craft, and he had indeed

committed the sin of overrehearsing the prisoners in the cage.
The story lacked convincing gaps and innocuous contradictions. Yet, he sensed that Houlihan's main interest lay not in Dorn's death but somewhere else.

"You sent this convoy to Königsee. You were supposed to catch up with it later. What the hell were you up to, Kruger?" The prisoner's English was passable. Good enough, Houlihan knew, to allow him to carry out the questioning with no other witnesses present.

The German gave him his gentlest smile. "Would you please speak more slowly?"

"Maybe you'll understand better if we talk about who killed Dorn instead of the convoy. It's up to you."

"I know nothing of these vehicles. I do not know why Lieutenant Dorn killed himself."

"You had him killed, because he knew about Bernhard." Houlihan leaned his face close to Kruger's.

The German stared resolutely ahead. His smile tightened imperceptibly.

"What was Bernhard?"

"So, Colonel, you have learned. of Bernhard." Now Kruger was smiling openly. "You impress me. It was an excellent operation of the SD. We forged all the papers for our secret agents abroad."

"That's a half-ass lie. You had Kraut couriers toting bags of British currency into Switzerland. Your boys dump some trucks into the Traun, and the next thing you know, five-pound notes come cruising down the river."

The German fixed his gaze determinedly out of the window.

"I'll tell you what Bernhard was. Bernhard was a counterfeiting operation. You were making British money. We turned those notes our boys fished out of the river over to the

British and they shut up like clams. It must have been good stuff."

He walked to the window, a satisfied smile lighting his face. "Of course, this is only my idea, you know. Putting two and two together." He turned about and faced Kruger. "The important thing is this. Now that Dorn's dead, how many of us are in on this little secret? The truck that got away?"

Kruger suppressed a gasp. The man was precisely what he appeared. He relaxed for the first time since entering the room. The Gestapo had been rife with the breed, venal fellows who exploited positions of trust for personal gain. They rented slave workers to industrialists and pocketed the profits. They diverted the jewelry and property collected in the solution of the Jewish problem to their own use. He despised them, but he understood them.

"Colonel Houlihan, I am a plain man. I will make no apologies to the victors for what I have done, out of duty, for my country ... unlike ..." his voice trembled, "those swine who deny today what they enjoyed so fully yesterday."

"I'm not knocking you, pal."

Kruger looked at him, momentarily confused. "I must understand one thing. Am I talking, how do you say, to a private person? In which case we may perhaps have some things to say to each other. Or am I talking to an American intelligence officer?" His mouth set tightly. "If that is so, then I will say nothing. Nothing!"

Houlihan gave him a knowing smile. "Let's say, like in my country, it's man to man. Okay. Now, suppose you tell me where I find that van."

"One moment, please. One more matter." Kruger raised a lecturing finger. "There are two classes of prisoners in the compound. There are good soldiers. Like you, my dear Colonel, they only served their country. Some of them you have already released, and they are going home to wives and children. Then, there are the others. Those you call, by a strange logic, 'war criminals.' What will be their fate, none of us knows at this moment." He stroked his chin meditatively. "You, Colonel, have it in your power to see that I am in that first class of prisoners. And I have it in my power to tell you what you want so much to know."

Houlihan felt a cold sweat of anticipation. He had not expected the German to join the issue so quickly.

"My dear fellow." Kruger cooed reassurance. "I know exactly what you are thinking. How can you do this thing for me without risk to yourself? Believe me. I am eligible for the *Persilschein.*" Kruger spoke of the document issued by Allied authorities declaring that the bearer had been investigated and found to have no Nazi affiliation or war crimes guilt. The Germans had immediately called it the *Persilschein,* "whiter than white."

Houlihan's face glowered. "You must think you're talking to some sap. An SD officer? You expect me to clear you?"

"Colonel, I think we can overlook the Nazi Party business." His tone was assured. "Like yourself, I was an intelligence officer. A professional. You have already detected my function, rather cleverly. Hardly a war crime, you must admit. I was never involved with the ugly business. The camps. The Jews. Be quite sure of that. All that I ask is for you to do sooner what will be done for me in the end anyway. In return, I am prepared to tell you what you want to know."

Houlihan returned to his desk. He made several attempts to light his cigar with a shaking hand. His voice was unnaturally subdued. "What exactly will you do?"

"Free me. Give me the paper that I am, as you say, 'denazified.' " He looked hard at Houlihan. "And I will take you to what you seek."

*

"Where are you going, my little Werner?" Erika leaned from her window, stretching in the late morning sunshine, groggily shaking off sleep. It was his first glimpse of her in days.

Goren was about to enter a battered Volkswagen abandoned by the German army which the Americans had given to Gluckhertz. Goren spoke without looking at her. "To Ramsau. Your father has sent me."

"Wait, I'll ride with you. Unless you're going to see a woman." She laughed and disappeared from the window.

They drove down the twisting road in the full glory of the alpine summer. Edelweiss, Butterblumen, and Enzian lined the roadside, composing a rich quilt of whites and reds, golds and blues. Goren stared straight ahead, holding the wheel stiffly, wordlessly.

"I think you are really going to see a girl friend." She gave him a teasing smile.

"Why do you mock me?"

"Oh dear. Aren't we sensitive today." She rested her head on the back of the seat and breathed deeply. "It's so good to get away. Why are we going to Ramsau?"

He pointed to a piece of greasy machinery resting on the stained back seat. "Pumps for the water. There's a man in Ramsau who might have parts."

They drove in silence through Berchtesgaden, then along the road paralleling the white, churning torrent at Wimbach Gorge fed by the snowfields of Hochalter Mountain.

"It's so strange." She spoke as to herself. "How can the world be so beautiful and all of us so unhappy?"

He continued to stare ahead. "You are unhappy?

"You are such a fool."

"I know nothing of women."

"Oh, God. How I wish I had the courage to leave. But I will not go back to Munich and be nobody again." Her face was briefly grim. Then she began to laugh. "You know that big American major, the one who calls you 'Sauerkraut'? The one who insists on sitting with me, following me all over? He says he wants to marry me!"

Goren blushed.

"He is going home soon. He wants to bring me back to Texas. Do you know what he does? He sells gasoline, along the Texas autobahn." She laughed hysterically. "Can you imagine?"

They fell into a long silence again until Goren spoke. "Do you need money?"

"No, you ninny. I don't care about money. I want freedom. I want to be free to leave this place. I want a handsome apartment with good paintings and clever friends to have coffee with me. I want to go to the opera. To fashionable shops. To dine with whom I choose. To vacation at Rapallo. I want dignity in my life. Oh God." She buried her face in her hands.

Goren pulled the Volkswagen to a stop on the shore of the Hinteresee. "Money is possible."

She rubbed her eyes and gazed out at the lovely blue water trapped between the peaks.

"Did you hear what I said?"

"No." She answered hollowly.

"Money is possible. A great deal."

She patted his hand gently. "You are a funny little man."

"Do you think you could like me? I mean like the old fellow. The fat one. Fritzchen?"

She was still staring out absently. "Of course, Werner, I always like you." Her voice was toneless.

"The money can be arranged." He told her about the secret of the storehouse, what he had found when he had recently broken open the trunk. His smile exposed the ferret's teeth up to the gums. He leaned over. She endured his kiss. She had not imagined it could be so unpleasant.

*

Goldhammer felt weak with hunger. He had walked the ten miles from Munich to Dachau. No GI had heeded his outstretched thumb in its uncertain imitation of the hitchhiking gesture. The day was hot. Goldhammer sweated under a thick GI greatcoat, not daring to leave it with Edelmann, who had forbidden his return. He passed by released German prisoners trudging home, some in bare feet. There had always been an intimidating sureness in non-Jewish Germans he had known. He looked for it in vain in these wan figures.

He entered a suburban town and picked his way through uncleared rubble. Everywhere knots of people, old and young, men and women, with shovels and makeshift tools, doggedly worked at putting their broken world in order.

He neared a point where the main road eased left and began to parallel the rail line. Here the devastation was total. An oddly unscathed sign on the only standing wall of the station proclaimed "Karlsfeld," much as a tombstone marks a departed life. Goldhammer sat down on a lone bench in the roofless, ruined building and gazed into the sun with squinting eyes. He reached deep into the pocket of the greatcoat and drew from it the last piece of bread Frau Blauvelt had gladly given him on leaving, thinking here was the last of the glum Jew. He nibbled furtively at the crust as a rat does. When it was gone, he licked the crumbs from his hand.

He slowly drew himself to his feet and followed the snarls of twisted railroad track toward Dachau. Along the way he passed abandoned freight cars, ancient stock with curved roofs and large, exposed narrow wheels, the pre-World War I equipment which had hauled his people to their death from all over Europe.

As he approached Dachau, he saw other camp survivors and DPs converging in a thin trickle on the main gate. GIs manning the sentry post in white helmets and black MP brassards ignored the questions uttered in a half dozen languages and motioned them all toward the same place, a low-slung barracks with a long line feeding into one end and spilling out the other, as from an intestine.

Goldhammer stood in line for two hours. From time to time someone in the queue would hide behind a coat collar and chew at something. Goldhammer's stomach rumbled. He shuffled forward a few inches. When, at last, he passed through the doorway, he saw a crowded rectangular duct, with a long row of GI clerks behind tables. The people filed past, speaking in cowed, pleading voices. The young Americans shouted casually to each other across the oblong. "What have you got on a Finkelbaum, Rosa, Treblinka?"

"Checking it out. Didja try the Auschwitz cross-listing?"

It was Goldhammer's turn. The clerk did not look at him. Goldhammer looked down on what appeared to be a child's curly head. "I want Kruger, SD Colonel, Wolf Kruger."

The GI turned a youthful, bored face to Goldhammer. "You know his number?"

"Number?"

"Number. Tattoo." The soldier gestured toward his wrist.

Goldhammer shook his head uncertainly. "He is no Jew. He is a war criminal!"

"Wrong office." The soldier spoke idly as he looked past

Goldhammer down the line. "Next, please."

Goldhammer felt his body quiver. He remained rooted. "What do you say?" He stammered.

"War crimes, buddy. This is Inmate Locater Service. You got somebody you're looking for, you come here. You got a war crimes gripe, that's E-2. Other side of the base. Come on. Move it."

It was then that something in Goldhammer's head flashed a searing red, before going black. He collapsed to the floor.

*

"That's what happens when you go to school on an empty stomach, sonny."

Goldhammer opened his eyes to a stout, jovial American medical officer, with a toothbrush moustache that twitched when he laughed. His eyes swept the surrounding starched whiteness. He saw his greatcoat flung over a chair and noticed that his shirt had been unbuttoned, exposing his pallid, hairless chest.

An orderly wheeled up a cart with a steaming soup kettle on it. At the smell, Goldhammer felt faint again. The soldier set a bowl before him.

"Here, sit up, man." The genial doctor slid a hand under Goldhammer's back and helped him rise. "Eat it all. And eat it slowly." It was the voice of a nursemaid admonishing a child.

The first spoonful seared his mouth. He began to cough. The doctor gestured for him to slow down. He turned to the orderly. "When he's finished, give him a couple of sandwiches and some Hershey bars. Then he can go." He turned a warm smile on Goldhammer. "You'll be fine." Then he left.

Goldhammer nodded dumbly and continued spooning the soup.

As soon as the doctor was gone, the orderly barked, "Come on, Mack. Put it away. We need the bed."

Goldhammer suspended the spoon in midflight and looked at the man fearfully. "The other food?"

"Don't worry. We ain't let none of you starve yet."

Outside, Goldhammer felt an unaccustomed lightness in his step. His head was clear and he entered E-2, the Central Registry building, with renewed hope. Most of the ragged petitioners sat at benches, puzzling over forms the Americans had ordered them to fill out.

The clerks stood at a makeshift counter before an anarchy of teetering cardboard boxes, stacked nearly as high as the room.

The clerk spoke in the unintelligible melodious slur which Goldhammer had learned meant an American from the south. "What's that?" The voice fairly flowed.

"Wolf! Wolf Kruger."

"Voolf?" The soldier hazarded Goldhammer's pronunciation. "Voolf ... Kruger." He spoke the names with a curious lack of inflection.

Goldhammer nodded eagerly. "Yes. You have him?"

The clerk resignedly disappeared among the leaning heaps of boxes. Goldhammer could hear his soft curses as he flung and restacked each case. "Goddamn it all to hell." A box tumbled from the top, spewing file folders across the floor. He continued shuffling, moving, swearing.

Ten minutes later, he returned to Goldhammer. "Nobody here by that name. We got plenty of 'Voolfs.' " He leaned on the counter. "But not your 'Voolf.' "

Goldhammer stared at him, his mouth open, unmoving. "I do not understand."

"Sorry, fellow."

Goldhammer nodded. He turned away and headed for

the door with heavy steps. He moved down the long drive, shaking his head. At the gate, he stopped and ran back toward E-2.

The soldier was now stretched atop the counter, his arms under his head, feigning sleep. Goldhammer tapped gingerly. The eyes opened a slit, large enough to emit the man's displeasure.

"Please. A question."

The GI reluctantly swung his legs to the side and pushed himself off the counter with a gymnast's grace. He leaned close to Goldhammer and fixed him with mocking, wide eyes.

"Your question, sir?"

"You have looked for Wolf?"

The young man gave a tolerant nod.

"You looked for Kruger?"

"That is what you said. Right?"

Goldhammer studied the clutter of boxes behind the counter. "You have looked like this?" He sliced a *W* through the air with his finger.

The clerk eyed him curiously, nodded, and mimicked Goldhammer's hand gesture.

"You must look *Ka!*"

"What?"

"*Ka!*" This time Goldhammer traced a *K* with his finger. He was smiling brightly. The clerk muttered and disappeared again behind the boxes.

He reemerged holding a rectangular card with holes punched in it. "Kruger comma Wolf. Hope we've got that much straight. Colonel, SD. Apprehended June 16, Obersdorf Commandant, D Wing, Oranienburg."

Goldhammer's face glowed with an insane glee. "Yes. It is him." He reached a trembling hand for the card. The clerk pulled it out of his reach.

"Where is this man? Tell me. Please!" The voice was gleeful.

The clerk studied the card. "He should be in the pre-screen cage. Colonel Houlihan's operation. You got to go over to E-1."

*

"Records sent him over, Colonel, they thought you ought to have a look at him." O'Day leaned into Houlihan's doorway. Behind the clerk-typist was a small bald man in shapeless, unmatched pants and jacket. His frayed, gray-white shirt was buttoned to the neck with no tie. He sat, round shouldered, his gaze bolted to the floor.

"I got no time. You know I'm leaving in ten minutes."

"I know, sir. But he has something to do with Project Bernhard." O'Day whispered it conspiratorially. "I squeezed that much out of him."

Curse you, you fairy bastard, Houlihan thought. He had never uttered "Bernhard" to O'Day. He grunted and made a motion waving the man in.

O'Day crooked a finger at the man. "Come, now. The Colonel doesn't have all day." As the stooped figure rose, O'Day leaned over Houlihan's desk. "His name's Goldham-mer. He's a camp survivor. A Jew."

"No kidding. Look, O'Day, you take the jeep over to the camp and pick up Kruger. Wait outside. I'll be out as soon as I've finished with this one." He closed the door, sat down, and left Goldhammer standing before his desk.

"You know something about Bernhard?"

The man looked up for the first time and nodded eagerly.

"Let's hear it."

"I sit down. Please. I come a long time from Wiesbaden for this kind opportunity to see you."

Houlihan waved toward a chair.

"Thank you. I begin?"

Houlihan nodded.

"I have important information on war crimes."

"Jesus." Houlihan sighed in exasperation. "I thought you knew something about Bernhard."

"Ah, yes." Goldhammer looked chastened. "I was werkmeister at Oranienburg. D Wing."

Houlihan stiffened imperceptibly.

"That is where we have done Bernhard. And that is where I know the war criminal . . ."

"Never mind that. Tell me what you did in Bernhard."

"We make English bank notes." Goldhammer seemed surprised at the question.

"What denominations?"

"Five. Ten. Twenty. Most five."

"How much?"

"In four years, maybe one hundred and fifty billion pounds."

Houlihan flung his head back and moaned sensually. "Jesus, Mary and Joseph! How good was it?"

The man appeared confused. "Good? My work was perfect. I did all they told me. I received the award." He got up, speaking in frantic bursts. "It makes no difference. In the end, he . . ."

"Slow down, Izzy." Houlihan held his hand up. "How do you know it was perfect?"

The man's head dropped. His voice was again empty.

"Major Vogel . . . he is not the man I come to speak of . . . Major Vogel said the British got suspicious. By 1944." He looked up with a sudden, mad grin. "But our work was too good. They could not distinguish it. So they pretend nothing has happened. They honor all British currency, not to make somebody mad."

Houlihan was smiling coolly. "And last April, ten trucks loaded at your plant. Right?"

"Yes." Goldhammer's eyes widened. "You know?"

"I want you to tell me where they were going and what they carried."

"I remember. The first three have money, one my plates. The rest, equipment, paper. Then after we finish ..." His voice broke. "That is what I come to tell."

"Where were the trucks going?"

"To the Berchtesgadener Land, to hide. To use again someday."

"That's real helpful, Mister Goldberg. The U.S. government thanks you. Really appreciate your coming in." He rose and opened the door. "That's fine. Thank you."

"No. No." Goldhammer was clenching his fists at his side. "That is not why I come. I come to give witness against the war criminal."

"Sure. You report out front to the reception. They'll give you an appointment with an interrogator for tomorrow. Say Colonel Houlihan sent you."

"Please, you listen." The clenched fists were shaking uncontrollably. "I have testimony against a prisoner. He is here. He sent all Bernhard workers to Buchenwald." His voice was tremulous. "He sent them to die!"

Houlihan blanched. "What are you talking about?"

"Kruger. Standartenführer Kruger. They have told me. He is here. In this camp. I have come to give testimony. He is a war criminal."

Houlihan's brow and hands went instantly damp. "What's your proof?"

"Proof? Proof?" The man stared at him insanely. "The proof of my eyes! My Hannah ... my Neda! Proof?"

"How do you know who sent you to the death camp?"

Goldhammer swayed dizzily. His mouth emitted odd, strangling sounds when he tried to speak.

Houlihan hovered over the small, trembling figure, his voice bellowing. "You come in here and start accusing someone of a crime without any proof? We got a little rule in my country. A man's innocent until proven guilty."

Goldhammer's eyes rolled back. His head jerked awkwardly.

"You're denouncing someone who's been investigated and cleared by the War Crimes Branch, 87th Division, Third Army. Kruger's denazified."

"Murderer! Murderer! You have freed a murderer!" He lunged toward Houlihan, who easily seized his thin wrists and flung him to the floor.

"MPs! Get some MPs in here!" the American roared. Two soldiers came trotting into his office almost instantly, pistols drawn. Goldhammer lay on the floor, his cheek pressed against Houlihan's shoe, making deep, guttural sobs.

"Take it easy on him, boys." Houlihan grimaced nervously as the MPs seized the man. "He's a nut. Poor devil cracked up in one of the camps. Just get him out of here. Put him on a train back to Wiesbaden."

Houlihan closed the door as the small whimpering figure was dragged from the room. He slumped at his desk, reached into the drawer, and felt for the bottle.

O'Day burst through the door, wide eyed and out of breath. He stopped short. Houlihan glowered at him.

"Sir, he's gone! Kruger's gone!"

The color drained from Houlihan's face. The corner of his mouth sagged.

"You dumb son of a bitch! How can that be? Prisoners don't just walk out of this compound!"

"He had the *Persilschein.* We sent it through the Provost Marshal's two days ago. Somehow Kruger slipped out of the camp between last night and this morning."

"Is the jeep out there?"

"Yes, sir."

"All right." Houlihan was breathing heavily, drumming the palm of his hand on the desk. "All right. You tell Colonel Waltham he's in charge until I get back. I've got to investigate this personally."

"Where shall I tell him you'll be, sir?"

"Königsee. Now get out of here."

He went to another drawer of his desk and drew out a file tabbed "Kruger, Wolf Ludwig, Standartenführer, SD." He seized a red pencil and scrawled "DEAD FILE" across the face of the folder, and stuffed it into a briefcase.

On his way out of the camp, he wheeled the jeep before the security incinerator. A sergeant stepped out and saluted him.

"Can I help, Colonel?"

"Sure, Sergeant. I've got some classified trash." He handed the soldier the folder. "Burn it for me, will you?" His smile was paternal.

*

Aubrey Tepley was strikingly handsome, almost a pretty man, until he turned his head. In August of 1940, Tepley was among the RAF wings thrown against over a thousand German aircraft in what was then the largest raid on London of the war. A rough division of labor governed their work. The faster Spitfires fought off the Messerschmitt 109 fighters, while the slower Hawker Hurricanes hunted enemy bombers.

Tepley was flying his third Hurricane sortie in thirty-six hours. His hand and eye moved reflexively, independent of his fogged mind. They had not moved quickly enough to evade the Messerschmitt that swept up beneath him as he closed on a Heinkel bomber.

The German caught his engine with a surgically precise burst. Flames sheathed the fuselage as Tepley lost precious seconds while contemplating the warning of his squadron commander. "Save the aircraft at all cost." At last, he shoved the bubble back and lifted himself out of the cockpit. He was unconscious of the searing heat as he pushed himself free and released the chute.

He had struck the ground with such force that the pelvic joint was shattered. He suffered burns over twenty percent of his body, with the left side of his face in the ravaged zone. A year of treatment and skin grafts had left him with a slight limp and an oddly halved appearance, which, he cheerily noted, "only frightens little children."

After he recovered, his father used his connections as a subcabinet official of the Churchill government to have Tepley transferred to MI 6 (v), British counterintelligence. Since 1943, he had been assigned to probe rumors that the Germans were counterfeiting British money. The war had ended with nothing proven.

The lead Tepley received at the Broadway headquarters in August of 1945 was neither more nor less promising than a hundred others he had run to the ground in the previous two years:

BUCHENWALD SURVIVOR CLAIMS TO HAVE WORKED ON SD PROJECT TO COUNTERFEIT BRITISH BANK NOTES. CREDIBILITY UNVERIFIED. HOLDING HIM PENDING YOUR INSTRUCTIONS. ERNSTWHISTLE. BREMEN.

Major Colin Ernstwhistle was a small, trim man in his early fifties with an unexpectedly resonant voice. Dapper was the inevitable adjective. He sat on the edge of his desk, legs folded, his hands clasping his knees. He looked down a long nose through a great bush of sweeping moustaches at the ridiculous figure wringing his hands in the chair before him. It was a deep, comfortable chair, yet the man sat on its edge as though he feared being seduced by comfort.

"Now, Mr. Goldhammer, please. No more gibberish. You've confused me quite thoroughly already. I haven't the faintest notion what you're talking about – geometric lathes, photo offset, albumin-coated something-or-others." What Ernstwhistle did not say was that Goldhammer's excitably sputtered English all but ruled out any sort of communication, much less technical jargon. "Luckily, we have something rather better to go on today."

He rose from the desk and moved toward a door. After notifying London of Goldhammer's arrival he had received a detailed cable from Tepley on how to proceed. He leaned out of his doorway, and in a rich bass called out, "I say, Boomer, would you bring me the pouch that courier chap delivered last night from Broadway? Thank you." He came back with a small leather briefcase. He set it on his desk and resumed his seat on the corner.

"Now there, Mr. Goldhammer, rather than all that mumbo-jumbo, I want you to tell me the identifying flaws in the bank notes."

"Flaws?" The voice was beseeching.

"Why yes, flaws, defects, small mistakes that will let us identify the bad stuff, don't you see."

Goldhammer swung his head slowly. "I have made no mistakes."

Ernstwhistle shook his head too, but rapidly, as though trying to shake off this tiresome fellow. "No mistakes, eh? Not the tiniest error over the genuine item produced by the Bank of England?"

Goldhammer looked up proudly. "They were perfect."

"I see." The voice had a nasal disdain. "Then I don't suppose Tepley's next task is going to help much. I have in this case several hundred notes. Some are authentic. Others, judging from their sources, could be counterfeits. Assuming there were any counterfeits." He gave Goldhammer a skeptical regard. "In any event, I am going to put you into that small room next door. You shall have all the time you need. I want you to see if you can tell which are counterfeits."

Goldhammer nodded. "I don't need so much time. I need the chemical." He struggled with the words. "Meth . . . yl . . . ene chlo . . . ride."

The deep voice rose to an incredulous falsetto. "What the devil for? And what is it?"

Goldhammer bowed his head. "To test if the watermark is true or printed. It is not possible without."

"Very well." Ernstwhistle went to the door again. He muttered impatiently to someone. "How should I know what it is? Don't be a bloody fool. And don't come back without it."

The chemical was not found until the next morning. In the meantime, Ernstwhistle was happy to be clear of the printer for a while. He had placed Goldhammer in the hands of an unhappy Jewish lance corporal named Pearlstone, who protested the assignment in a heavy Liverpudlian accent.

"Come now, Corporal. Be a good chap. See that Mr. Goldhammer enjoys the unparalleled delights of Bremen." He gestured sweepingly toward a window looking out over the shattered port city's ugliness.

Major Ernstwhistle sat back in the huge swivel chair, his toes not quite touching the floor, while great clouds of smoke rose from his cigar. He had established Goldhammer and his bottle of methylene chloride in the small room next door, several hours before. He was determined not to interrupt, but found himself getting restless. He went to the door and cocked his ear. He heard nothing. He paced the room, went back and gently eased the door open.

Goldhammer sat amid a maelstrom of scattered bank notes, his bald, pink pate sweating.

"Now, old chum. What do you have to tell us?" Ernstwhistle was stroking his generous moustache with a long, luxurious sweep of his thumb and index finger.

Goldhammer looked up, a stupid terror on his face. "All good. There is no Bernhard bank note here." He was close to tears.

Ernstwhistle took the briefcase smugly and began to stack the notes into it in neat piles. Goldhammer, his jaw hanging slack, stared at the floor.

"Thank you. Thank you so much, Mr. Goldhammer." Ernstwhistle finished the packing. "Let me show you out." He took the printer by the arm and edged him toward the door. Goldhammer resisted weakly. He spoke over his shoulder as Ernstwhistle pressured him forward.

"You must believe me. There *are* counterfeits. What do we do now? We must not stop."

"Of course not. Just leave an address where we can find you. There's a good fellow." He had Goldhammer through the door and left it open wide enough only to extend his arm for a quick handshake. That done, he returned to his desk and to his cigar.

*

Aubrey Tepley's scarred face broke into an amused smile as he read the cable:

BUCHENWALD SURVIVOR INTERROGATED PER YOUR INSTRUCTIONS. GENUINE SWISS MOVEMENT. CUCKOO. CUCKOO. SAYS FORGERIES HAVE NO IMPERFECTIONS. SAYS WORK OFFSET, NOT ENGRAVED. UNABLE DISTINGUISH FAKES IF ANY AMONG YOUR SAMPLES. RELIABILITY RATED F. FULL REPORT FOLLOWS VIA POUCH. CHEERYBYE. ERNSTWHISTLE.

He started to get up, stopped, pursed his lips in meditation, then reached for the telephone. "Ring up Bletchley for me, will you please? Dr. Shepard-Jones. Yes. Thank you." He hung up and dug into a pile of correspondence. He was scribbling a response on a letter when the phone rang.

"Hello there, Shep. What's new at dirty tricks? What? Of course I am. Still on the trail. Soft bed, eh? I find it rather a bore. Yes. I imagine we will close shop soon." Even as he spoke, he could see the shadowy arm and hear the squeaking as a workman removed his painted name and title from the frosted pane of his door. He had been advised to expect a smaller office.

"By the way, Shep. Let me check out one very, very long shot with you. Interest of thoroughness, you know. No, I'm not sure this is any more promising than the last goose chase. Just tell me. Is there any possibility that offset work could pass as engraving? ... Of course not. I admit I don't know anything about printing. That's why I'm permitted foolish questions. I could answer my own foolish questions if I knew. Not possible, eh? Thought as much. Thanks all the same. Ring me up when you're in town, won't you? Lunch? Of course. Thanks so much, old man. Goodbye."

It was winding down. It was just as well. Still, the

incompleteness bedeviled his neat mind. He hated to leave the
job unfinished. His last clerk had been demobbed two weeks
before. There would be no replacements. Tepley rose and
shook the pain and stiffness from his leg. He took the cable
and made his odd, dipping walk to the file cabinet marked
"Investigated." He pulled open a drawer labeled "1945" and
yanked up a folder with the tab "Goldhammer." He let
Ernstwhistle's cable slip to its clerical grave. He looked up to
see the last of his painted title disappearing under in the
workman's solution.

*

London was filled with war-commissioned MI 6 and
SOE intelligence types. The last thing most of them wanted
was to return to the solicitor's office or the brokerage on
Throckmorton Street. For Tepley, the transition was equally
distasteful and in his physical state, less possible anyway. Still,
he wondered how he was to parlay one failed case, a scarred
face and a game leg into a career billet, with the war now
ended. The Soviets, he assumed, were the best card, though he
expected he was not the only one contemplating this angle.

And so he had arranged the luncheon at the Carlton
with Featherby, Eastern Europe, and Hotchkiss, Communist
Parties, both decent sorts and old friends. The Bolshies were
becoming nasty. It was a ground-floor situation at Broadway.
He'd bring the subject around, somehow at lunch. Still, in the
back of his mind the unfinished matter of the pounds rankled.

*

"They swallowed the Baltics practically for breakfast,
now, didn't they?" Featherby virtually snorted. He was a florid
man, with greased gray hair parted cleanly down the middle as

though by an axe. He had recently returned from cover in the transportation section of the Embassy in Moscow. "And mind you. Don't expect Uncle Joe to give up Poland, Yugoslavia, anything from the Baltic to the Adriatic."

Hotchkiss, a renegade academic in a rumpled wool suit, had a bemused, supercilious smile and pale, skeptical eyes. "Be fair, now, Featherby. What we call expansionism is our friends' protectionism. They obviously can't have a hostile Poland as their buffer with Germany. That's why they insisted on the Lublin government. I think they've gone more than the extra mile taking in Mikolajczyk, that professional peasant." Hotchkiss snorted equally well.

Featherby's face flushed a full-bodied burgundy. "I swear, Freddy, you sound like a damnable dupe. I can't imagine the Russians needing any apparatus here as long as we have enough silly buggers like you on our side."

"See here!" Hotchkiss stiffened and wagged a professorial finger.

Tepley, whose thoughts had drifted off, broke in. "Suppose we have another brandy." He signalled the waiter, who brought the bottle and promptly spilled some of the amber fluid over Tepley's shirt cuff.

"Terribly sorry, sir." He spoke with well-rehearsed contrition. "A spot remover will do nicely there. I'll fetch it straightaway." Tepley stared at the spreading splotch as though mesmerized. He jumped up. "If you'll excuse me." He spoke distractedly.

"Aren't you going to wait for the fellow to clean you up a bit?" Featherby called after Tepley's retreating, limping footsteps.

Hotchkiss looked pained. "I do hope he remembers to sign first."

The scar tissue itched maddeningly, as it always did when he was stimulated. He was speaking into the telephone with petulant impatience. "Well then, find him! He can't have vanished. He's obviously somewhere. I'll wait here at my office until you have." He slammed down the receiver.

The perspiration on his brow and palms was a cold, unpleasant sensation. He went to the file cabinet and tore the folder from the drawer. He read the cable again, for the third time, all the while tapping his foot, a toothy grimace on his face. He sat down, only to get up, then sat down again.

His hand grasped the buzzing telephone like a trap springing. "Shep! Where on earth have you been? ..." His voice rose angrily. "Of course I know what time it is. Yes, and I know the bloody war is over." He calmed himself. "Shep, old man. Believe me. I do apologize. And I wouldn't put you to all this bother if it weren't terribly important. Here it is. I want you to go over for me one more time, slowly, my dear fellow, slowly, exactly how the watermark is produced." The voice at the other end fairly crackled. Tepley jerked the receiver from his stinging ear. "No, you insufferable ass! That's not the only reason I'm calling."

He spoke now with cold, angry precision. "Just do as I say ... Yes ... yes ... I see. No ink involved at all, then. All in the texture. Thank you. God bless you for patience. Now. Do as I tell you. Do you remember the bundle we sent out to the laboratory? The waterlogged lot. Yes, those the Yanks fished from one of Jerry's lakes. I want you to put a solvent to them ... Yes. To the watermarks. No. I haven't gone daft. How should I know what solvent? Paint remover! Any bloody solvent you've got out ..."

*

He had actually been able to fall asleep stretched out on the lumpy, red leather couch. A large tumbler of gin had helped. The telephone jangled several times before he stirred from a drugged slumber. Starlight silvered the darkened office. His bad leg had gone stiff. He hopped awkwardly to the desk.

"Yes. Of course, I'm awake." His tongue was thick. "And I am sitting down. God! No!" A beatific smile spread across the good half of his face. "Dissolved the bloody watermark? Extraordinary. Simply extraordinary." His voice was hushed.

5

ALOIS GLUCKHERTZ HAD NOT SEEN NUDELMANN
since the war had ended. In his position as village party chief,
the innkeeper had found the local numbskull useful. The
Führer had noted, quite rightly, it turned out, that the
Nudelmanns of this world were essential to any political
movement, understanding nothing, obeying everything.
Gluckhertz had used Nudelmann to run messages, sweep out
the meeting hall and inform on his fellow villagers. Now,
Nudelmann was among the people he wished never to see
again. But here was the fool at the Bonalpina telling
Gluckhertz, in a self-important, conspiratorial whisper, that a

high-ranking SD officer was in Königsee eager to see him.

Gluckhertz excused himself from a knot of American officers who were telling him incomprehensible jokes in English at which he laughed uproariously. He brought Nudelmann to the small, airless office he kept off the kitchen.

"What are you talking about? And be quick about it."

"I tell you, Alois, he's Spiderweb."

"What are you talking about, man?"

"Spiderweb. The movement to resurrect Germany."

"Get out! Get out of here, you fool." He spoke through clenched teeth. "And don't let anyone hear you speak such foolishness again, if you have a particle of sense."

"He wants to talk to you about an SD vehicle."

Gluckhertz put his hand over his eyes and cursed softly. He shut the door to the office. "Where is this man?"

"He is my guest." Nudelmann beamed.

Gluckhertz thought a long while before speaking. "Tell him I will be by in the morning." His voice was defeated. "Now, get out of here."

Gluckhertz pasted the innkeeper smile back on his face and rejoined his American guests.

*

"So you see, I regard myself as a keeper of the flame."

Gluckhertz listened to the white-haired man's seductive phrases with colliding emotions. From the moment he had entered Nudelmann's dreary lodgings and this fine-looking gentleman had seized his hand warmly and called him "Herr Zellenleiter," he had felt a forbidden nostalgia. Once an association with Wolf Kruger would have swelled him with pride. Now it made him sweat profusely.

"You are a businessman, Herr Gluckhertz. So much the better. You will understand completely. There were wise men in the party, as early as '44, who faced up to the possibility of a purely military defeat. They met, I can tell you exactly where, in the Hotel Maison Rouge in Strasbourg. They drew up the original plan for the Spiderweb. And now we are putting it to work. But money is everything. Money is the oxygen. It keeps the flame alive. And you, I, Herr Nudelmann," he gestured toward the grinning man, "we must be keepers of the flame.

"Those now in hiding need help, support for themselves and for their families until we can manage their escape. Those already out of Germany must lead secret lives. An expensive business. They need our help, too. But more important. They must be bound in brotherhood so that their faith does not wither in exile.

"We have gold in friendly banks, particularly in Switzerland. We have reichsmarks. But their value declines daily. We know the Allies will soon replace them with a new currency. That is where my role comes in. It is my responsibility to get the British currency that was in SD possession . . . I need not go into details now. But that is where you come in also."

Gluckhertz struggled to look composed while the sweat trickled in tiny rivers into his sodden collar.

"Ah, my dear man. I understand the doubts you feel. It's natural enough. The Fatherland appears crushed, beaten. But look at what is happening already. At Aachen, those Russian swine, Displaced Persons, they broke out of their camp. They robbed. They murdered. They raped our women. The Americans have reported tens of thousands of cases of rape by Russian soldiers and these DPs since the war ended. And now the Bolsheviks are accusing the Americans of forcing Russian prisoners to Africa to join the French Foreign Legion. Do you realize what all this means, Gluckhertz?"

The man shook his head.

"It means that it has already begun. They have started to claw at each other. One day they will start to tear at each other. Then they will war on each other. And that is when we shall return!"

The evangelical fervor evaporated as quickly as it had appeared. He spoke calmly. "Gluckhertz. Where is that van?"

Gluckhertz felt his collar strangling him. He ached to flee from the spell of this persuasive lunatic.

"Is it necessary, Herr Standartenführer, to have Nudelmann remain?"

"But Nudelmann is the good soldier." Kruger, smiling, gestured expansively toward his host. "Nevertheless, if you are uncomfortable. Nudelmann, old fellow, would you please give us a few minutes alone?"

Nudelmann glowered at Gluckhertz and reluctantly left the room.

Kruger rose, locked his hands behind him, and paced. "Please, Gluckhertz. Don't think I am insensitive to your situation." He turned around and placed his hand on the innkeeper's shoulder. "You sense danger in seeing me. That is unnecessary. You must have no fear. Do you know why?"

Gluckhertz stared at the man blankly. Kruger's hand tightened on his shoulder as he leaned close to him.

"Because I have been denazified!" He released his grip and exploded in insane laughter. "Can you believe it, my dear Gluckhertz? I . . . am . . . denazified!"

Gluckhertz gave a sickly, baffled smile.

"You and I, we can stroll arm and arm through König-see to the lake. Take the boat to St. Bartholomew. Have a wonderful picnic. You have not a thing to fear from your new American clients." The faintest contempt invaded his smile.

"Look. I have the paper, my *Persilschein,* attesting that I

have had no association with the party." He showed Gluckhertz the document and laughed gaily.

Gluckhertz felt a nauseous rolling in his stomach.

Kruger was up and smiling quite pleasantly again. "I
don't intend to waste another minute in the life of a busy
man." He glanced at his watch. "You must be preparing
lunch for your guests, I know. Assure me only of this. You do
have the English money?"

Gluckhertz coughed. "May I ask you a question, Herr
Standartenführer?"

"Of course, my dear fellow."

"When your affairs are finished here in Königsee, is it
your intention to leave?"

"Ah, you see. Another man might interpret that as a
veiled discourtesy. But I understand you perfectly. Unfortunately, the work of the Spiderweb cannot be conducted
from this charming oasis. No. It is my intention, when, as you
say, my affairs are finished, to continue my work from my
home. I will be returning to Nuremberg as soon as you have
performed your last duty to the Fatherland."

Gluckhertz rose, the resignation of a condemned man in
his face. "I know nothing of English bank notes. But I believe
I know something about what you seek. Come to the Bonalpina at eleven o'clock this evening, to the small entrance in
the rear. Wait for me there."

"Splendid, Gluckhertz. Splendid."

As Gluckhertz reached for his hand, Kruger gave him a
warm smile and a casual Party salute.

*

"You can't really blame me now, can you, Tepley? I put
him through the paces, just as you asked. Weird duck, I must
say. One never felt comfortable with him. Tedious on the

subject of the camps. Although, I don't suppose we can blame him. Can we?"

Tepley and Ernstwhistle were seated in the back of a Humber staff car, driven by a sergeant in the Coldstream Guards, on the autobahn leading to the Ruhr where they would turn south to Wiesbaden.

Tepley patted Ernstwhistle's arm. "Not blaming anyone, old man. You did precisely what I asked. I've made a career of false starts these past years. You can't imagine how many times I've rendezvoused with the shadiest blokes possible in Lisbon back alleys. All blind, needless to say. Not to mention high-principled Swiss who had the answer for us for the right price. I'm afraid I'd have dismissed your crazy little Jew, too. Trouble is, are we going to find him now?" He was gazing pensively out the window as Germany's prostrate industrial heartland rolled past, resembling the skewered bowels of an iron monster.

"We do have the address. Fortunately I kept that." Ernstwhistle said it with a trifle too much self-satisfaction. He was eager to salvage something of his standing. The younger man had impressed him deeply. He was surprised at how quickly he had become used to the face. "Of course. He wants tit for tat. Kept insisting we had to help him find this fellow who supposedly ran the show."

"Kruger?"

"Yes. That's the one. Our little friend is practically gaga on the subject. He must have said a dozen times that the Yanks are in bed with the Nazis. Freeing war criminals. That sort of thing. That's when I started to bail out, I'm afraid."

"Had he lost anyone?"

"Oh, yes. Wife and kid. Haven't they all?"

"Obviously, we can accommodate him on Kruger." Tepley looked to Ernstwhistle, expecting agreement.

"Oh. How's that?"

"Same quarry, different reasons."

"Yes. Quite so. But Kruger's gone. We can't very well scour all of Germany for the fellow."

Tepley sighed and nodded. "We'll have to take whatever loose thread we find and start tugging at it. For the moment that means your friend Goldhammer."

"Damn slender thread, I dare say."

They fell into silence as the skies darkened and they approached the burned-out hulk of Dortmund, no beauty in the best of times.

*

"Damn! Damn! Damn!" Tepley jammed the fist of one hand into the palm of the other in rhythm with his curses. He had come out of the office of the Chief of Intelligence, 87th Division, Third Army, at Dachau. He leaned into the back seat of the Humber where Major Ernstwhistle waited. In the front, next to the driver, Julius Goldhammer sat in a catatonic reverie.

They had found the printer with astonishing ease. Arriving in Wiesbaden, they had gone directly to the Blauvelt address Goldhammer had left with Major Ernstwhistle. Frau Blauvelt's cooperation had been unstinting when she learned they hoped to take Goldhammer away with them.

The Coldstream Guardsman translated for them. "The crazy. I know where to find him. Go to the Americans. The War Crimes at Dachau. He is always there, driving them mad. If they haven't thrown him out today. You want me to pack his rags?"

Tepley and Ernstwhistle exchanged amused smiles. "Tell her, Sergeant, we would be most grateful," Tepley said.

The first sentry they asked gave an exasperated nod.

Goldhammer had already worked his post that day and would
probably be badgering the detail at Gate Able, by now.

*

Though Goldhammer's memories of Ernstwhistle were painful, he had immediately agreed to join the search for Kruger. They had begun by retracing Goldhammer's steps to Colonel Daniel E. Houlihan at Dachau.

"Trail's run cold." Tepley shook his head ruefully. "We're dead ended."

"What did they say, Tepley?"

The younger man opened the car door and flung himself morosely into the back seat. "I talked to this Houlihan fellow's clerk. Lovely little creature." He made a small, contemptuous laugh. "In any case, the man's gone. He doesn't know when Houlihan will be back." He shook his head. "Something odd about it all."

"How so?"

"I asked this clerk fellow, bit of a twit, you know, what he might tell me about SD Colonel Kruger."

"And?"

"And I was informed there are eighty-two thousand Germans being screened here."

"Helpful."

"Quite. He suggested I consult their central files."

Ernstwhistle raised a questioning brow.

"I did. They don't have a scrap on any Colonel Kruger."

Ernstwhistle gave an accusing glance to the back of Goldhammer's bald head in front of him. The head turned.

"Mr. Tepley." Goldhammer spoke in halting, measured tones. "This man. This Houlihan. They have told you where he has gone?"

"Off to some resort town, it seems. I suppose he's

exacting the spoils of war from some pliant Mädchen."

"Where is this place?" Goldhammer's short neck craned about uncomfortably.

"In the Berchtesgadener Land, the fellow said. Königsee, I believe."

Goldhammer nodded his head. "Yes. That is where we must go."

"What the devil for?" Ernstwhistle spoke impatiently.

"You will see." Goldhammer kept nodding.

*

"Take your time, Corporal. Don't sweat it." The huge, gravel-voiced officer who had come barging into the duty room said it with menacing impatience. The corporal cranked the telephone nervously. He wondered if his forehead revealed the sweat he felt.

"We're lucky, sir." He gave an appeasing smile. "The only working line to that town is to our MilGov unit."

"That's just swell. You keep at 'em, boy." He gave a joyless laugh, accompanied by insistent foot tapping. Houlihan eyed his watch. He calculated the remaining driving time to Königsee at two and a half hours. The idea had struck him after he had left Munich. These hours could be working for him. His line of authority was tenuous. Still, slippery terrain was his habitat. The less authority in hand, the more authoritative the manner. It was his rule. He had marched into Military Government at Rosenheim and demanded to see the duty officer. When the appropriately cowed young lieutenant arrived, Houlihan told him to have his duty clerk call the unit in Königsee. At that point he sat down, lit a cigar and exuded impatience.

The corporal clapped his hand over the mouthpiece. He

was nodding eagerly. "Got him coming on, sir," he informed Houlihan. The soldier then barked into the phone. "Rosenheim Military Government here. I got Colonel Houlihan, 87th G-2. He wants to speak with your C.O. Now! You better damn well find him." The corporal turned beamingly to Houlihan. The colonel returned an approving nod.

"They're looking for him, Colonel."

Houlihan puffed more casually now.

"Lieutenant Wheeler? Colonel Houlihan coming on the line." The corporal handed the receiver to Houlihan. He took it in a great, enveloping fist.

"What's it? Wheeler? All right, Wheeler. You listen real close. This comes in two pieces. First, put a search party out for a Mercedes paneled van, Wehrmacht gray. Should have some sort of SD markings. Scour the village and environs. No, you don't call me back. I'm on my way to you. In a few hours. Got it. OK. Number two. I also want the town searched for a German national. Party suspect. Name, Wolf Kruger. K-R-U-G-E-R, former SD colonel. Maybe five-ten. Midfifties. White, wavy hair. Ruddy, pink complexion. Blue eyes . . . Can't tell you. Probably civvies. Right. Good man, Wheeler. OK. Move it."

He hung up. And sat quietly for several moments. Then he jumped to his feet. "Have that jeep gassed up and check the spare gas can." He also wanted to ask if the O club bar was open yet. He checked his watch again and decided against it.

"Good work, son." The smile now was genuine. "Oh yes. One more thing. This is G-2 business. No paper trail. Got it? Tell that duty officer, too. What was his name?"

"Musante, sir?"

"Yeh, Musante. Tell him no log entries."

"What about the gas? Sir."

"Charge it to post allowance."

The young corporal was grinning now. "Gotcha, Colonel."

"Sure, kid."

*

The Königsee Burgermeisteramt amused Houlihan. Hansel and Gretel, he thought. He pulled the jeep directly in front of the gaily painted town hall where an MP started to wave him off, got a look at Houlihan and thought better of it. Houlihan returned a minimal salute, left the door open for the MP to close and ambled with hands-on-hips authority into the building where he encountered another MP. "Get me Wheeler, kid."

"Yes, sir!" The words stood at attention.

Houlihan measured Lieutenant Wheeler. He was tall and lanky, and spoke in flat, clean midwestern accents. There was a transparent wholesomeness to the young fellow. Houlihan instantly disliked him.

"Nice slot, Lieutenant. How'd you land it?"

Wheeler smiled shyly. "German major, University of Minnesota."

Houlihan snorted. "All right. What have you got for me?" He walked possessively into a room over which a freshly stencilled sign hung: "C.O. AmMilGov." He sat himself down in a chair opposite the neatly arranged desk from which Wheeler ran the town.

Wheeler sat at his desk. "Colonel, we've found your vehicle. At least a vehicle matching the description you gave."

Houlihan raised an inquiring eyebrow. "And the fugitive?"

Wheeler nodded carefully. "A lead. That's all."

"What about the vehicle?"

"My search party located it about an hour and a half ago. It must have gone off the road. We found it down a hillside."

Houlihan's eyes narrowed to hard beads. "Go on."

"I guess the buzzards got there first. Picked clean. Tires stripped. Except on one jammed wheel. Tank drained. Battery gone. No papers. No cargo, either."

Houlihan's brow wrinkled. "And Kruger? What have you got?"

"Yes, sir, Colonel. If you'll come with me."

The officer rose and led Houlihan down a vaulted hallway. "We picked up this old fellow an hour ago. Someone matching the description you gave has been seen coming in and out of his place the past couple of days."

"What else?"

The young officer looked back over his shoulder. "Nothing, I'm afraid. He's not too bright. But he's a tough old bird. He won't say anything."

They stopped before a door where an MP stood posted outside. Inside, the room was bare. The windows had been barred. The lone furnishings were a U.S. Army cot and a chair on which a small, hunched figure sat. He did not look up at the two men who entered.

"Name's Nudelmann, sir. That's about all we got."

"Did you give him an incentive?"

Wheeler looked puzzled. Houlihan was unbuckling his holster. His face had an icy grin. He drew the .45 and touched the end of the barrel to Nudelmann's temple. In the silence of the room, the click of the safety catch fairly exploded.

"All right, college German major." Houlihan's voice had a throaty hoarseness. "Translate this for me."

The little man's knees made a soft, batting sound as they pounded together. Sweat had popped onto his brow instantly. His mouth hung open and he made low, moaning sounds.

"Ask him who the man was."

Wheeler translated. His colorless midwestern speech assumed in German an authority that surprised Houlihan.

Nudelmann's eyes rolled insanely. Still, he said nothing. Houlihan moved the gun barrel directly into the old man's ear. Nudelmann's body began to shake convulsively.

"Standartenführer Kruger." The rasping, terrified voice was barely audible.

"Ask him where we find him."

"I don't know. He is gone. I don't know where." Nudelmann's answer tumbled out in a babble.

Houlihan pressed the barrel deeper into the ear.

Nudelmann strained to bring his eyes around so that he could see his tormenter. He driveled out more words.

"He says he left earlier this evening," Wheeler again translated.

"Where? Goddamn it!" Houlihan shoved hard on the gun barrel. Nudelmann groaned. The words now came in a torrent.

"I think you can take the gun away, sir. He's flowing pretty freely now."

Houlihan gave Lieutenant Wheeler a contemptuous glance. He sheathed the weapon. "You always got to give 'em an incentive. Understand? What's he saying now?"

"He doesn't know where Kruger was going. And he doesn't think he's coming back. He took one small piece of luggage with all his belongings and he badgered Nudelmann all day to find a larger suitcase for him. As soon as he found it, Kruger left without a word."

"What did he put in the big one? Ask him."

"He says nothing, Kruger took it empty."

"Jesus!" Houlihan's eyes flashed.

Nudelmann began babbling again. The voice was now

hysterical. Tears flowed down his wrinkled cheeks. His whole body shook as he stole frightened glances at the bulging holster on the huge American's hip.

"What the hell is bugging him now?" Houlihan muttered.

"He says it's always the same. Always the little guy who gets it, while the big ones get off. Why are we scaring him to death? Why are we going to kill him? He's nobody. Why don't we go after the big shots, like Gluckhertz?"

Houlihan held up his hand to stem the continuing tide of Nudelmann's babble. "Who is this Gluckhertz?"

*

The man set the suitcase on the ground and flattened himself against the wall of the Bonalpina. In the moonless night, with the felt hat pulled over his face and dark raincoat, he formed little more than a blur. From within the inn, he could hear the cowboy yelps and drunken singing of the Americans. Outside, the stillness was disturbed only by the shrill plaint of cicadas and the hooting of night birds.

The rear door of the inn swung open and an orange-yellow globe invaded the darkness. Gluckhertz came out carrying a kerosene lamp in one hand and a crowbar in the other. He jumped at the sound of Kruger's voice.

"What took you so long, Herr Gluckhertz?"

"I couldn't find the flashlight. We must go quickly, before they notice I am gone."

They followed the light along the rutted path, around the curve to the storehouse in the clearing.

"Take these." Gluckhertz handed Kruger the bar and lamp.

The cluttered key ring was attached to Gluckhertz's belt. He fiddled impatiently with the rusted lock, then shoved the door open. "Please. Let me have the light." He took the lamp, held it up and let its soft illumination suffuse the room. "There." He pointed to the loosely stacked bales.

Kruger began to push the bales aside until the outlines of the trunk emerged. Gluckhertz brought the lamp up close. They peered down at the dull gray surface of the container. Gluckhertz moaned. Kruger glared at him menacingly and tightened his grip on the crowbar. "I don't understand. Believe me!" Gluckhertz's voice was desperate.

The seals were broken and the locks on the trunk had been sprung.

"Shut up!" Kruger jabbed the crowbar at the lid of the trunk and flung it open. In the glow of the lamp, the neatly bound notes gleamed.

"Thank God!" Kruger fell to his knees and embraced the trunk.

"Thank God," Gluckhertz gave a deeply relieved sigh.

On top of the bank notes was a flat, oblong tin case. Kruger seized it and opened it. "The plates! Even the plates!" He smiled at Gluckhertz. "Now. Quickly. To work." He opened the suitcase and began to stack the bank notes in it, while Gluckhertz held the lamp.

"Herr Kruger. There is not going to be enough room in your bag."

"Then I will have to trust you to look after the remaining account. Won't I? The Königsee branch bank of Spiderweb, eh?" He made a small, tight laugh as he continued stuffing the notes.

Gluckhertz was contemplating this uncertain blessing when the door creaked. He looked up into the barrel of a U.S. Army .45-calibre pistol.

The lamp threw the shadow of a colossus against the wall. "Keep packing, Kruger." Houlihan's bulk obliterated the doorway. He stood with legs wide apart.

Kruger turned slowly, his mouth contorted. Then it curled into a waxen smile. "Congratulations, Colonel. You are a persistent hunter."

"Thank your friend Gluckhertz, here. Some of his old cronies don't like him much."

Kruger seized the crowbar and in one motion had smashed it against Houlihan's knee cap. The American let out an agonized howl. Kruger lunged at the staggering figure, seizing the arm that held the gun. Houlihan struggled to free himself, stumbling backwards over the open trunk. They wrestled each other to the ground. The older German possessed unexpected strength. Gluckhertz gaped at the writhing figures, unsure where to ally himself.

Kruger had his thumb pressed against Houlihan's eye and was driving it in with a force that made his hand tremble. The American made ugly, horrified noises. He dropped the gun in order to pull Kruger's hands from his face, Gluckhertz reached uncertainly for the .45. The two men released each other and dove at him simultaneously, knocking Gluckhertz over and sending the lamp careening along the stone floor. For an instant the room went black. Then small tongues of flame leaped amidst the scattered hay. Gluckhertz got up and ran for the doorway. The two men continued to wrestle as smoke began to envelop the storehouse.

Kruger let go of Houlihan and reached his hand into the trunk for the oblong metal case. Houlihan ground his heel into Kruger's wrist. The engravings fell back into the trunk, and the men continued to struggle, coughing, gagging, their eyes filmed with tears as the smoke thickened and waves of heat rolled over them.

The fire had reached the trunk. The top layer of bank notes curled crisply. The two men freed each other and crawled toward the doorway, trying to stay below the now overpowering heat. Outside, they collapsed on the ground, gasping and gulping in the cool night air. Gluckhertz was standing back from the building, shaking his head and muttering, "Mad! Mad!"

They could hear the voices of the crowd, drawn by the flames, coming up the pathway from the Bonalpina. Kruger glanced at Houlihan who still lay on his back, propped on his elbows breathing noisily. The German slowly edged himself back out of view, then quietly got up and slipped into the woods.

The flames now curled out of the windows and licked at the sides of the storehouse. The wooden eaves formed a ring of fire. The patrons from the inn came closer and recognized their host. "Hey Putzi, how much insurance you got on that barn? . . . You going to have a fire sale? . . . Who's your arsonist? The Mafia?"

Gluckhertz returned a sickly smile. His face was flushed and sweat streaked from the heat of the blaze.

Houlihan shook his head as though to revive his fogged senses. He noticed the approaching crowd, and immediately looked about for Kruger. His face was smeared with soot and his uniform patched with sweat. He rose slowly to his feet and limped away from the oven the storehouse had become. He could hear the masonry cracking as the flames scorched the structure. He spotted a young lieutenant, alone and apparently more sober than the rest of the spectators.

"Kid. Come here!"

The young man stiffened. "Yes sir, Colonel."

"Get into town. Find Lieutenant Wheeler at MilGov. Tell him to get a security detail out here right away to cordon off this building. I want a twenty-four-hour watch."

Houlihan turned to the crowd. His voice was hoarse and his eyes bloodshot. "All of you. Go on back. Get out of here. This area's off limits, order of 87th Division G-2."

The tipsy spectators stared at the disheveled, limping, sweat-soaked officer. There was something in his bulk and dead seriousness that still commanded authority. They began to drop back. Among them was Werner Goren, who watched the consuming flames with an enigmatic smile.

Houlihan was still breathing deeply, replenishing his lungs with the fresh air. He ambled over to Gluckhertz with deliberate casualness, his hands on his hips. "Sorry you lost your property, Herr Gluckhertz." The voice had a cop's practiced sympathy. He spoke loudly enough for the retreating spectators to hear. "There was no avoiding it. This case has been a son of a bitch. I think we've got it licked now." He lowered his tone and spoke with his lips barely moving. "Don't worry about your Nazi Party business. Military Government's got my orders to lay off."

Gluckhertz listened to this confident giant with confusion or respect. He was not sure which.

*

Gluckhertz trembled as he banged on the door of the room he had provided for Houlihan at the Bonalpina. The morning was radiant, with shafts of sunlight piercing the hall windows and shining on the scrubbed floors. Houlihan did not answer. The German cautiously urged the door open. Houlihan lay spread-eagled on the small bed. His forearm shielded his eyes from the light streaming through the window. Gluckhertz could still smell the smoke in the khakis Houlihan had not bothered to take off. The American was snoring rhythmically. Gluckhertz shook his shoulder.

"Colonel Houlihan. Please. It is important."

Houlihan grunted and rolled over on his stomach. Gluckhertz shook him harder.

"Go away. I want to sleep." His words were thick and clotted. Gluckhertz saw a nearly emptied bottle of American whiskey on the dresser.

"There are some British police here to see you."

The man wheeled around and sat on the edge of the bed. His head hung down and his thick brown hair obscured his face. "What police?"

"Two are British Intelligence. Another one looks like a workman. They came here just now, this morning. They came from your office in Dachau to see you. They are asking about the fire. Will there be trouble?"

Houlihan lurched to a sink. He filled it and plunged his head in.

"Trouble?" The water dripped down the soiled khaki shirt as he dried himself. "I just broke a hell of a case for these Limeys." He gave Gluckhertz a harsh smile. "And don't you forget it, buster. You were there."

"Of course. Shall I tell them you will be down?"

"Yeh. Give me ten minutes."

The three men at the table on the sunny terrace of the Bonalpina looked up at a huge figure in newly starched khakis, his hair slicked back and his skin pink from a fresh shave. Only the blood-streaked eyes contradicted an image of recharged vitality. Houlihan looked down to see a curious half face smiling serenely at him, also a smaller man in the uniform of a British major and a man it took him several seconds to place as the little Jew who had hounded him at Dachau.

The scarred man rose, still smiling, and took Houlihan's hand. "Terribly good of you to see us, Colonel. Tepley, MI 6 (v) London. This is Major Ernstwhistle, MI 6 chief at Bremen.

And I believe you've met Mr. Goldhammer. Won't you please sit down?"

"Gentlemen, it's a pleasure." Houlihan shook Tepley's hand, then Ernstwhistle's. He ignored Goldhammer, who had not yet raised his eyes from the table. He seated himself. "I see Putzi has taken good care of you."

"Herr Gluckhertz has been most kind." Tepley gestured toward the steaming pot of coffee and thick slices of bread, jam and butter. "Königsee seems to have been spared the war."

"That's right. It's a different world outside of the cities. Except for the ones trying to make a buck off of you, you still get an arrogant kraut in these mountain towns."

Houlihan turned to Werner Goren, who hovered nearby. "Bring me some black coffee, Katzenjammer. A pot of hot, black coffee." He sat back, smiling fixedly. Seconds passed.

Tepley broke an awkward silence. "It seems we missed a rather good show. Last night, I mean."

"Yes." The smaller Englishman with the church organ voice spoke up. "We were apparently late for the fireworks." He laughed hollowly.

Houlihan sat with arms folded, still smiling, saying nothing. Again, a stiffness settled over the table.

"Colonel Houlihan. British Intelligence, not to mention Scotland Yard's Counterfeit Branch and the Bank of England, would be terribly grateful if you would let us inspect the site of the fire. As I'm sure someone in your position is well aware, for some time now we've been pursuing the possibility that the Germans were counterfeiting our money." Tepley waited for a response, which was not forthcoming.

Ernstwhistle picked up the flagging effort. "We wandered up to the site of the fire when we arrived in town late last night. Your chaps, quite rightly, wouldn't let us near the place."

They both looked to Houlihan.

His voice was determinedly casual. "Why did you come to Königsee?"

Tepley and Ernstwhistle looked at each other, then to Goldhammer, who was gazing off.

Tepley spoke, his usual grace only faintly strained.

"Ah . . . yes . . . Mr. Goldhammer, as you know, claims to have been rather deeply involved in an SD counterfeiting operation. He convinced us that if we found this chap, Kruger . . . ah . . . through you, we could solve our case."

Ernstwhistle leaned forward eagerly. "Precisely. That's what brought us to your headquarters at Dachau. We gathered from your man, O'Day, that you were up here on the same hunt for Kruger."

"That's it?" Houlihan eyed them cautiously. First Tepley, then Ernstwhistle. "You were just looking for Kruger?"

"That's all." Tepley smiled. "And now we've stumbled onto this fire."

Goren came, set Houlihan's place and poured the hot coffee into a large cup.

Houlihan blew noisily across the surface of the coffee and drank. He was nodding and smiling. "Gentlemen. Your case has been solved, courtesy of the 87th's G-2 officer, personally. If you'll just give me a chance to finish breakfast, I'm going to show you one hell of a sight."

*

The storehouse was gaunt and hollow-eyed. Its black-streaked walls stood in harsh contrast to the billowy blue sky and vivid green of the trees. The air was still pungent, and wisps of smoke rose from fallen timbers. The MPs had roped off the building and a guard was posted at each corner. A small knot of curious villagers and American soldiers stood about. The ruined storehouse looked smaller to Houlihan than it had the night before.

He returned the MPs' salute and depressed the rope with his foot to let Tepley and Ernstwhistle step over it.

"May we have Mr. Goldhammer with us?" Tepley asked. "It would help so much."

"Sure." Houlihan turned to the MP. "Let him in."

Inside the storehouse, the burnt hay had a strong, rather pleasant bite. Scorched beams littered the floor, but the trunk was easily identifiable with the remains of Kruger's suitcase next to it. The notes had burned as a book does. The edges of the stacks were charred and curled, the centers still intact.

"Why don't you take a look, Mr. Goldhammer?" Tepley turned to Houlihan. "Would you mind awfully, Colonel?"

" 'Course not. Go ahead."

Goldhammer moved cautiously toward the trunk and removed a bundle of five-pound notes. The singed wrapping band fluttered off.

"What do you think, Mr. Goldhammer?" Tepley asked.

There was a tenderness in the man's handling of the paper. He fanned the bills with a practiced motion, then set the stack aside and picked up another. He held it close to his eyes. "I have no doubts." He smiled wistfully. "These numbers we used. These wrappings we used. This trunk I packed." His eyes fixed on a scorched metal box on the floor. He picked it up and opened it reverently. He walked over to Tepley, a crazed smile illuminating his face. "You see? The plates. My engravings of pound notes."

Tepley took the case. He gazed at the contents for a long time. His face had the misty look of a voyager home at last.

The thin metal sheets were streaked and blackened with soot, but their design was hauntingly familiar.

"Lovely. Simply lovely. Isn't it?" Tepley held the plates for Ernstwhistle to see. He turned to Houlihan. "Colonel, I needn't tell you how extraordinarily important all this is to our country." He continued to look fondly at the engravings. "We are going to be asking your government for authority to dredge up those other two lorries the Jerries ditched in the Traun. Then we'll have it all. Won't we?"

Houlihan's surprise was poorly concealed.

"Oh, yes. We learned about that matter as well from your man, O'Day. Really quite a bright young fellow. Most helpful."

Houlihan muttered inaudibly. "A real bright son of a bitch."

"What's that?" Tepley smiled quizzically. "The important point is that the master engravings have been recovered. That might have been sticky. And now, I'm going to ask if you would be willing to turn this material over to us, as representatives of His Majesty's government. You've done a splendid job, absolutely extraordinary, in breaking this case. Worth at the very least the MBE. Wouldn't you think so, Major Ernstwhistle?"

Ernstwhistle stammered.

"In any event. That's the recommendation I intend to make." Tepley swept his fingers affectionately over the engravings.

Houlihan beamed while searching their faces for any trace of jest. Both Englishmen were now smiling warmly. Tepley extended his hand. "Congratulations, Colonel Houlihan."

Houlihan coughed modestly. "It was a hell of a case, let

me tell you. Fifteen years a cop, before I went into the law. And I never had a tougher one."

Goldhammer was tugging at Tepley's sleeve and whispering in his ear.

Tepley nodded. "Colonel, and what about Kruger? Our friend wants very much to know."

Houlihan gave Goldhammer a cursory glance, then swaggered. "I don't think you got to worry about that bastard anymore. I whipped his ass all to hell and back. And not ten minutes too soon."

"Yes, no doubt." Tepley smiled tolerantly. "But do you know where he's off to?"

"Thrashed him to a pulp." Houlihan winked. "I'd look for him in the hospital."

Tepley suppressed an exasperated sigh. "In any case, Colonel, I take it you will turn all this evidence over to us?"

"Certainly. That was my plan all along. As soon as I had the case wrapped up."

"Goodo. Why don't we go back to the inn then, celebrate with a drink, and arrange some sort of proper receipts." Tepley was now effusive.

As Houlihan led the way through the crowd of the curious, Ernstwhistle pulled Tepley aside. "The MBE, Tepley? A bit rich, isn't it?"

Tepley gave his marred half smile. "Come now, Colin. It's a small price."

Gluckhertz waited at the entrance to the Bonalpina, his innkeeper's smile less than ordinarily convincing. "Gentlemen, I hope that you will be my guests for lunch." He was rubbing his hands and sweat beaded his brow. Before they could respond, he had seized Houlihan's sleeve and pulled him aside.

"That weasel. Werner. It was he who broke into the trunk. I knew it. And now he is gone." The innkeeper's face was an unhealthy maroon. His whispering hissed like steam. "He has run off with my Erika. My daughter!"

The two Englishmen watched Houlihan whispering into Gluckhertz's ear. The innkeeper's head was bobbing. Houlihan returned to them with a determined casualness. "You fellows excuse me? They need me down at MilGov. I'll be back in no time." He disappeared into the Bonalpina. The two Englishmen eyed each other uneasily.

The screech of tires came from around in back of the inn. Tepley hobbled to the corner of the building in time to see a jeep disappearing around a bend in the road.

"Colin, quickly. Into the car. After him."

"I, too?" Goldhammer hurried alongside them with a flat-footed waddle. The three piled into the Humber, where the driver was already gunning the engine.

*

The road from Königsee to Berchtesgaden swayed madly. Houlihan pushed the stubby machine to its limits, his huge body banging hard against the seat as he took the curves. At Berchtesgaden, villagers went fleeing as he barreled through the twisting streets, honking incessantly.

The faster, sleeker Humber caught sight of him as he was pulling out of the village.

"Shall I overtake him?" The sergeant in the Coldstream Guards shouted over the roar of his engine. Beside him, Goldhammer sat rigidly.

Tepley leaned forward. "No. Just keep him in sight."

Beyond Berchtesgaden, the road began to twist tortuously. Houlihan wrestled the wheel to maintain control. He caught sight in the rearview mirror of the trailing staff car and cursed softly. He skirted the edge of the raging Wimbach Gorge, lodged between two stone mountains. He slowed briefly to negotiate the tiny village of Ramsau, again scattering townspeople like fallen leaves. The Britishers maintained their distance as though an unseen cable linked them to the jeep ahead.

In the distance, Houlihan caught the glint of a blue jewel nestled amid the steep mountains. The road seemed to hurtle toward it, wheeling to the left, careening to the right. He stole a glance over his shoulder, went momentarily off the roadbed, and fought furiously to muscle the jeep back on course. The road now headed directly for the Hintersee. Houlihan worked the brakes frantically as the vehicle bounded from side to side, kicking up puffs of dust. He managed to bring it to a stop on a stretch of stone ledge that dropped directly into the lake.

The wooden guard posts were freshly snapped. Four people standing there gesticulated at him, spewing out words he could not understand and pointing to the lake. An old couple, with the same craggy faces as the surrounding mountains, set their bicycles down and continued their excited babble. A young boy and girl, also with bicycles, peered into the Hintersee's lovely cobalt waters.

The Humber pulled up alongside in less than a minute. Its passengers piled out.

"I say, Colonel. What the devil's going on here?" Tepley asked it with polite distress.

Houlihan hitched up his trousers and lumbered over to them. "Anybody know what these people are yapping about?"

Goldhammer spoke respectfully to the old couple. The two young people joined in the answer.

"The boy and the girl. They have seen an automobile go into the lake." Goldhammer translated into clunking, mechanical English.

The boy spoke rapidly to Goldhammer, eyes ablaze with excitement. "This has happened one half an hour. The boy and the girl saw from up there." Goldhammer pointed to a high overlook of curving road.

Houlihan spoke to Goldhammer. "Find out who they saw in it."

Goldhammer glared at him then asked the boy. "He cannot see from up there who is in the auto, he says. Only he knows it was a Wehrmacht Volkswagen."

The boy pointed beyond the shattered guard posts.

"That is where the Volkswagen is. In the lake." Goldhammer now spoke to Tepley and Ernstwhistle.

Houlihan turned to the two Englishmen with ponderous authority. "It looks like the U.S. Army's got a dredging job on its hands."

Major Ernstwhistle regarded the American with a look poised between perplexity and annoyance. "Do you suppose, Colonel, that you might tell us just what this is all about?"

*

The tow truck and the divers did not arrive from Rosenheim until after dark. Even in summer, the night air in the mountains had a biting chill. The headlights of the vehicles, parked around the tow truck, threw a harsh, unnatural light over the now black lake. The huddled, silhouetted figures, the pitch darkness, violated by cones of illumination, gave the lake shore the appearance of a frigid corner of hell.

The two Englishmen stood with collars upturned and hands jammed into pockets. Goldhammer, beside them, made

no attempt to block the cold and stood shivering uncontrollably. Houlihan moved between them and the tow truck crew, a
cigar clenched in his teeth, occasionally bellowing instructions
and reporting progress to the Englishmen. "Tell him to move
out another twenty feet and over to the left." A sergeant on
the bed of the truck cupped his hands and relayed Houlihan's
orders to a figure in the lake, bobbing amid the converging
headlights.

The voice came back, a hollow, otherworldly echo. "Pay
. . . out . . . forty more feet . . . Real . . . slow." Then the diver
disappeared.

Houlihan returned to the Englishmen. "You fellows
could be up at the Bonalpina swilling Putzi's hooch instead of
freezing your asses down here."

Ernstwhistle gave him a puzzled smile. "I don't imagine
Herr Gluckhertz is much in the mood to regale his guests at
this point, Colonel."

Tepley gave his countryman a quick, warning glance.
"Actually we're enormously grateful that you've allowed us to
come down here. We'd hate to discover a loose end just when
we thought we had the matter buttoned up."

"No trouble." Houlihan flicked his cigar ash and headed
back to the truck crew. "Christ, can't you see, he's jerking the
line!"

The diver's head broke through the slick, reflecting
surface. He made a pumping gesture with his right arm. The
truck engine started. The winch screamed and whined as it
wound the steel cable around the drum. Two GIs helped
the diver onto the rock ledge. He ripped the rubber mask from
his sweat-drenched face. He was gasping. "I . . . got a good
grip . . . She . . . ought to hold."

The water parted and a large hump rose up from it.

Everyone moved closer to the water's edge. A silence prevailed except for the slow, steady groaning of the winch and the truck's engine. The upper windows were now visible as the vehicle was drawn toward the shore like a glass-eyed sea monster. When it was finally pulled clear of the water, the Volkswagen seemed terribly small, almost toylike. Water spouted from its seams and windows, as a half dozen soldiers maneuvered the car onto the stone ledge.

Houlihan was first to it, with the Englishmen immediately behind him. He shined a flashlight inside the auto. The dead-white face of Werner Goren floated up before them.

"He's sure as hell alone in there." Houlihan nodded his head.

"No possibility another body might have gotten out, Colonel?" Tepley asked.

"Nah. Look. The windows are shut tight. None of them broken."

As the last of the water drained from the car, the soldiers set the body aside and pulled a sheet over it.

"Search him and the vehicle."

They responded hesitantly to Houlihan's gruff order.

Within minutes a corporal came over to the Humber. He handed Houlihan a ring of keys, some damp reichsmarks, and a Wehrmacht jackknife. "That's all was on him, Colonel. Nothing at all in the Volks."

"What do you suppose the poor beggar was running after?" Ernstwhistle's rich bass asked.

"Or from," Tepley added.

Goldhammer spoke up. "It is possible I know."

"Well, out with it." Tepley drew close to him. "What do you know, Mr. Goldhammer?"

The little man for the first time looked directly at Houlihan.

"Something is gone when we look in the trunk in the fire. It is not in the metal case where I have put it."

"My God! You mean we still don't have everything?" Tepley's voice was anguished.

"You have everything for you, Mr. Tepley. It is the Americans."

Houlihan glared at Goldhammer."What do you mean?"

"The other plates were missing."

"What other plates?"

"The twenty-dollar note of American money. I have just finished the engravings at the end at Oranienburg. It was my masterpiece."

6

GEORGE HORNING STOOD AT THE RAIL OF THE *Queen Elizabeth.* The wind stung his face and threw his hair into stiff swirls. No one else was outside this raw January morning. The *Queen* was the first of the great liners to resume Atlantic service since the war and was making Le Havre as well as Southampton. He looked out at the French coast, a smudge on the horizon. Horning imagined how his return might appear in a film. A montage of flashbacks: winter gray dissolving to that June morning eighteen months before; squawking sea gulls turning into fire-spitting aircraft; the merriment of passengers in the ship's lounge shifting to taut GI faces aboard a lurching LCI.

He shivered and turned away. He yanked open the reluctant hatch and moved quickly past the countess' stateroom. At least she had introduced herself as a countess. It made no difference to Horning, except for the barroom anecdotal value. He had known where the evening would end the moment she had said at the captain's table, with a playful smile at Horning, how much she had enjoyed her four-year exile in America. The men were so charmingly naive. Just marvelous little boys at heart.

He imagined her as he had left her earlier this morning—a rather overripe body for a Frenchwoman, the sheet forming wrinkled drifts around her body. She had stirred a cold, mechanical desire in him. His lovemaking had driven her to shrieking eloquence in French-accented American obscenities. Horning wondered who her tutors had been. Afterward, he had felt a compulsion to get away, the same hollowness he had known since coming home to Sally after the war.

Horning skipped steps up the ladder to his stateroom. He was a large man of unexpected grace and speed, qualities of the athlete, which indeed he had been.

*

George Maynard Horning had been recruited into the Secret Service after graduating from Sewanee in 1938, where his name figured as a halfback choice in several All-American polls. To this son of a dirt-poor farmer, growing up in Depression Tennessee, the Secret Service held out a rare combination, adventure with security. And Horning, with unfashionably high grades for a football scholarship student, looked equally attractive to the Secret Service.

He was assigned to the White House detail. His father, a congenital Democrat, was transported to know that his son breathed the same air as Franklin Delano Roosevelt. The father was forever pressing newspapers into the faces of neighbors at the feed store. There, in blurred wire service photos, behind the jaunty figure with the great, handsome head waving from the '39 Lincoln touring car, part of the face or a shoulder of George Horning could be distinguished.

Horning spent six months standing outside of doorways at the Oval Office, Hyde Park and Warm Springs, until he began to sympathize with the Pinkerton who had abandoned his post for a drink the night Lincoln was shot. His request for a transfer had struck the chief of the White House security detail as impertinent and ungrateful.

*

"Afternoon, Congressman." Horning smiled and nodded to a pouch-cheeked, white-suited visitor being ushered in to see the President. The man barely nodded, then backed up before he went through the doorway.

"Horning, ain't you? Goddamn! Buster Horning." He seized the young man's hand. "I heard you was over here, Buster. Had a bunch of constituents over from the district the other day. They told me. Got to go in and do me a little horse trading with the fellow in the wheelchair. Good seeing you, boy." He squeezed Horning's arm and winked as he entered the Oval Office.

Horning assumed that Congressman Yancey was currently useful to the President. The man had been invited to the White House three times in two weeks. Back home in Humphreys County, Horning knew him only as Dam Yancey for his ability to wangle public works projects for his district.

Horning's telephoned request for an appointment with Yancey had been granted instantly by a secretary, who immediately aroused his interest with a suggestive voice and the accents of home.

"Go right on in, Buster. The Congressman's waiting for you." The suggestive voice, Horning found, belonged to a plump, fiftyish woman, who claimed she had gone to school with his mother.

"Don't mind if I don't get up, son. I'm tuckered out." Yancey held out a limp hand. The Congressman then sat back, took off his glasses, and wiped them with a monogrammed handkerchief. The removal of the glasses left a void in his face. He leaned his head back and closed his eyes. Horning observed the flaccid cheeks and putty-colored skin.

"I'm so tired of dealing with that boss of yours." He shook his head. "When he wants something, he's downright shameless. I swear. That man could knock up your wife, then tell you how 'delighted' he was to have a Roosevelt in your family."

Horning laughed on cue.

The Congressman put his glasses on. "What is it, boy? What do you need from old Yancey?"

"Sir, I hate to be taking up your time . . . "

"Come on, boy. When's the right time? Let me tell you a little something. A politician's favors are like horseshit. The more you spread around, the more you reap. And we get the manure free anyway."

He appreciated Horning's hearty laugh. "Let me tell you another thing. If you want somebody's favor, ask him as soon as he's asked you for one. And do it before you say yes. That's how I play it with the Squire of Hyde Park. Not that I don't respect the man. I truly love him. He's a great President."

Yancey shook his head. "But he sure loves to play the game. And he don't respect anybody who can't. Now, next week, after he gets my committee on board on this court bill of his, he won't remember my name. Until next time."

"I want out of the White House detail, sir."

Yancey took off his glasses again and looked at him with his oddly naked eyes. "Out? How far out?"

"I'm bored silly holding up the walls of the oval office and riding around on running boards. I'd like to go over to the Secret Service Counterfeit Detail."

"Let me see. I guess I've got about another week at Santy Claus's knee. That's when my committee reports the bill out. I might as well put you on the Christmas list. Let's see what I can do."

Horning stood up and reached for the Congressman's hand. "Thank you, sir." He was grinning broadly. "But you just violated your own rule."

The old man looked baffled.

"You agreed to my favor before hitting me with one of your own."

"The hell I did." He made a giggling laugh. "You handsome young sonofabitch, you're going to take my daughter, Sally, out to lunch when she gets here in ten minutes, 'cause I just don't have the time or energy."

*

The transfer to the Counterfeit Detail came within six weeks. Horning thrived. It was a game, and playing games had been his habitat. The deductive intelligence required, the rewards of intuition, the rogue artists they stalked, all of it fascinated him.

He won a citation in his first year for the library scheme.

It had been simple and successful. While awaiting his transfer, Horning had spent his free time in the Library of Congress reading about the production and counterfeiting of money. He had made a curious observation. Among the hundreds of thousands of catalogue cards on file, none appeared more thumbed with wear than those dealing with counterfeiting.

Six months after he had gone to work for the Secret Service, his suggestion had been adopted that major libraries in the country report the names of borrowers of these books to the Secret Service. The reports from the New York Public Libarary alone had led to five arrests and three convictions in one year.

Horning completed nearly three years with the Counterfeit Detail before the war came along. He enlisted immediately and did what seemed most natural to him. He applied for infantry OCS. If one were going to fight a war, the infantry seemed to Horning the starting lineup.

On leave in Washington before going overseas, Horning had done something else that seemed right for the era of "I'll Walk Alone" and "Saturday Night Is the Loneliest Night of the Week." He married Sally Yancey.

He thought later, much later, that he had probably married her because her refusal to go to bed with him during the six months they had been engaged suggested something fine in her character that he did not fully grasp. She had given him, however, every other possible relief. The moral nuance between acts she would perform and the one she would not escaped him. But Sally Yancey had been raised by a mother who taught her that a well-brought-up Southern girl saved her most beautiful gift for her husband on their wedding night. Or, as Dam Yancey counselled his daughter, "Who'd buy a chicken if they can get free eggs?"

They had honeymooned in New York City before Horning went overseas, three days that had blurred in his mind into a montage of beds, bathrooms and hammering flesh. He could not remember a word they had exchanged.

George Horning led his company ashore with the First Army's First Division at Omaha Beach on June 6, 1944. From the moment men had dropped around him and failed to rise, the comfortable metaphor of combat-as-sport failed him. He thereafter fought a cautious war and achieved his sole ambition, to survive it.

By August of 1945, Horning was mustered out of the Army, back with the Counterfeit Detail as Assistant Director, and living with an acquaintance who was also his wife. In time he came to know her better and did not particularly like the woman he met.

Sally was oblivious to the flat convention of their lives. Horning was there for her, more than presentable. He had a faintly glamorous position, and was part of her due, like their Kalorama apartment, the membership in the Congressional Club that her father had arranged and her charge account at Garfinkels. She needed nothing more. Her priorities surfaced early. Reading, politics, heavy conversation were a bore, sleeping with her husband a pleasant enough duty and the shopping excursion with her mother the acme of Sally's week.

*

Cyril Patterson saved him. He had called for Horning on a Friday afternoon late in December of 1945. The Special Agent in Charge of the Counterfeit Detail was ten years older than Horning, an ugly, engaging man with a scythe of a nose and a ring of unruly curls semicircling a bald head. He was the father of seven children.

"I don't know what the hell took so long. The British

tipped us off last July. George, this could be a disaster. Do you know how good the British stuff was?"

"Perfect, they say."

"Can you imagine a harder-nosed bunch being taken in by the Nazis? Swiss bankers. Slippery Polish double agents. The Bank of England itself. Think of it. Out there, somewhere, are engravings of American bills produced by the same operation. That's the biggest blank check anybody ever held against the U.S. Treasury. And we don't know who's holding it."

"What denominations?"

"Twenties, at least as far as we know. That was bright, too. Big enough to be worth it, small enough not to be conspicuous." He laughed. "Remember that dumb son of a bitch before the war. Counterfeiting nickels? We figured out his production costs."

"I remember." Horning smiled. "I think it worked out to six cents each."

"We're not dealing with that breed here. Somewhere in Europe a bomb is ticking that could blow a hole in the American economy. Suppose those plates got into the Russians' hands?"

"How much do we know?"

"Not a hell of a lot. British Intelligence got onto our problem while they were investigating their own case. They notified our embassy in London. Then the whole business slipped through the cracks somewhere between State, Army G-2, and the FBI. By the time it got here, where it belonged in the first place, we'd already lost six months."

Patterson rose and came around to sit on the corner of the desk. He folded his hands over his knees. "George, you don't have to take it. You've been home what, four, five months. Christ, I've got guys on the staff who spent the war at the Pentagon gym. You've got that knockout wife. You probably want to get started on a family soon. I'm talking to you for only one reason. You're the best man, and you'd wonder what I was up to if I didn't at least ask."

"I'll go, Cy."

"Maybe we could give it to somebody like Foster. And you could supervise him from here."

"I said I'll go."

Patterson studied him curiously. "How will the wife take it?"

"It doesn't matter." He was quiet for a moment, then shrugged his shoulder. "It's no good."

Patterson nodded. "I'm sorry. I had no idea."

*

He told Sally over dinner at the Shoreham. He had chosen the main dining room Friday evening when he could count on a large crowd to discourage a scene. He need not have worried. She had reacted, it struck Horning, more in annoyance than sadness, as though learning her favorite hairdresser was moving out of town.

"George. I just know Daddy can get you out of it."

"I don't want your Daddy to do a damned thing."

*

The village of Muhlbach lay at a point where the Bavarian Alps paused briefly before resuming their steep march. On the edge of the village was the white-plastered farmhouse of the widow Knebel, and in the attic of the widow's home was a tan leather valise. Frau Knebel had thought it a shame to leave such a handsome piece of luggage there unused. But that was what her niece had insisted.

Frau Knebel had last seen Erika six months before

during that brief, disturbing visit. Her niece had arrived in the
night.

"You look thin, child."

"I'm fine, Tante."

"And so tired."

"Believe me, I am fine."

"Even so. You are still a beautiful thing." She held
Erika's face in her hands. "Always, since you were a child."

Erika patted the woman's work-coarsened hands.

"Just stay a few days to let me fatten you up and let my
neighbors see my elegant niece."

"No, Tante."

"But eat something. You haven't touched the *Knö-
delsuppe.*"

"Really, Tante, I'm not hungry. I'm just very tired. I
would like to go to bed now, if you don't mind."

"Sometimes I am so lonely here." The old woman
sighed. Tears welled in her eyes. "My dear boys. One in Africa.
What is the other place? Stalingrad? Places I have never heard
of." She dabbed at her eyes with a corner of her apron.

"I know, Tante. I understand. I'll come back and visit
you soon. And I'll write where you can reach me in Munich. I
promise."

She had left as early as possible the next morning. Frau
Knebel took the valise to her attic. She would not have
dreamed of opening it, although she had squeezed it and
shaken it. It was locked, anyway.

As months passed, she wondered if perhaps she should
ask Alois about Erika. But she knew the distance between the
father and his daughter. Besides, her brother always treated her
impatiently and made her feel terribly stupid. Still, she wrote
to Gluckhertz of his daughter's visit. But she said nothing of
the tan leather bag.

*

"You really are a schmuck! I can't believe it. A schmuck! A schmuck!"

Julius Goldhammer cringed under the huge American's lashing. He was tired and ached to leave the room. The lieutenant ceased his pacing and slumped morosely into the chair behind a cluttered desk. He squeezed his temples fitfully.

"I'm starting to understand. Really, for the first time. You're all so docile. So scared. So stripped of guts from four thousand years of ass-kissing. No wonder they slaughtered you like cattle."

"Please. I can go now?" Goldhammer feared this angry, powerful young man. He had not known such Jews. The officer had thick, coal-black hair, which he periodically flung back with an impatient motion. For all his burliness, he appeared to pounce rather than move. His nose lay bent to one side, the badge of an intercollegiate heavyweight boxing championship. Everything about Milt Kantrowitz intimidated Goldhammer.

Kantrowitz was a Chicagoan and a lawyer out of Northwestern. When the opportunity to join the war crimes prosecution staff came up, he had leaped at it. He had been impelled not by a thirst for justice, but by the chance to hang Nazis.

Kantrowitz had been assigned a case that whipped him to a delicious fury. Army Counterintelligence had unearthed an organization for spiriting fugitive Nazis out of Germany. Some arrests had been already made, including a minor cog named Ferdinand Moser. Kantrowitz was preparing the prosecution case. The idea of stamping out the last, hiding bacteria of Nazism excited him. He had a strong potential witness against Moser, but the man was suddenly and maddeningly refusing to cooperate.

"In all Germany, there's a handful of you left. You're practically extinct. They blot out three hundred thousand German Jews. And you won't testify against one of the bastards?"

Goldhammer fidgeted. "Please. I don't want to say more. Some things we cannot explain."

Kantrowitz radiated frustration.

"I can go now?"

The lieutenan nodded wearily, and Goldhammer rose to leave. Kantrowitz watched the stooped shoulders, the listless steps of the departing figure with a feeling he could not distinguish between pity and hatred.

Goldhammer stopped at the doorway and turned his head slowly. "I know, Mr. Kantrowitz, you try to help me. But this man you have is nobody. He is not the one important to me."

"I know. You told me. But your Colonel Kruger has disappeared."

Goldhammer nodded sadly and left.

Outside, Goldhammer stood at the gate beneath a sign reading "Central Suspect and Witness Enclosure, U.S. Third Army, Wiesbaden."

Smart, white-gloved MPs directed traffic in and out of the gate. A soft snow pelted Goldhammer and began to soak through his thin, worn shoes. He gestured clumsily at a personnel carrier pulling from the compound. The vehicle passed him. Soon he was chilled through and coughing. A teenaged corporal pulled up in a jeep and waved him in. *"Sprechen Sie Englisch?"* The accent was oddly soft and the words drawn out.

"Only little."

"Get in anyways, before you freeze."

Goldhammer pulled himself into the comparative warmth of the canvas-covered cab and immediately fell asleep.

The events that had brought Julius Goldhammer to Lieutenant Kantrowitz at Wiesbaden had been triggered by a news story appearing in the *Wiesbadener Kurier* on January 9, 1946. He had returned to the city the previous July after the trail to Kruger had dead-ended at Königsee.

The two Englishmen, Tepley and Ernstwhistle, had solved their case, and while grateful for Goldhammer's help, had no interest in his quest. They had dropped him off at Frankfurt on their drive back to Bremen and had given him a supply of English tinned meat for bartering. From Frankfurt, Goldhammer had covered the eighteen miles to Wiesbaden on foot. He had gone directly to the Blauvelts' house, seeking Jacob Edelmann.

Edelmann greeted him like a bill collector. He informed Goldhammer that it was not possible for him to move back because the Blauvelts had taken in two more DPs. Edelmann agreed that he would continue to check the Crowcass register from time to time to see if Wolf Kruger were rearrested. But, given what Goldhammer had told him, it seemed hopeless.

Edelmann also gave Goldhammer several addresses where he might find lodgings. He located a room with a stout, unsmiling war widow who took his canned meat in place of rent and thereafter never spoke a word to him.

During his first month back, he had hounded the War Crimes offices, the G-2 section, and Military Government until he had been banned from all U.S. installations. With the coming of winter, he reluctantly sought work. Goldhammer was employed by Druckerei Krause, a printer prospering under a contract with the American occupying forces. The manager had seized at the opportunity to exhibit a Jew on his payroll.

Goldhammer was treated by most of his fellow workers as a harmless crank and gifted craftsman. In some of them he sensed the old attitudes lingering, but in the winter of 1946 no German with a job was prepared to indulge the luxury of anti-Semitism.

He had seen the newspaper story on Ferdinand Moser while sitting by himself in the company's canteen lunching on carrot soup, black bread and potatoes. Had it not been for the rather muddied photograph, he would not have recognized the name. Moser was reported to have been arrested by American counterintelligence in Nuremberg on charges of falsifying documents for Nazis trying to escape Germany. He was identified as a former SS sergeant at Oranienburg, and was now in the compound at Wiesbaden.

Goldhammer had gone limp and the pounding of his heart made him dizzy. He went back to his table in the shop, took off an ink-stained apron, put on his army greatcoat and left Druckerei Krause without a word.

The guard at the main gate had thrown back his head and groaned. "Oh, Jesus. Not you!"

Goldhammer had persisted. His dogged insistence that he had information on an important suspect was all that had prevented him from being thrown out bodily. Ultimately, he had been taken to the intelligence officer assigned to the Moser case, Lieutenant Milton Kantrowitz. The American had seized on him.

"Look, Mr. Goldhammer. Here's the way I see it. A helpless old man is walking alone down a street. A bunch of toughs work him over for no reason, just for the hell of it. Just because he's a Jew. But the old Jew happens to have a young, tougher son who comes on the scene and takes care of the bastards. That's how you've got to see us, especially a Jew like me."

Goldhammer eyed him dubiously. "He is not important, this man. He is not what you think."

"Let me be the judge of that. Please? Now, tell me. How did you know Ferdinand Moser?"

Goldhammer recalled the man, a thin, sallow-faced braggart who talked loudly and never seemed to be taken seriously by the other SS guards. He had been as arrogant and abusive as the others toward the prisoners. But there was a caricatured quality to Moser's swaggering, and he had never laid a hand on a prisoner. Moser's chief responsibility was to pack the bundles of English bank notes and to arrange their shipment. It was Moser who had supervised the loading of the vehicles the previous April.

"Are you ready to testify against this man?"

Kantrowitz's intensity unsettled Goldhammer. He averted his gaze.

"I want first to talk to him."

"What for? All you have to do is tell the court what you've told me so far. We need you only to establish Moser's earlier connection with the counterfeiting business."

"I would like to speak to this man."

Kantrowitz reluctantly arranged the appointment for an afternoon in mid-January. Goldhammer was taken into a onetime SS barracks. The place was now a silent, concrete cavern, divided down the middle by a finely meshed screen. Raw illumination glared from high, unshaded lights dangling from the ceiling. The building was empty, except for two MPs posted at each end.

Goldhammer was directed toward a row of folding chairs lining one side of the screen. He stared dully at the doorway on the opposite side guarded by a white-helmeted MP.

The door opened. A shrunken man in prison gray stepped through, his hands in handcuffs. He squinted at the lights. His sleeves exposed bony wrists. His trousers were unbelted and the fly sagged halfway to his knees. The guard motioned for him to sit opposite Goldhammer. Goldhammer felt a sharp stab of recognition.

The prisoner resigned himself to another interrogation. He bowed his head toward Goldhammer and mumbled, "Good afternoon, Herr Doktor." The guard ordered him to sit down. He positioned himself on the edge of the chair.

Goldhammer looked him full in the face. "Moser, don't you know me?"

The man returned Goldhammer's searching gaze and shook his head.

"I am Goldhammer. The werkmeister at Oranienburg. Certainly you remember?"

Moser looked about uneasily. He turned to the guard, his bound hands turned up in a gesture of incomprehension. The guard made no response. Moser fixed his eyes downward.

"Moser. They want me to testify against you."

The prisoner looked up slowly at Goldhammer, his face twisted. Then he looked down again. The voice was whining and indignant. "I have never done anything against your people. That was not my responsibility."

"You put us on the train to Buchenwald. Do you remember, Moser? I remember. You put the women on the train that same morning."

Moser looked steadfastly away.

"You put us on the train. You sent us to the death camp. I will testify to that at your trial."

The man made as if to seize the wire mesh in his constricted hands. "I did not know they would kill you. Believe me. I was only a clerk." He looked up imploringly. "Thank God, man. At least you can tell them the truth."

"You are with the Spiderweb?"

Moser started at the word. "I had no work. No money. Do you know a Party member can only hold a laboring job under the occupation?" He looked at Goldhammer helplessly. "I have a wife, children. They came to me. The Spiderweb. Months ago. They thought I could help with false documents because I had been with Bernhard. Believe me, even today, they still frighten a man. And I had no money. What was I to do? Can't you understand?"

Goldhammer felt exhausted. He did not want to look at Moser anymore. He forced up the image of his dead wife and child to stiffen his will. His words came in a bleak monotone.

"I will not harm you, if you tell me what I must know." Goldhammer leaned forward. "Where is Kruger?" He whispered.

Moser's head dropped. "Oh God, I am safe nowhere. They will kill me."

Goldhammer's voice took on an unaccustomed hardness. "Listen to me, Moser. There is an American officer on your case. He is a Jew. He wants to see you hang. At this moment, he only knows of the Spiderweb and Bernhard. He does not have to know you shipped the prisoners to die, if you tell me where Kruger is."

The man turned his thin neck about as though searching the room before leaning close to Goldhammer. He whispered. "Outside Nuremberg, in the country, near the village of Feucht."

Goldhammer reported back to Lieutenant Kantrowitz. He risked the man's formidable wrath and refused to testify in the case of Ferdinand Moser.

It was at that point that Kantrowitz had lost his temper.

"But, Lieutenant. I give you a more important criminal. And I have told you where you find him."

"And that's your last word on Moser?"

"Yes, I am sorry."

Kantrowitz shook his head. "I'll wire an alert to War Crimes at Nuremberg on Kruger. That's all I can do. It's outside our jurisdiction."

Goldhammer had faith in this fine, strong American. But, he decided, he must also go to Nuremberg himself.

7

HORNING SAW HIS MEETINGS AT INTERPOL headquarters in Paris as payment on an overdue debt. He had gone ashore on D Day, but missed out on the delirium of liberating Paris. Horning's battalion had bypassed the city to continue pressing the westward offensive. Then they had stalled for months against the Siegfried Line. As the stalemate dragged on into December, Horning had wangled a four-day pass to Paris. On his second day, the Germans chose to launch what history would call the Battle of the Bulge. Horning was immediately recalled to the front. Paris remained for him an unsatisfied hunger.

Inspector Dussellier was a bleary-eyed, distracted man who chain-smoked until his lips were cracked and blistered, mostly cigarettes cadged from Horning.

"What more can I tell you?" He gave a shrug. "Our cooperation with the Scotland Yard Counterfeit Currency Branch, it is excellent. But, British Intelligence? They have revealed nothing to anyone for three hundred years, least of all to us French." Again the shrug. "You will have to see this man, Aubrey Tepley, of their counterintelligence. The British have kept Bernhard a military matter."

Horning had stretched his dealing with Dussellier unconscionably. His nights he spent with Josette, Dussellier's secretary, an older woman with arresting streaks of gray interrupting glistening black hair. She was the widow of a Frenchman who had fallen in June of 1940 at the Weygand Line. Horning found her an enthusiastic, knowledgeable guide to the city late into the night and a demanding Venus into the early morning hours. He decided that he had learned as much as possible from Dussellier when Josette's appetite began to give him an unaccustomed sense of masculine inadequacy.

In London, Horning met Aubrey Tepley for lunch in the lobby of the Carlton Club in Pall Mall. The Englishman rose in obvious pain, yet smiled broadly.

"Delighted you're here, Horning. Absolutely fascinating case you're on."

Horning looked at the scarred face self-consciously.

"The club's a bit worse for wear. Took one of Jerry's five-thousand-pounders during '40. Blew out the façade. Sent the entire ceiling down on the members' heads." He laughed gaily.

"Come along, let's have some lunch. Cottage pie Tuesdays. Really quite respectable."

Well toward the end of the meal Horning recognized that this marred, affable Englishman had extracted from him a thorough explanation of how the American Secret Service functioned.

"You must be tired of hearing me go on about our operation, Mr. Tepley. Especially after you've just cracked the toughest case."

Tepley gave an amused smile. "It might have helped somewhat if we had, as you say, 'cracked' it during rather than after the war."

"Can we talk a little about this Colonel Houlihan?"

"Oh, yes. Not the sort one forgets easily." He smiled enigmatically.

"Did Houlihan know about the American engravings?"

"I'm afraid so. Now, mind you, Ernstwhistle and I had no tangible reason to suspect the man's motives. As Ernstwhistle put it, tawdriness is a fault, not a crime. However, we did feel a responsibility to have someone on your side, besides Houlihan, aware that these engravings were at large. That's when I went to your embassy, after I'd returned to London. And now, as a result, here you are." He caught the waiter's eye. "Suppose we drink to that." He ordered two brandies.

They finished lunch and were leaving.

"And Goldhammer. Where do I find him?"

"I can't say exactly. Odd sort. Really quite a tedious fellow. We left him at Frankfurt. I believe he planned to push on to Wiesbaden."

"I'll start with Daniel E. Houlihan." Horning drew a small addressbook from his inside coat pocket and thumbed its pages. "G-2 officer, 87th Division, Third Army War Crimes Investigation Center, Dachau."

"He has a pretty little clerk named O'Day. He can be

rather useful, if you handle him properly." Tepley gave a knowing smile.

"He probably prefers foreign men."

Tepley looked at him, surprised, then laughed. "Quite. In any case, when you find Colonel Houlihan, give him my fondest regards. I'm quite sure he'll remember me."

*

Erika Falkenhausen girded herself for the visit to her late husband's parents soon after she returned to Munich. She had found few friends left in the city, and had quickly exhausted her money. She looked on the secret of the tan leather valise at her aunt's farmhouse as a last, desperate resource, one which she was too frightened to exploit, even had she known how.

It had been a rash, impetuous act. Having done it, she tried to rationalize her gnawing anxiety. Of what crime was she guilty, other than betraying that disgusting little creature, Werner? The engravings, if they were anybody's, belonged to a defeated regime. Obviously, they were of great interest to the Americans. Most likely she would offer them to the occupation authorities for a reward. In any case, the engravings had already served their prime purpose. They had provided her the courage, however irrational, to break away from Königsee. Still, the possession of them left her little peace. She must dispose of them soon. In the meantime, she needed the Falkenhausens.

*

"We are delighted to see you again, child." Erik's mother, aristocratically slender, with a glasslike fragility in her speech, still struck Erika as more Englishwoman than German Frau.

She poured Erika coffee, and with the opening amenities discharged, looked at the younger woman with a prim, patient smile.

Erika had always found Falkenhausen civility as stifling as a tomb. She went quickly to her point. "I come to ask your help."

"Of course." Erik's father looked like chiseled granite, with his flat, steel-gray hair and a grave but not unkindly expression. At this moment the expression was muted anxiety. "How can we help?"

She could almost see into his mind. The *Schulschiff*, the training vessel. They would assume that she wanted entrée into that world of respectable but down-on-their-luck German women who were maintained by young German men of good family. Erik had explained it all to her. Training vessels were invaluable in keeping high-spirited sons physically satisfied, more or less within their own class, so that their passions would not lead them into socially disastrous involvements. Erika had no desire to become a *Schulschiff*.

"I must find work. I ask only your help."

Herr Falkenhausen's relief was visible.

"Of course. I will do whatever I can. Please tell me where you can be reached, and you will hear from me." He smiled. His wife smiled. The audience had ended.

*

She had not heard directly from her former father-in-law. But, shortly after the visit, she received a note from one of Falkenhausen's agents suggesting that she call on a Herr Dollmann at a fashionable address on the Marienplatz.

It was a testament to the resiliency of the rich that a dealer in objets d'art dared reopen his shop barely three months after Allied bombers had flattened Munich. Erika met a short, waddling pigeon, with a few slicked strands of hair pasted like a doily over his naked pate. Dollmann spoke with a high-pitched, fussy voice and never failed to introduce "Frau Falkenhausen" to his wealthy clients. He paid her a pitiful salary.

Erika had been with Dollmann for five months when she returned to her small room on Veterinarstrasse to find a man waiting for her. He introduced himself as "Doktor Wolf Kruger."

*

Houlihan's intoxication had stabilized at a slurred garrulity. He had insisted that his visitor follow him on his customary rounds. The starting point was the officers' club bar in a building that had once served a similar purpose for a crack SS infantry regiment headquartered near Munich. Houlihan first drained two scotches. He picked up the third and waved for Horning to follow him to a small room alive with the whirring and clatter of one-armed bandits.

Horning shook his head in wonder. "I was fighting a war in this country nine months ago."

Houlihan inserted the first coin and yanked the arm with a thick, bristled fist. "Right. To make the world safe for slot machines."

Houlihan played with single-minded intensity, cursing softly as the rotors coasted to a halt. He issued a joyless laugh whenever the machine's mouth disgorged coins. He handed his empty glass to a young German waiter posted in the game room. "Fill it, Heinie!" After half an hour, Houlihan gave the machine a rude shove. He had exhausted his coins. Horning, he noticed suspiciously, had assembled a sizeable pile.

"You got to cash them in for military scrip." Houlihan guided Horning to a cashier's booth outside the game room.

A sinuous German girl behind the window wordlessly counted Horning's winnings.

"Hey, *Weibstuck,* how about you and me . . ." Houlihan held up his arms, danced an elephantine tango step and winked at her, ". . . when you get off tonight." The woman returned Houlihan a look of glazed disdain and smiled invitingly at Horning as she counted out his scrip.

Houlihan led his guest back to the bar. "Look, Horning, you won't use up all that scrip if you're leaving here tomorrow. I'll give you fifteen dollars American green for it." It was half the value of the scrip. Horning eyed Houlihan with amused disbelief. He pushed the scrip to Houlihan. "Here, Colonel, you just take it. Now, do you suppose we could sit down, have some dinner, do some talking?"

"Sure. In a minute." Houlihan quickly pocketed the scrip and ordered a drink. "You're not a lawyer, are you, Horning?"

Horning shook his head.

"I am. The army got a cop and a lawyer when they got Daniel Houlihan." He emptied his glass and ordered another before beginning to trace his rise from South Boston to his present eminence. Horning could not maneuver him into the dining room for another hour.

"You know what burned my ass most?" Houlihan held his fork upright in one hand, the knife in the other. "The Limeys never showed any gratitude. None! Now, you got to admit. I broke the big one for them. Not a word. Not a letter of commendation. The scar-face son of a bitch talked about the MBE!" Houlihan belched softly and gave Horning a knowing leer. "I got zip. We know why too, don't we?"

Horning's head had begun to throb, as much from Houlihan's yammering as from the drinking. "Colonel. Do you have any idea where I might trace this woman, Erika

Falkenhausen, Gluckhertz's daughter? Tepley thinks she's my best lead."

"I turned the whole damn works over to him." Houlihan was leaning low over the table, his eyes wet and glistening. His dark hair had tumbled over one eye. The voice was low and coarse. He swung his arm expansively, perilously close to the wine bottle. "Can you imagine some Englishman named Aubrey Tepley," he pronounced the name in a deep, mocking bass, "giving credit to a Boston Mick? In a pig's eye! You talk about your Secret Service! Your biggest case was like pissing in the Pacific compared with what I did for the English." He looked up at Horning with a maudlin smile. "Hey. I didn't mean that personally."

"Colonel Houlihan. You are a crock. And you *can* take that personally!" Horning shoved back his chair and rose unsteadily. Houlihan stared after him like a stunned ox.

Horning moved out of the club with excessively prudent steps and down a short road to the guard post, drinking deeply of the cold night air. The girl from the cashier's booth was standing there with her neck buried in the fur of an upturned collar. "It's so silly." Her English had a husky timbre. "I have no way to get home."

*

Horning woke up trembling. He pulled the odd cover over his naked body. It was a huge pillow, encompassing the entire bed and wonderfully warm. His head ached and his mouth was thickly coated. He stared at the wall. The room was neat to the point of sterility, and frigid. The girl was gone. He remembered only that she had begged him to be quiet during the night, though she had responded to him with shuddering cries.

He wondered if he was now alone in the house. He

forced his legs over the side of the bed. The door to the room was open. He walked to it. He peered down a wooden staircase as mercilessly scrubbed as the room. At the bottom, a stout woman with braided hair spied him and quickly turned her head aside. He returned and studied his face in the mirror above the dresser. His eyes were pouched. He needed a shave. It would have to wait until he returned to the hotel. He began to dress quickly. Horning shivered as the stiff coolness of his shirt touched his skin.

He spied a note on the dresser. He had difficulty with the looped, European hand, but made out ". . . return 2 P.M. You will wait, please. You are a beautiful man." It was signed "Gerda." He crumpled it and started to throw the paper on the floor, then stuffed it into his pocket.

When he reached the landing at the bottom of the stairs, the plump woman and a gaunt, middle-aged man were eating at a table. They did not look at him as he walked out.

8

GLUCKHERTZ WAS PREPARED FOR HIS VISITOR. He had hurried to Military Government in the Königsee Bürgermeister's office on getting word that the colonel wished to speak with him on the telephone. Houlihan, with scant subtlety, had reminded him that his party affiliation was no problem as long as he handled Horning right. Did he understand? Of course. He did understand.

In March of 1946, the Bonalpina was no longer the quaint billet of transient American officers. Most of the men who had passed through the summer before were now mustered out and back home. Alois Gluckhertz's clientele was

reduced to occasional GI skiers on leave and successful German black market entrepreneurs with a taste for alpine vistas.

He eagerly received this impressive fellow who informed
Gluckhertz that he was an official of the U.S. Secret Service.
Horning had emphasized that he was concerned only with
solving a counterfeit case. But Gluckhertz was not so easily
deceived. The words *secret service* had a clear and awesome
connotation to a German of Gluckhertz's generation.

He escorted Horning through the charred shell of his
storehouse and, with rolling eyes and exuberant gestures,
described that night the previous July.

"And that mouse, Werner. He was the cause of it all.
Now he is gone. It is over. Soon after, your army has, how did
they say, 'delisted' me from temporary BOQ. Ah!" He threw
up his hands in resignation. "Here you see me, Mr. Horning, a
poor innkeeper struggling to survive in this unfortunate
land." The face was that of a suffering, corpulent saint.

"But Erika? Your daughter?" Horning persisted.

Gluckhertz shook his head pitifully. "Mr. Horning. You
are a father?"

"No, I'm not."

"I raised that girl alone. I am a widower. I sent her off for
an education. That is not done among these mountain people.
What is my reward? She was poisoned by crazy Socialist ideas.
Her father was ..." He rolled disbelieving eyes, "a petit
bourgeois! That is what she called me. That was my reward."

"But where is she?"

"It is not surprising. But it breaks my heart. She has
disappeared, into the Soviet zone. Vanished. I wish I could tell
you more." The voice had a weary helplessness.

Horning searched the sweating face with its pitted, pig-
skin surface.

"And Colonel Houlihan ..." Horning began.

Gluckhertz interrupted. "A fine officer, a wonderful American."

"What was his relationship to Erika?"

"He did not know her. She was already gone that morning. Before sunrise. I learned later from one of my maids. She left before that fool, Werner. No. Colonel Houlihan never saw Erika."

Horning had a sense of doors slamming around him. He said nothing for a time. Gluckhertz remained the injured parent.

"Herr Gluckhertz. Let me ask you one more thing."

"Certainly. Anything I can do. I am at your command." He smiled an eager, pathetic smile.

"A picture. A photograph of your daughter?"

Gluckhertz did not stir immediately. He rubbed his hands together and pursed his lips. Finally he raised his heavy body from the chair. Horning followed him up a steep stairway and down a hallway into a bedroom. It was larger than the others in the inn, with a solid sense of permanence about it.

Gluckhertz pulled open the bottom drawer of a large oaken wardrobe. He quickly brushed aside a red and black armband, trying to conceal the swastika. He rummaged among old notebooks and drew out a large, embossed leather album.

He sat down on the bed. Horning hovered over him. He turned the black pages. Photographs, freed after years from dried mucilage, began to fall out. He settled on a page and began to extract from it a fuzzy picture of a girl who appeared to be about fifteen. Horning stayed his hand and went to a large head and shoulders shot, evidently of the same girl in her early twenties.

"This one will do fine, Herr Gluckhertz." He shoved it into his breast pocket. He studied the innkeeper's gross face and marveled at nature. Gluckhertz's daughter was an undeniably beautiful woman.

*

Horning fidgeted with the message. Cy Patterson's last words had particularly stung him. "Do you need any help?" He knew Patterson's unstated meaning. He could not blame him. Horning had just returned to Munich after three weeks in Berlin. The U.S. High Commission had been horrified at the thought of involving the Russians in a search for Erika Falkenhausen. His queries to the home office had produced the same caveat. Stay away. If the woman were in the Soviet zone and had the plates, it was too late. There was nothing to do but wait and try to contain the damage. Soviet cooperation in this matter, they told him, was laughable.

He wadded Patterson's message and flung it angrily and accurately into a wastebasket of the chilly hotel room. Obviously, he could not stay on indefinitely. The fragile chain of evidence had snapped at Königsee. Now Patterson was telling him, in effect, if you can't do it, let someone else.

He jumped up from the bed and brought his fist down with a resounding crack on the dresser. The glass top split the full width. He felt ridiculous. He would run out his last few desperate leads and then pack it in.

*

"Jesus, I'm sorry." Houlihan gave a mirthless laugh. "You really been bird-dogging it, haven't you? I figured you'd gone back home. Still here. And not a damn thing to show for it. That's too bad." They were sitting in the colonel's office, Horning having declined an invitation that they catch Happy Hour at the club.

Horning addressed him with painful civility. "Colonel, what do you make of Gluckhertz's story?"

"Oh, sure. Erika was that kind of dame. You know, lefty, pinko. A lot of them university krauts were Red until the Nazis took over."

Horning's eyes narrowed. Otherwise his face maintained a mask of sleepy ease. He rose lazily and extended his hand. "Sorry to put you to all this trouble, Colonel. You've been damned good about it."

"Hey, fella. What trouble?" Houlihan was now on his feet grinning broadly. Two large hands joined in a hearty, overly long shake.

"I'll be saying so long now." Horning waved and headed for the door. "Oh. Just one little thing. To kind of wrap it up. Gluckhertz gave me a picture of the woman. Would you take a look? Just for a confirmation?" He handed Houlihan a photograph.

Houlihan glanced at it. "Good-looking bitch. That's her, off with the Commies. Imagine!" He handed the photograph back. "You going back to the States now, Horning?"

Horning gave a slow smile. "I was. I don't know. I kind of got stuck on that Königsee country. I just might give it a few days more."

Houlihan smiled uneasily. "Great country."

Outside, Horning slid the photograph back into his billfold. He had shown Houlihan a picture of Sally.

*

Gluckhertz retreated backwards, stumbling over chairs, bobbing his head and grinning desperately. "What a pleasure to see you again, Mr. Horning. Such a pleasure." He caught himself as he started to fall over a table. Plates smashed onto

the floor. Still Horning moved relentlessly until Gluckhertz
was trapped against a wall. His eyes bulged as the powerful
hands gripped his neck.

"Where is she?" Horning rammed Gluckhertz's head
against the wall until the crockery perched on the carved
moulding began to crash down. "Where is she?" Gluckhertz's
head thudded after each repetition. Two chambermaids stood
in a doorway clapping their hands over their mouths, shrieking. Gluckhertz was too terrified to speak. Horning released
him.

He gagged and took in noisy gulps of air. He staggered
to a chair and collapsed into it. "I . . . Oh, God. Don't hurt
me, I don't know." Horning's fists moved toward him.
"Please. No! Believe me, Mr. Horning. I don't know."

"Who put you up to it? Why did you lie?"

"Please. Don't hurt me. I will tell you all I know."

"Talk, you stuffed Nazi sausage."

Gluckhertz's chest heaved uncontrollably. Horning
feared that the obese man's heart might fail.

"I have talked to my sister. Only she has seen Erika. But
that was nine months ago, the day. she ran off." He paused,
panting lugubriously. "Erika told Bertha she was going to
Munich. Believe me. That is all we know."

"Christ. Under my nose," Horning muttered as he
stormed out of the inn.

On his way out of town he called on Lieutenant
Wheeler at the Bürgermeister's. "Don't you know you got a
goddamned card-carrying party member up there?"

The bespectacled young officer flushed. "Why, yes, sir.
But Colonel Houlihan told us . . ."

"I can damn well imagine." He shook his head in
exasperation and left.

9

THE DERELICT, UNHEATED TRAIN FROM NUREM-
berg to Munich had taken four hours with two breakdowns en
route. The shabbiness of their dress and the apathy in the faces
of the passengers had depressed Kruger. That Germans should
be reduced to the same spiritless misery as Slav refugees he had
seen during the war pained him. All the more motivation to
press his mission.

All had not gone as expected. Months had passed since
the war had ended and still no clash of the West and the
Soviets. Instead, the Allies had joined to perpetrate what

Kruger saw as a *Justizskandal* against his countrymen.

Since November of '45, the surviving leaders of the Reich had been placed on trial in his own city of Nuremberg. War criminals, they called them. Kruger marveled at the depravity of the human mind. That patriots who had fought for their country should be tried by a court possessing no legal authority and treated like common criminals was to Kruger the ultimate war crime. Thank God, he thought, as the train rolled past the stricken land and shattered cities, the Führer had been spared this infamy.

At least, Kruger comforted himself, the Spiderweb was functioning. They had three working escape routes. Argentina had proved a paradise. A second line spirited people into the Middle East. The route through Italy and then by ship to Spain relied heavily on several abbeys run by Franciscan friars. The brothers helped out of a sense of Christian compassion. It was the least they could do, Kruger felt. They had done the same for the Jews during the war.

He imagined, as he shivered under his overcoat, his countrymen sunning themselves on Spain's Mediterranean shores. Still, someone had to carry on the work. Kruger had no complaint. The Jews had survived as a dispersed people for millennia. The party faithful could certainly do the same for a few years.

It had been no simple matter for Kruger to make the journey to Munich. He had quickly made himself indispensable to Major Kincaid. On his return in August of 1945, he had found Nuremberg much the same as other German cities. Streets were mere paths between the rubble. Almost nothing worked, not the postal service, streetcars, refuse collection. What did function had been monopolized by the victors. Phone lines were reserved to the military. Undamaged first-class railroad coaches were confiscated. The ancient coach Kruger was now riding to Munich had no doors and most of the windows were smashed. Fortunate Germans rode these rolling wrecks. Others thronged the roads atop farm wagons or on foot.

Allied military government officers searched desperately for Germans with administrative talent to impose order over this anarchy. Most experienced administrators were former party members and thus ruled out of all but menial jobs. Anti-Nazis who surfaced after the war proved largely to be cantankerous nonconformists or Communists. When a man of Kruger's executive talents appeared, bearing the coveted *Persilschein,* Major Cooley Kincaid recognized his good fortune. He had hired Wolf Kruger on the spot.

Kincaid's job was to allot the scarce resources of Nuremberg. In the winter of 1945–46, German coal production was a fraction of what it had been during the war. Whole carloads of fuel disappeared between one railyard and another. Wolf Kruger became Coal Allotment Administrator for the American Military Government of Nuremberg. He quickly demonstrated utter reliability and organizational flair. Major Kincaid came to depend on Kruger not only in parceling out coal, but wherever experience and judgment were demanded.

Kruger, after an initial wariness, had found Major Kincaid a man whom he could talk to with considerable openness. Kincaid had told him, early in their association, that he came from a part of the United States that understood the problems certain races could create. Mind you, he didn't endorse the German solution. But some people didn't fit. Why deny it?

"Why are the Americans so naive about the Russians?" Kruger had dared the question after a day in which he had pleased Kincaid by unearthing an extra hundred tons of coal for the officers' quarters.

"Damned if I know."

"I have always been amazed. The British, you Americans. You never understood that Adolf Hitler's cause was your cause. I remember," his eyes went dreamy, "we were sixty kilometers from Moscow. Can you imagine? Just sixty kilometers. I was there." He gazed at Kincaid with fierce pride. "What a world it would have been if we had succeeded. Bolshevism crushed!" He caught himself and spoke penitently. "I'm sorry. We Germans have no right to speak of politics now."

"Hell, man. Don't worry. Look. Back home we got Republicans and we got Democrats fighting over who gets the tit. Here it's Nazis and anti-Nazis. What's the difference? It's just politics."

"Major Kincaid, you are a philosopher of startling clarity." Kruger smiled.

His post with the Americans had bitten heavily into the time he could devote to the Spiderweb. But it had provided exceptional advantages now that the work was becoming increasingly difficult. Money was the crux, as the value of the Spiderweb's cache of reichsmarks continued to fall. The German currency now fluctuated between ten and twenty to the dollar. But, somewhere, there was an untapped fortune for the cause. He had never entirely abandoned the hope of finding it. He had written to that faithful fool, Nudelmann, in Königsee and learned roughly where to expect his prey.

He had been aware, on opening the trunk in Gluckhertz's storehouse that insane evening, that the American engravings were missing. He discovered, through Nudelmann, the abrupt and unexplained disappearance of Gluckhertz's daughter. Village speculation was that she had probably returned to Munich.

*

"Major Kincaid, this is the sort of matter I never wanted to trouble you about." Kruger stood rigidly, the faintest diffidence in the proud face.

"Come on in, Wolf." The drawling speech managed to stretch the name to three syllables. "What's up?"

"May I sit down?"

" 'Course."

"I hesitate to bother you with a personal matter."

"Don't mention it."

"Thank you. You are kind." He lowered his eyes and spoke quietly. "I have never had much family, Major Kincaid. I never married. I had but one brother and sister. They were both . . ." There was a faint catch in his voice. ". . . They died in American air raids."

The taut features of the Major softened. "War's hell. Both sides."

"Yes. So true." Kruger nodded. "All I now have left in this world is my niece, my sister's child. I have tried without success to locate her. The mails are still hopeless, as you know. Their home in Munich, in any case, was destroyed." He looked squarely into Kincaid's eyes. "I have no right to ask you this. But is it at all possible that you might help me to find her through your colleagues?" He smiled modestly.

Kincaid picked absently at his teeth with a fingernail. "Maybe we can do something. I suppose I could query Military Government in Munich. They could run a check on ration card holders there. Something like that."

Kruger brightened. "That would be terribly kind. It would mean so much to me."

"OK. Suppose you give me your niece's name, for starters."

Horning stood looking out the hotel window at Munich's streets in the gloom of early spring. He glanced down his rolled-up sleeve at powerful, hairy forearms. He laughed bitterly. Did Secret Service men, football stars, combat veterans get desperately lonely? Rather, were they permitted loneliness? No, he knew. They sauntered into barrooms, made quick friendships. Swapped tales of conquest. Boozed. Picked up women. Played cards. He had had his fill. Horning felt a deep, rootless longing. He hated the town. The country. Mostly its dour, defeated people. He wished he were . . . where?

He opened the window and let the cold, damp air assail him. On the street below he heard tipsy GIs haggling with whores.

"Du fucking cheap-shit-son-bitch-ass-hole. Shove your GI scrip! I take dollars, soldier!" The woman stomped off. A staggering GI shouted something incomprehensible after her. It amazed Horning. He had noticed the same thing in France, the quick ear of prostitutes for the vernacular. He slammed the window.

His memory leafed through an album of the dead. Delbert D. Perry, a goddamned kid, nineteen. Lived five miles from Horning's hometown. Freddy Dambrosi, the first New Yorker he had met in the outfit, a onetime piano player. Warren Bellerman, a whining pain in the ass. Always writing the Red Cross about a sick wife and two kids in some half-ass town in Illinois. All gone, along with a dozen others whose names had faded. Yet the faces were sharply etched in his mind, each in a frozen pose. This was what it had all been about?

He slumped down in a chair and buried his chin in his hand. Patterson was pressing again. Military Government had been useless in the quest for Erika. They told him that what he wanted did not involve them, it was an intelligence affair. How did he explain his reluctance to work through the Munich G-2 chief? What really did he have on Houlihan? Some lies. As much loathing as suspicion.

In the end, he had fallen back on a cop's elemental resources. The Munich phonebook, for one thing. In this case, an outdated edition where the numbers identified a heap of rubble more often than a building. Still, he had found something. And the next day he would make a last stab at "Falkenhausen, Dealers in Fine Art."

*

Major Kincaid had the telephone cradled between his neck and shoulder. His feet were on the desk, and with his free hands he thumbed through a shaggy copy of *Collier's* magazine.

"You heard me right, fellow . . . that's it . . . not a damn thing. I'm not going to do anything." His face flushed. He threw the magazine on the floor, sat upright, and seized the phone in his hand.

"I don't intend to do anything because you haven't given me one good reason why I should . . . that's why. Listen, friend. Herr Kruger is the best man I've got . . . I hear what you're saying. Then it's just your word against another officer in the U.S. Army.

"Look. You jokers may be having one hell of a time playing avenging angel. But we've got a real job here. We got five thousand Americans to run a zone with seventeen million people, not counting a couple of million pain-in-the-ass DPs. We're supposed to feed everybody, clothe them and house them in a country that's on its goddamned knees. . . .

"Hold on, man. Don't start giving me that music about

why we're here. I put more time in the front line than you put in the chow line. . . . Anyway, you're still giving me hearsay . . . I got a copy of a statement in my files by Third Army dated, Christ, nearly nine months ago, says this man was investigated and cleared. . . . Can't you understand? . . . He's denazified. Are you serious? If we got to fire every kraut who ever saluted Hitler, we'd have to wait for the next generation to grow up to run this country.

"You call that new evidence? Kruger's already told me everything you just told me. Yes. He said he was SD. That's intelligence, right? . . . Same thing as you're in, right? Come on. You're reaching now, aren't you? . . . An intelligence officer was gassing Jews? Listen, what's your name again? Kantrowitz. OK. Lieutenant Kan-tro-witz. You people are getting your pound of flesh. Every Nazi bigshot left in this country is on trial here at Nuremberg with his head in a noose. And there's some pretty smart lawyers who aren't sure these trials are what you'd call Kosher."

Kincaid swung his legs back onto the desk and twirled the long telephone cord with his free hand.

"That particular war is over now. We've gone into something else. Wait a minute. Don't try to tell me a Nazi is any worse than a Communist. . . . Of course, you might want to take exception."

He put his feet on the floor again. "You listen to me, Kan-tro-witz. We've got a country to build up here. And I'd damn well rather have sixty million tough krauts between us and the Commies than fill the jails with a bunch of ex-Nazis. Yes . . . that is my last word. Wolf Kruger stays on my payroll, unless you can produce something resembling evidence. Goodbye, Lieutenant."

Kincaid hung up the phone and muttered to himself. "Know-it-all Hebe sonofabitch."

10

NEVEGASSE HAD BEEN THE HEART OF JEWISH LIFE
in Nuremberg. It was not the street of Jewish bankers,
physicians and university intellectuals who had imagined
themselves assimilated into German society. Nevegasse was a
neighborhood of bakeries, tailor shops, of fishmongers and
small jewelers. It had been a ghetto perhaps, but an island by
choice rather than force where old patterns of life and belief
could endure.

When Julius Goldhammer arrived at Nevegasse in Feb-
ruary of 1946, it was a picked carcass. The shops were boarded
up. Smashed windows of abandoned flats and stores looked

out onto streets strewn with debris. Doorways hung from broken hinges and rattled as wailing winds blew through the streets.

Goldhammer picked his way through the shattered glass, moulding sofas, wheelless baby carriages, and splintered table legs. He spied a twisted menorah in an alley. He set down his cardboard suitcase and kneeled to the ground to pick it up. He wiped the dirt from its tarnished limbs and tucked it under his arm.

A handful of haunted old men and women moved silently through once teeming streets. Goldhammer tugged at the sleeves of strangers, asking for Chaim Katzman. He was met with suspicious stares and shrugging shoulders. Then an old woman mumbled directions.

Goldhammer stood before the corpse of a butcher shop. Loose slats hung from the boarded front. Goldhammer read the sign in Hebrew proclaiming the dead establishment and the name of its long departed proprietor. He tapped on the door leading to the flat above. Then pounded heavily. He shook the handle and the door swung open. He walked up the landing to another door. Its once polished surface was now peeling and the panels split as though someone had forced entry.

Goldhammer heard a droning from behind the door. The mournful incantation of the *maariv* struck him with almost unbearable familiarity. An image of his long dead father shot through his mind.

He rapped repeatedly on the doorway before the praying finally stopped, followed by shuffling footsteps.

The door opened a crack. "What do you want?" The flesh of the old man's face hung like a faded, wrinkled garment. The beard was a mat of yellow-white strands. The voice had the dryness of sand.

"I am Goldhammer. Julius Goldhammer. Your nephew, Jacob Edelmann, sent me. Did you get his message?"

The door opened wider. Chaim Katzman's frame was bent. He wore a frayed yet carefully pressed suit of dark serge with a tightly buttoned vest. In his hand he carried the siddur.

The old man had lost his wife and three sons to the death camps, Edelmann had told Goldhammer. He had survived because a favored customer of his tailor shop, a popular actor at the *Schauspielhaus,* had taken him in as his personal valet, in effect hiding Katzman to the end of the war.

The tiny figure motioned wordlessly for Goldhammer to follow him as he padded down a dim corridor. He fumbled for a key in a long leather purse.

The door opened on an airless, unlit room. Its only window was boarded. The old man groped about for a bead chain, and a single bulb glared from above. A huge chifferobe of a deep stain dominated one entire wall. The bed filled much of the rest of the room. It was covered with an aged, wine-red silk spread. Goldhammer was instantly uneasy. It was as though he had violated the sanctity of his mother and father's bedroom.

The old man grinned through spaced, yellow teeth and pointed to a corner of the room. Goldhammer saw a small enameled table, a chair, a gas stove and a water tap. Katzman bobbed his head eagerly and cited a price. Goldhammer nodded back absently and wandered to the boarded window through which a plane of bright sunlight shone. The old man trotted after him and Goldhammer turned to face an outstretched palm.

"Do you want American or gold?" Goldhammer asked it in Yiddish.

Katzman looked at him as though he were mad. "Gold!"

Goldhammer fished a gold piece from his pocket, which

he pressed into the old tailor's surprisingly firm hand. Katzman handed him the key and left him alone.

Goldhammer sat on the edge of the bed and stared into the heavy carved doors of the wardrobe towering over him. He pulled his suitcase onto the bedspread. He released the cheap, tinny catches and opened it. His hand rummaged slowly among the clothing until it withdrew a cold, hard object.

Goldhammer held the gun as though he expected it to explode. He had traded three of his cans of English tinned beef for it in the black market of Wiesbaden. The previous owner was a limping veteran who wore a shabby cloth cap of the Afrika Korps.

"Do you know what you're getting?" The man's voice had been reverent.

Goldhammer had stared at the weapon stupidly.

"It's a Walther PPK. A police pistol. The best made." The old soldier rubbed the wooden handle grip sensually. He opened the chamber. "Look. An eight-cartridge repeater." He grinned at Goldhammer.

"Will you show me, please, how to use it?" He had said it reluctantly.

Now, as he sat on the bed in which Chaim Katzman and his wife had conceived three sons, Goldhammer's thoughts turned to Lieutenant Kantrowitz. Surely that fine, strong young Jew would approve his decision.

Three weeks before, he had gone back to the Wiesbaden War Crimes Center to learn what the lieutenant had done with the information he had provided on Wolf Kruger.

Kantrowitz had seemed uncharacteristically subdued as he explained to Goldhammer his telephone conversation with Major Kincaid.

That the Americans had refused to take legal action against Kruger had driven Goldhammer to an insane fury.

But the latest information Kantrowitz provided, that the German had actually been hired by the Americans, transcended any outrage left in him. This knowledge had driven him at last to cold, clear-headed reason. There was no justice to be obtained in books, or laws, or courts. It was then that he had taken his tins of beef to the black marketeers of Wiesbaden.

He felt someone watching him and looked up to see the old man staring from the doorway.

"A Jew? A gun?" Katzman shook his head.

*

Erika had found him on her return from Dollmann's shop, a distinguished figure with his white, waving hair and casual bearing, chatting with the elderly concierge of her building. The concierge had evidently been quite taken by this gentleman, and on her arrival was earnestly confiding to Kruger that he had been the Party warden for the apartment house. "Spine of the movement!" Kruger had nodded gravely.

"This is the lady." The concierge nudged his visitor when Erika appeared.

Wolf Kruger rose immediately. He bowed and spoke in an elaborately courteous voice. "My dear Frau Falkenhausen. You must forgive the unexpected intrusion."

She was startled, yet disarmed by the courtly manner.

"Your father asked that I bring you news from home while I was in Munich. We are old friends, Alois and I." His smile revealed small, even, white teeth.

Erika's heart began pounding. Her throat tightened. "I'm afraid I'm terribly tired."

Kruger remained unruffled. "Of course, Frau Falkenhausen. Your father was especially eager to know if your marvelous engravings had arrived safely." He watched the color drain from her face.

The concierge strained to catch the flow of conversation. "Do you suppose we might chat for just a few minutes? The Café Mozart on the corner seems quite pleasant. I passed it on my way here."

Erika nodded numbly and turned to leave. The concierge raced ahead and opened the door, with a smile for Kruger.

She felt relieved that he chose a large, crowded place. Kruger guided her to a small table. He pulled out a chair for Erika, then sat down, studying her with an unremitting smile.

Kruger had long imagined himself possessing an attraction to women like that of a handsome priest, absorbed in his calling, seemingly inaccessible, and yet . . . to an enterprising woman? He acted on this image, not selfishly but to further his objectives. At times, both meshed happily. Here, with Erika, he felt the situation unfairly reversed. He gazed at her and he knew that he must discipline the fire she had stirred.

"I am a bachelor, you know."

She looked at him quizzically.

"Oh, I would have liked to marry, but it was quite impossible."

"Herr Kruger. What is it that you want of me?" She knotted her handkerchief endlessly.

The usually hard, glinting eyes were now wide open, taking in the outlines of her face. He sipped carefully at a glass of dark beer. "I was proprietor, with my brother, you see, of a pharmacy in Furth. We lost it during the Weimar Republic. That's right. I was once a simple druggist." He looked at her as though anticipating disbelief. "You are too young to remember those days. The party was my salvation. I have had little time for anything else. It is no exaggeration to say that the Party became my wife. I have been married to a cause." He turned his cupid-mouth smile on her, expecting to see some small disappointment in this hint of his unattainability.

Erika barely moved. She did not touch the *Cremeschnitte* he had insisted on ordering for her.

The bitch was not responding. Kruger's expression hardened. "And now, restoring the party and my country are the sole objects of my life." Quickly the softer manner returned. "That, my dear, is why it is so important that we talk."

She dared not look directly at him.

"Frau Falkenhausen. I am a simple man. Contrivance is not my style. You are an intelligent woman. You have something in your possession that is vital to our cause." He could not help himself. He saw her hand trembling and took it tenderly into his own. "Now, now. You must trust me."

"Why?" she murmured, withdrawing her hand.

"Why? Because I can help you ... or I can hurt you." His eyes chilled her.

"What is it you want of me?"

"What you took from Königsee."

"I took nothing from Königsee."

He looked pained. "I told you, Frau Falkenhausen, I am a direct man. I know about the contents of your father's storehouse. Indeed, I was responsible for their being there."

Her throat ached. She had difficulty speaking. "And suppose I go to the authorities. To the Americans?"

He laughed. "You are such a beautiful young woman. And clearly not stupid. Let us look at your alternatives clearly. What will you do with this advantage you possess? Will you actually deal with the Americans? Let us assume they are grateful. They give you a reward. Perhaps a thousand American dollars. Oh, yes. And a position selling cigarettes at one of their post exchanges." He sniffed. "Let us consider a second

possibility. The Americans become suspicious. Ungrateful.
They investigate you. They confiscate the engravings and jail
you."

Erika felt a fierce tension hammering against her forehead.

"I haven't finished the possible alternatives, my dear. Let
us say you displease our organization by refusing to help." His
face assumed a musing malice. "You know, this business has
already cost the life of one foolish young man. It was quite
sad."

He sat back, arms folded. "Or, you may quite simply
turn over the engravings to me. Never mind that you will be
doing it for the Fatherland. I do not try to move you with that
argument. But you will be well taken care of. I personally
would see to that." He turned an admiring smile on her, and
briefly the hard, agate eyes were again idolizing.

She raised her head and looked directly at him. She
managed a firmness in her voice, although her heart was
thumping and her legs beneath the table twitched involun-
tarily. "You must come to this place two nights from now, at
the same time. You will bring me five hundred gold Napo-
leons. I will accept nothing less. Then, you shall have what
you want."

Kruger studied the lovely face with its mouth now set so
determinedly. "You are as wise as you are beautiful. I shall
keep my end of the bargain. However, if you do not keep
yours . . ." The smile now suggested shark's teeth, and he
shook his head as though shuddering at the alternative.
Kruger rose, reached into his pocket, and deposited a small
pile of reichsmarks on the table. He moved quickly out of the
café, while Erika fought to subdue her trembling body.

*

"My dear Helga, I am not sure that was at all wise." Dr. Falkenhausen frowned deeply, the gray moustache bristled his disapproval.

Frau Falkenhausen viewed the stern face with amused tolerance. "My dear Friedrich. What did you expect? You were not in town when he called at your studios. He was insistent. He came directly here. And he *is* an official. In present circumstances, would it have been wise to refuse to see him?"

Her husband sat down opposite her. A servant entered. "Would Herr Doktor care for something before dinner?"

Falkenhausen shook his head and dismissed the man with a wave of his hand. He did not speak again until the servant was gone. "That is not my point. You are quite aware."

His unrelenting rectitude was testing her nonchalance. "She can't have been up to any good, could she? And so I told this Horning fellow that we had not seen her for years. Since Erik died. Why else would the American authorities want her? I can't imagine how our getting involved could help."

"I have always respected that young woman. I felt a certain affection, too."

"Nonsense, Friedrich. We hardly knew her." Frau Falkenhausen's handsome features hardened.

"Yes. You made quite sure of that."

"You know as well as I that she was not for Erik." Her eyes filmed. "Ah, so impetuous." She dabbed at her eyes lightly with a handkerchief. "I am truly sorry if I have handled it poorly. Nothing prevents you from informing the Americans that your foolish wife made a mistake." She looked at him with a helpless smile.

"That would certainly make us look foolish." He rose and paced the room with his hands linked behind him. "No.

We will do nothing more. It is done. We leave the matter
where it is."

*

Kruger pulled the concierge's shirtfront into a tight
knot and shoved the old man against the wall. "What are you
talking about?" His voice had a low, rasping menace.

"I don't know. The landlord is angry with me, too.
Yesterday morning she was gone. Her clothes. Everything.
Without a word." The man's eyes bulged. His unshaven jaw
quaked. "I have no idea what has become of Frau Falkenhausen."

Kruger suddenly remembered the roses for her, still
clutched in his other hand. He mashed them into the concierge's face and stormed toward the door.

*

Horning could delay no longer. The trail was not simply
cold. It was dead. The day before, he had paid a final call on
Colonel Ferretti, deputy to the chief of Military Government
for Munich.

"Look, Ferretti, I'm not that long out of the game
myself. I know all about channels and chickenshit. I played
the game for forty-four months."

Ferretti was a large, rough man with a rumpled, genial
manner. They had played against each other once on a long-
ago Saturday afternoon. "What was your outfit, George?"

"First Army, First Div."

"Oh, man. Omaha Beach. The Bulge. Remagen."

"You got it. The works. Look, Pete. You know I've been
here on a hell of a sensitive matter. My ass is riding on this
one." He found his speech slipping into the good-ole-boy
cadence that amused and disarmed Northerners. "I surely wish
I could give you a little more of the details. I just can't. I only

ask you this. I know you got to go by the book. Just add another page for me. If any leads come through Military Government, just let us know at the same time you inform G-2. All right? Will you advise Secret Service in Washington?" He gave a big, sheepish grin. "I guess that is asking a special favor. But I sure as hell will appreciate it."

The colonel's large jaw worked rapidly. Finally he nodded. "OK. Will do."

Horning rose and put out his hand to Ferretti's. He slapped the other man on the back. "That's damn white of you, Pete." He couldn't remember the last time he had used the expression. "I'll be at the Vier Jahreseitzen at least one more day, tying up some loose ends before I head home. You stop by. Y'hear? I'll buy you a drink. Hell, I'll buy you a whole dinner." They grinned like mutually respectful opponents after a tough game.

*

The loose ends were tied up, quite literally. Horning tugged at the leather straps of his last suitcase. He tossed it from the bed to the floor and went to the telephone.

"Will you get my bill ready, two-twelve? And have someone up here to bring the bags down. Right. Thanks." He slipped on his jacket and went to the window. It was late afternoon. The sun was setting behind gutted buildings, and its red-yellow glow shone hellishly through empty windows. On the street people moved along, shoulders hunched, pace rapid as though trying to escape the grimness.

Horning was making a last-minute check of the closet. There was a light tapping at the door. "Come in."

"Herr Horning."

He turned around, expecting the bellman.

The voice was deep and musical. "I am Erika Falkenhausen."

*

Kruger had terrified Erika to the marrow. She had passed
the night after seeing him in sleepless dread. She knew she
would find no peace until she had rid herself of the plates,
though it could never be through the Nazis. Still, she felt a
self-loathing at her reluctance to exploit her advantage. That
little fool, Werner, would have been more cunning. Would
she now simply throw herself onto the mercy of the Americans? She thought of the hateful Kruger's warning. And even
if the Americans welcomed her cooperation, what would have
been the point of it all? The day after, she would still be
selling Dollmann's precious junk.

She resolved the matter as impetuously as she had entered into it. She had set out for the main Munich headquarters of Military Government with no clear idea of what might
happen next. She had to get herself under a protective wing.
She knew that. If she could turn the occasion to profit as well,
so be it.

The Americans had taken over the partially restored Nazi
Party Administrative Building on Bienerstrasse. She remembered long ago the cool disgust of Erik's father in describing
these brute edifices. "Troost's tombs" he had called them, after
their creator, Hitler's pet architect. She was directed by a fresh-
faced American MP to the Führer Building across the street.
As she walked the wide, scarred avenue, she remembered that
a tunnel ran beneath it connecting the two main buildings. It
had been the refuge of Party bigwigs during the great air raids,
a deep, safe shelter, barred to ordinary civilians.

"Help you, Ma'am?" The soldier sat behind a lone desk,

shrunken and incongruous in the massive, echoing foyer.

On entering the building, she had seen a directory posted on a wall and had randomly chosen a name near the top. She gave it to the soldier.

"Up the left-hand stairway. You got to hike it to the third floor. Elevator's still kaput."

She passed what had once been the office of the Führer's adjutant. Now an American general's name graced the doorway. She entered the anteroom. A GI slouched at a desk working a crossword puzzle.

"He's up in Augsburg today. Was he expecting you?"

Erika spoke with cool confidence. "Then I will see his assistant."

"His deputy," the soldier-receptionist corrected. "Colonel Ferretti. He's two doors down on the right."

The officer had greeted her amiably. Her name was instantly familiar to him. "I got somebody who's going to be pleased to meet you, pretty lady. But you're going to have to hurry to catch him."

Ferretti had asked few questions of her. She left to find Horning with her options still agreeably open.

*

Why did she have to be dressed so wretchedly? The thought had flashed through her mind the instant he opened the door. She wore a once stylish gray gabardine suit, the lapels now limp from repeated cleanings.

Horning found her attractiveness disconcerting. "I think we better talk downstairs." His usual easy manner had turned self-conscious. "The hotel restaurant is quiet now." They stepped out of the grilled elevator cage. Horning excused himself and went to the desk, where he quietly informed the clerk to hold his room.

The maitre d', in shabby, shining black, shrugged imperceptibly at the untimely arrival. Odd, these Americans. He showed them to a table next to a window overlooking the street. "Just have the waiter bring us a couple of drinks." He looked at Erika. "Scotch?" She nodded.

Outside the passersby clutched their collars against the chill. The women wore heavy stockings and bulky coats. Most of the younger men wore some remnant of shapeless field gray, still looking to Horning much like the endless files of defeated Wehrmacht he had seen along the autobahn in those last weeks of the war.

He turned his gaze from the window after the waiter set the drinks down and left. "Fraulein Falkenhausen." He eyed her intently. "Do you want to start?"

"Frau."

"Yes. Excuse me. Frau."

The dreary room accented the gray cast of her eyes. Her face appeared calm, but she tortured a napkin endlessly.

"I can help you." She said it quietly, eyes downcast.

"Oh, I'm sure you can." The sarcasm was genial.

"You are looking for something, no?"

Horning smiled tolerantly.

"I know someone who perhaps can help you find what you want."

"Frau Falkenhausen, I'm a country boy. No games, OK?"

She blushed.

"Do you have the plates?"

The blush deepened. She was now twisting the napkin furiously. She set it aside, almost as an act of will, and firmly pressed her hands into her lap. "I know someone who perhaps can lead you to them."

"How do you know about all this?"

She lowered her eyes again. The lids formed delicate almond ovals. "I learned of it from an SD driver. I knew him briefly at the end of the war."

"I see." Horning nodded sagely. "He has them?"

"I would have to find out. Perhaps."

"Frau Falkenhausen. Why have you come to us? It might create problems for you. For your friend."

"Problems? Why problems?" Her eyes widened. She was twisting the napkin again. "I thought you would appreciate help."

Horning gave her a mysterious half smile. "How do you want that appreciation expressed?"

She turned away from his insistent gaze and did not answer.

"Who is this man who can help us?"

She looked at him uneasily. Her voice wavered. "I prefer not to compromise him."

"Come on." He raised his brow in mild impatience. "If you want us to appreciate your help, let's have some evidence of good faith."

She found a compelling force in the man's deep, soft-cadenced speech. She was drawn to the rugged features, the intelligent eyes. She felt a powerful inclination to abandon the game. Still, he had spoken of appreciation. She must go on. "What does it matter? But, if you must know, his name is Werner."

"First or last?"

"Werner Goren."

Horning broke into a slow smile. He shook his head. "Frau Erika Falkenhausen. You're a beautiful woman, but a terrible liar."

Her eyes darted quickly. "I'm afraid I don't understand."

"No?" His smile took on a mocking edge. "Your friend,

the one who is going to help us, Frau Falkenhausen, Werner
Goren. He's dead."

She made a soft, painful moan. Her head sank. Her hands trembled.

"I'm sorry," Horning said, wondering why he should be. This elegant lady had lied in her teeth. Her obvious humiliation touched him, he supposed. "All right. Suppose we start over."

She nodded wanly. Her eyes were now closed.

*

He surprised her. Outwardly, he seemed the sort of American she had known at the Bonalpina, the lightly carried masculinity, the offhand manner, the familiarity toward clerks and waiters. Under the casual surface, he had proved a relentless prosecutor. She felt wrung out. "And now what will you do with me?"

"Or for you? You mean our appreciation?"

A proud anger flashed across her face. "That is not what I meant. I have asked for nothing. I only wish I had known how. I am useless for that sort of thing."

Horning's searching eyes appeared to be gauging her sincerity.

"You must understand, Mr. Horning. I am a frightened woman. I expect no gain from you. But what of my life? Need I tell you, these are dangerous people."

Horning leaned back and drummed his fingers on the table. "Why didn't you come forward before? What was your angle?"

She closed her eyes and breathed slowly and deeply. "I think this is hopeless." She made as if to leave. Horning motioned her back into her chair.

"Will you make me a common thief?" The lovely gray-green eyes flared. "I don't believe you understand. We are a defeated nation, a broken people. We have nothing. Everything has been destroyed. Our wealth, our pride. I think your people have little idea what war really is."

In her mounting excitement she did not notice Horning's jaw setting grimly.

"I was looking for security. Something that could save me in this . . ." she gestured helplessly, "this graveyard."

The soft accents vanished. His voice became tight, harsh. Horning spoke through nearly clenched teeth. "Who made it this way? Who asked for it? And what the hell makes you think I don't know about this war?" He jabbed a finger out the window. "Somewhere out there in this hellhole there's some men I knew. They never wanted to come here. They were fine where they were. They came here and they died because of your poor, poor, suffering Germany." He stopped short, embarrassed by the outburst. It was not his style.

They avoided each other's eyes.

When Erika next spoke, it was in quiet, measured tones. "I do not question what you say. No German has that right. But we are human, Mr. Horning, believe me. We are as strong and weak, as selfish and unselfish as any others. Just as you and I can make a shameful, terrible mistake, so can a nation. But you must not think, Mr. Horning," her voice broke, "that it is somehow less painful to lose those you have loved because the cause was not noble. That is a terrible reason for a beautiful life to be wasted. It increases our pain. It does not make it less."

Horning found himself unwillingly transfixed by the beauty deepened now by her evident pain. His emotions battled within him. His mind conjured up and quickly dismissed a vacuous image of Sally.

Erika slumped back. "Then I can expect no protection

from you now that you have learned what you wanted? I am simply to walk back into the street?"

"You'll be taken care of, safe quarters." He answered gruffly.

They sat without speaking for several moments.

Guests had begun to drift into the crystal-chandeliered dining room. Horning's eye idly traced deep clefts wrought by American bombs in the carved ceiling. The guests were high-ranking American officers, occupation officials, diplomats. A few were elderly Germans. Horning was amused by their stiff Bismarckian posture.

He watched Erika follow the waiters' trays from the corner of her eye.

"Hungry?"

She smiled and nodded.

"I guess you've sung for your supper."

The smile disappeared instantly. "That is not a very pretty phrase."

Horning regretted it. He signalled a waiter.

Conversation during the meal was desultory. How far was Muhlbach? What was the best way there? How long would it take? Should she contact her aunt?

When the dinner was over, Horning asked, "I suppose you're worried about going back to your room?"

She found his expression curious, but smiled openly for the first time.

"I must confess to you, I am frightened to death." She laughed playfully. "Will you put me in your American jail?"

"You don't have to worry about going back. You'll stay with me tonight."

She eyed him coldly. "I am afraid, Mr. Horning, you have misjudged me badly."

11

GLUCKHERTZ COULD HEAR THE ELEGANT HUM of the engine before the automobile came into view. The sight of it brightened him. He stood alone on the balcony of the Bonalpina. The inn was virtually deserted. An unaccustomed shabbiness veiled the exterior. Nothing so fine as the approaching Daimler Benz had arrived since long before the end of the war. Gluckhertz's vocational smile began to wreathe his beefy face.

And then it froze. A tall, powerful-looking man emerged from the driver's side. His passenger was Wolf Kruger.

Kruger spotted Gluckhertz and waved gaily as he got out of the car. He pounded his chest and breathed in the cool alpine air. He took bounding steps up to the balcony. "Gluckhertz! My dear fellow. How good it is to see you again. Allow me to present my colleague. Untersturmführer Feuerbach." Gluckhertz felt his pudgy hand crushed in the man's grip. The hair was close shaven at the temples. The face had a chilling vacuousness. The dull blue eyes seemed to see nothing.

Gluckhertz's rictus grin remained in place. But he could not speak.

"Ah. My good man." Kruger was gazing out over the blue-gray lake flanked by plunging walls of stone. Again he pounded his chest and exhaled noisily. "One forgets the beauty of this country too easily. Extraordinary. It is simply extraordinary." He turned to the innkeeper. "Aren't you going to ask us in?"

The words tumbled out with a frantic gaiety. "But of course, Herr Doktor. It is just . . . I am so surprised. And . . . and so pleased. Yes, of course, pleased." He was hopping about in an aimless frenzy. "May I take your bags? That is, if you are staying. Will you be with us a few days?"

"Ah, no. I fear not. But we would be delighted if you could serve us a modest lunch"—he gave Gluckhertz a smile of dazzling menace—"and help us with a few matters. Then we shall be on our way."

*

Gluckhertz uncorked and placed the second bottle of Auslese on the table. Feuerbach had consumed the first steadily, morosely, almost alone. Kruger's glass was still half full. Gluckhertz had rushed about fussily, preparing and serving the meal himself. He had quickly produced a heaping *Berner Platte,* steaming mountains of sauerkraut capped with chops, bacon, beef, and sausages. This too Feuerbach consumed with a methodical absence of pleasure. Kruger ate heartily, savoring the dish and lavishly complimenting the chef.

Kruger patted his heart-shaped mouth with a frayed napkin. "And now, Otto, will you please move down? I want our friend, the good Zellenleiter, to join us." He gestured Gluckhertz to take the seat that Feuerbach hastily vacated. The innkeeper sat down uneasily between them.

"Business could be better, my friend, couldn't it?" Kruger oozed sympathy.

Gluckhertz shrugged and threw up his hands. "One hopes for better times."

"I am afraid your Americans were fickle friends."

A lumpy peasant woman appeared and began to clear away the dishes. Kruger's small, hard blue eyes darted about the room. "Who else is here?"

"Only her. Unfortunately, I don't need much help at the moment."

Kruger smiled pleasantly. "My good woman, please leave us alone for a while. Go on about your business somewhere else."

She scampered off like a chased cat.

"Your daughter, dear Gluckhertz. She is not with you, either?"

The perspiration was now running freely down the innkeeper's face. When he spoke, the voice was reedy and uncertain. "I have not seen my daughter since . . . for almost a year."

"How difficult that must be for a father." Kruger shook his head as the cold eyes continued to drill Gluckhertz. "Where is she these days?"

"I tell you the truth, Herr Doktor Kruger. I have not seen my daughter nor have I had one word from her in all this time. I have no idea where she is."

Kruger's eyes switched quickly to Feuerbach. The younger man's body tensed and his long hands moved to the table. Gluckhertz caught their movement from the corner of his eye. Kruger made a barely perceptible nod of the head. Instantly Gluckhertz's arm was twisted behind his back. His cry was stifled by Feuerbach's other arm hooked around his throat. His eyes bulged and rolled crazily.

Kruger leaned his face close to Gluckhertz, almost hissing as he spoke. "What did your daughter do with the plates?" Feuerbach tightened the arm another notch. Gluckhertz tried to move his lips, but no words came.

Kruger motioned to Feuerbach, who released the grip slightly.

"Believe me." Gluckhertz was gasping desperately. "I don't know anything you are talking about." Feuerbach jerked the arm up sharply. Gluckhertz let out a piercing shriek. "I don't know! I don't know!"

The voice was now pitiful and whimpering. Tears streamed down his cheeks. "Please." The words struggled from his throat. "Please. Let me go. I will talk."

Kruger nodded to Feuerbach.

Gluckhertz slumped back in the chair, wheezing noisily, clutching at his heart. The stout body trembled. "She left the morning after the fire. I never have had a word from her since then. I don't know if she is dead or alive."

"She lives. I can assure you." Kruger said it with a vague disgust. "But, go on. I want you to trace her movements after the fire."

"I know only this. She went first to my sister."

"Where?"

"To Muhlbach."

"How do you know that?" Kruger snapped at him.

"Erika spent only one night with her. Then left. Bertha became worried. So she wrote to me."

"She went to Muhlbach. So remote. For one night? Muhlbach." Kruger mused aloud.

He was suddenly affable again. "This sister of yours, dear Gluckhertz. What is her name?"

On the way out, Kruger drew a wad of reichsmarks from his pocket and threw several large notes on the table. "Excellent lunch, Herr Zellenleiter. Really, the Americans were quite foolish to abandon you." He smiled.

*

The MP checked Horning's credentials with maddening thoroughness.

"Something wrong, Sergeant?"

"No sir. But we don't get many civilians. OK. Looks fine." He handed back the leather billfold, which Horning replaced in his breast pocket. In the meantime, a stream of uniformed Americans filed into the train, casually waving papers at the MP.

Horning took Erika by the arm and started to help her aboard.

"Just a minute, sir. She going, too?"

Horning exhaled his impatience. "She's a material witness in an investigation. And if we don't get aboard soon, we're not going to make it." The train had indeed started to move. The MP looked appreciatively at Erika and gave Horning a knowing smile.

Most of the passengers were young replacement officers going to take up occupation duties in Innsbruck, Salzburg, and Vienna. They too eyed Erika. But an unspoken authority in Horning's bearing kept their glances chaste.

They entered a compartment where three young men and a grizzled tank corps major were sitting together. The major began to move to the other side of the compartment so that Erika and Horning could sit together.

"That's all right, Major." Horning waved him back and sat next to the man. Erika sat on the other side next to a towheaded second lieutenant who made Horning feel suddenly ancient.

The two officers facing each other nearest the door quickly resumed a gin game, which from their pattern of bickering appeared to have started somewhere in the States.

"Play a few hands, fellow?" The major spoke to the young blond officer next to Erika. He asked it with a hearty bluffness. His left breast pocket was a mosaic of ribbons and battle stars. Horning read the man instantly. Commissioned out of the ranks. Enjoyed hell out of the war. Found a home in the army.

The young officer answered shyly. "I'm sorry, sir. I don't know how."

A faint trace of disbelief crossed the major's eyes.

"Deal."

The major looked to see Horning smiling broadly at him. "Goddamn. That's more like it." He reached into a back pocket and produced a veteran deck.

Horning pulled a sheet of paper from his briefcase. "What's your name, and what's the stakes?"

"Spriggs. Penny a point."

"Major Spriggs. You're on."

Erika studied the masculine interplay. Horning was obviously on familiar terrain. In her distraction she did not hear the blond lieutenant at first.

"What is that?"

"I asked if you were American?" he repeated. "I guess you're not." He checked Horning out of the corner of his eye and smiled at Erika with the expression of a small boy daring big game. Horning appeared oblivious of the young soldier's attention to her.

"It's beautiful country." The young officer looked off in the direction of the distant Kitzbüheler Alps.

She laughed lightly.

"Why are you laughing?"

"Oh. Nothing. I never hear any of your people confess that." She looked reflexively toward Horning. "Where are you from, Lieutenant?" He answered, and soon they were engaged in animated conversation.

As Erika and the officer chatted, Erika and Horning occasionally stole wordless glances across the compartment. She had enchanted the kid. Horning could see that.

The train crawled into the Rosenheim station where Erika and Horning would switch to a small trunk line to Muhlbach. She rose and extended her hand to the young officer, who was looking at her with adoring eyes. "And I want you to promise me, before you return home, that you will learn to speak German."

"Ja, Ja. Ich ... werde ... Deutsch sprechen." He pumped out the words with labored eagerness.

Horning was extracting several bills from his wallet, which he handed to the major. "Damn expensive ride, Spriggs."

The older officer gloated contentedly. "It sure bothers me to clean out an old ground pounder." They laughed and clapped each other on the back.

*

The Rosenheim station still bore its war wounds. Erika and Horning made their way over the main track and through temporary underpasses to a crumbling platform where they would catch the next train. Overhead, the sky had become an unlovely black.

Horning was the only American at the station, except for a lone MP at the end of the platform. He felt the sullen, oblique glances of the other travelers, sitting in dour silence on broken benches.

The women, their heads wrapped in kerchiefs, had a resolute dowdiness. The men, whatever their age, wore the inevitable cast-off military garb mixed with rumpled civilian clothes. Horning, an indifferent dresser, felt conspicuously elegant. Erika was the object of disapproving stares. She maintained an unconcern that Horning admired.

"Hey! Joe! Look." The boy was no more than fifteen, with a wizened, unsentimental face and the lightest hair Horning had ever seen. He hobbled toward them on a crutch, his empty left pant leg pinned at the knee. He wore a bulging Eisenhower battle jacket and one combat boot. He unbuttoned the jacket to reveal the corner of a camera. "Rolleiflex! What you say, *mein Herr?* One carton?" The accent was comic opera.

"You better go play somewhere else, Fritz." Horning gestured up the platform to the American MP. *"Polizei."*

The boy laughed coarsely. "That *schmutzig* son of a bitch MP? I just sell him a nice Luger. Gives me a lousy pound of coffee. Come on. What you say? Beautiful camera. *Schöen, nein?"* He begged Erika in German to tell this rich bastard what a deal he was getting.

Erika studied the warped near-child with maternal longing. She looked at Horning. "Is he guilty, too?"

The boy stared at both of them blankly. "Rolleiflex. The best. *Verstehen Sie?*"

"No sale, Fritz. Beat it." Horning smiled good-naturedly and tossed the boy a cigarette. He lunged for it, but his crutch restricted his reach. It fell to the ground. Erika picked it up and handed it to him with a smile.

He looked puzzled, then broke into a grin. "No sale?" He laughed. *"Ja, ja.* No sale." He savored the sound. *"Das ist gut!* I like, 'no sale!' " He rebuttoned his jacket and thumped down the platform out of sight.

In half an hour, the train arrived. It was now raining heavily.

*

It was a third-class coach with wooden benches and no window left unviolated. The cars still bore the splintered punctures of aerial strafing. Yet the scarred and limping machinery was immaculate.

The passengers gave Horning and Erika a wide berth, staring at her with malevolent eyes.

"The left side, please." Erika said it with pretended Teutonic authority.

"Why?" He reacted with slight irritation.

"So that you can better see the Inn."

"What Inn?"

She smiled tolerantly. "The Inn River. It is quite beautiful. Please, you sit by the window."

The marshy southern reaches of Rosenheim gave way to gentle rises, then to sharply mounting ranges. As the terrain became more rugged, it reminded Horning of the hill country of his native Tennessee.

They had spoken little since leaving the hotel in the afternoon. Horning had gone off earlier in the morning to get

the authorization and arrange tickets for the journey to
Muhlbach. Before leaving, he had first tapped at Erika's door, which adjoined his room. The clerk had assumed he was to make that arrangement.

Horning had been struck by the effect of a night's sleep on her. Her face, beautiful but tormented the night before, was refreshed and radiant.

"Yes?"

He had stared at her blankly. "I just . . . "

She had regarded him with amusement. "You just wanted to be sure I was still here. Really, Mr. Horning. I have no place to go. I am your prisoner." She had smiled with no particular joy.

He had looked chastened. "I'll be back in about three hours. Can you be ready?"

*

The train made a stop at a town called Brannenburg. "How much longer?" he asked.

"Not more than fifteen minutes, I should imagine. If we don't break down again." She leaned back as comfortably as the unyielding bench permitted. "It is all so familiar to me. I remember coming here in better times. To visit Tante Bertha. You will like her. She has not had an easy life. Yet her spirit is so strong. She is everybody's *Mutti*."

Horning found himself drawn into the melodious orbit of her voice.

"Her oldest son, Lothar, was in Munich, a student, when I was there. I thought my cousin the most handsome boy. He was quite brilliant. He won the *Preis Universität* for architecture. Lothar wanted to build churches. He had the idea that he could take Gropius's concepts . . ." She turned to him. "What does it matter. I am sure this is not of interest to you."

Horning had been studying the way her hands moved in patterned gestures when she spoke. "Where is he now?"

"He died at Stalingrad. Two months later his younger brother was killed in Africa. Walther had been a medical student.

"My aunt was badly shaken. But it did not break her. I suppose that is why I am so important to her. She always made a terrible fuss over me, even as a little girl. She had no daughter. I was always so happy to visit her. My mother died while I was a student at the university. After that I spent all my holidays with Tante Bertha rather than face Papa and his Party friends." She shuddered. "God. They were awful. Pigs with power."

"Then Gluckhertz was a Nazi."

She laughed. "A Nazi? He would have been a Monarchist, a Free Mason, a Mohammedan. Whoever paid the piper. Although I think there was something in the way the Nazis bullied people that appealed to him."

Horning shook his head. "This was supposed to be a civilized country. I don't understand."

"Oh, it was quite simple. Hitler may have been a swine . . ."

He stared at her, startled to hear the words from a German.

"But he was a genius. Can you imagine finding out that someone else is responsible for all your troubles?" She made a sweeping gesture with her hand. The rumpled figures in the car watched her with mute hostility. "All the rotten things that happened to you, someone else was to blame. The terrible Allies after Versailles. The filthy Bolsheviks. And, of course, the Jews." She looked at him, smiling ruefully. "Brilliant? Don't you agree?"

Horning again shook his head.

She looked out the window. "We will be there soon. You have brought an appetite, I hope."

"Oh?"

"Oh, yes. Tante Bertha will fold her arms over her huge bosom and she will say, 'that young man must have some *Zellerschwartzkatz.*' Then she will set a cool pitcher before you. I assure you, it is delicious wine. Then, while she warms the potato dumpling soup, she will set out a thick *Landjäger* and some *Leberkäse* with the bread she makes herself."

"What happened to the war?" Horning was now smiling warmly at her.

"It was quite different in these country towns. They felt nothing. Oh. Perhaps a village or two at the very end. In fact, our beloved Führer kept most of the home front happy too, until your bombers spoiled it."

Erika felt the pressure of Horning's shoulder against her and did not move. By the time they pulled into the station at Oberaudorf, they were laughing easily.

Outside the rain was descending in cold sheets. "Maybe we can get a taxi?" Horning turned up his collar against the driving dampness.

She looked at him as though he were a foolish child. "Taxi! Come along." She took him by the hand. "It is only one kilometer to Muhlbach. We can walk."

Their shoes were quickly soaked through. The rain made great swelling stains on the shoulders and down the backs of their clothes. It was still early evening, but the glowering skies had obscured all light. They passed a few villagers on the unlit streets who invariably turned to stare after the strangers. To Horning, Muhlbach in the rain, with its distinctive roof and spires, was a macabre Bavarian tableau.

"There it is." Erika pointed off to a house on the edge of the village. Its façade made a lonely silhouette against the horizon. Horning could make out a dim, yellowish light in an upper story.

Erika held Horning's hand more tightly. "It looks so still." The rain had matted their hair and trickled down their faces. She felt a quick shiver under her drenched clothes.

Erika hesitated before the door, looking about uneasily. She reached for a chain that rang a cowbell hanging above the doorway. She paused, then rang again, then again. Horning tested the latch and the door creaked open. A pale, thin light streamed down a staircase.

They walked in and Erika turned on a lamp. They were in a large, warm, solid room with dark-stained, heavily crafted furniture.

"Tante Bertha!" Erika called out in earnest cheeriness. "Tante! It is me, Erika." She looked to Horning, puzzled.

"Wait here," he ordered. Horning went noiselessly up the stairway and disappeared from Erika's view. She went after him. As she reached the top, Horning was already coming back. She saw his face and stifled a sharp gasp with the back of her hand. He was ashen.

"Don't come any further. Go back downstairs. I'll be down in a minute." His voice was dry and toneless. He went back and retraced his steps to the attic.

The woman's gray hair was tightly braided, giving her the aspect of an old child. A few white hairs spiked a mole on her chin. She lay on her back, her hand still clutching the tan valise. It had been ripped open and was empty. Her throat was bright crimson from ear to ear.

*

The wind was sharp and biting on the rock-strewn hillside next to the church. The wind knifed through the mourners. Murder made for large funerals, he thought. The language of the priest, uttered in the local dialect, struck Horning as less harsh than what he had been accustomed to in Germany. The Catholic service here in Bavaria surprised him. She was right. He knew nothing of the country.

With the funeral over, the few intimate friends of the widow came by and expressed sympathy to Erika, giving Horning suspicious glances as they departed. She had managed a black veil, but otherwise wore what she had on the journey from Munich. She met each mourner with simple dignity. Her quiet grief gave her beauty a haunting quality.

Horning feared Tante Bertha's violent end might have shattered her. Erika had instead reacted stoically. "We have lived close to death for years," she told him.

Erika went about closing the book on the old woman's life with calm competence, seeing the priest, the police, an undertaker in Oberaudorf, arranging a lawyer to handle the woman's small estate. Horning tried to be helpful, but could do little more than stand by her. He also prepared a long report for Patterson on the Muhlbach development while he waited, and told his superior that he now intended to focus on tracing Kruger.

Erika had managed to get word to her father of his sister's death. Gluckhertz sent a message soaked in *Welt-schmerz,* professing that the only good to come out of this crushing blow was the knowledge that his dear daughter was safe. He had even hazarded a badly hashed allusion to the prodigal son. Regrettably, however, affairs at the Bonalpina prevented his coming to Muhlbach.

They left the cemetery and were driven by the local police chief, a petty bureaucrat, to the Gasthaus Marienquell up a steep hill outside of Muhlbach. The policeman fairly slavered in Horning's presence.

They had spent the two previous nights at the inn in

separate rooms. Both their rooms opened onto a small, common patio offering stunning views of the Pyramidenspitze and the Elmhauer Halt, two early prefaces to the towering Alpine range that lay just over the horizon.

As the small vehicle ground out the last kilometer to the Marienquell, Horning saw Erika's mask begin to crack. She stared ahead fixedly, her lips faintly trembling.

They went up the stairway, to their rooms. Minutes later, as if on signal, they both appeared on the patio. Erika stared silently toward the mountains, then gave out a wounded cry. She flung herself into Horning's arms. He felt the slim body heave with her sobs.

"Go ahead. Cry. You can now. It's over." His hand smoothed her long hair with gentle strokes.

She lifted her head from his chest and looked into his eyes. She took his face between slender fingers and raised her head to kiss him.

"You have been so good." She held him closely as she spoke. "I could have done nothing without you beside me these days." She began another gentle kiss, but Horning engulfed her in his arms and made the kiss deep and burning. He felt the sudden limpness in her body, the slackening of her open, wet mouth. She spoke in hot, quick whispers. "We will go inside."

Inside her room, Horning advanced toward her. She held up her hand. "No. Not like that." She did not take her eyes from him as she began to unbutton her blouse. "You too." She gave him a soft command. They stood, their eyes consuming each other as clothing dropped to the floor. She stood before him, proud and naked, and took slow, graceful steps into his embrace.

*

They did not emerge from the room the next day. Their meals were brought up to them. The following day, with a theatrical brazenness that amused Horning, she demanded that the proprietor produce suitable walking shoes for her and a warm sweater. The cowed man expropriated them from a grumbling daughter.

They walked over the bridge at Oberaudorf to the base of the Pyramidenspitze. Horning felt long neglected leg muscles ache after the trek from the village. "This is terrific." He said it doubtfully. "What now?"

"We climb it, silly." She gave him a playful kiss. "Come." They began the steep ascent. Horning made an incongruous figure in a tieless business suit and overcoat topped by a feathered Tyrolean hat, which Erika had also confiscated from the proprietor.

At the summit, they gazed out at neighboring peaks, rough green cones narrowing to gray, cutting the sky with jagged, white-capped teeth. He took her in his arms and they kissed. Horning trembled in the cold, even as he felt the heat of Erika's mouth. The hike up had passed under clouds in a raw wind. But as they clung to each other, the sun burst forth.

"Do you dare?" She had an impish expression that surprised and amused him.

He looked around the bare, now sun-bright summit, and shook his head, laughing. "We'll get pneumonia."

She guided him by the hand to a place between two great rocks that cut the wind, yet caught the sun. The ground between the rocks was resilient with a deep green moss.

She gently urged Horning down onto this natural bed and unbuttoned his overcoat. She drew the coat flap over her and began to pull her dress above well-molded thighs. They could hear the wind moaning, but no longer felt it.

*

"Do you want to see the river?" She motioned to a seat on the right side of the train.

Horning appeared distracted. "Uh. What? Oh, yes, it doesn't make any difference." He had been preoccupied since they had left the Gasthaus Marienquell that morning. "Can you tell me, my dearest, what is troubling you?"

"I'm all right." He had set his jaw grimly. "Just going back to reality."

As the engine groaned northward, Erika settled against Horning. Her hand rested lightly on his arm, her head against his shoulder. She soon fell asleep. He gazed ahead vacantly. Late that afternoon they were back at the Vier Jahreseitzen. This time in one room.

12

KRUGER CREDITED HIMSELF WITH AN INTUITIVE
feel for the ebb and flow of movements. He had not called the
Nuremberg circle of the Spiderweb together for weeks and for
good reason. The spirit of his men was fragile, lifted or dashed
by ever shifting American attitudes toward denazification. In
an earlier meeting he would have faced nothing but awkward
questions. Now, he had answers.

They had gathered at the modest country house Kruger
had taken on a tree-covered knoll five miles from the city. A
black Daimler-Benz was parked in the rear. Only Kruger's

association with the Americans had made it possible to maintain the powerful automobile.

The five men were seated in the bauernstube, the peasants' room, low-ceilinged, rudely paneled and furnished in rough, country-style pieces. The room was warmed by the white-plastered dome of the fire chamber, something like an oven protruding from one wall of the room.

They sat around a thick plank table with Kruger at the head. He wore the gray, green-trimmed loden dress of Bavaria. Behind him stared the official party portrait of the Führer. Kruger had hung it just before the arrival of his guests. It would go back into hiding when the last man left. The others did not know that Hitler's image appeared so briefly, and they admired Kruger's courage in displaying it. They also saw the photograph as tacit acceptance of their operation by the Americans. After all, Kruger worked for them.

Kruger knew they enjoyed the snugness of the bauernstube, particularly this fuel-short winter. Still, they would be querulous at first, full of recriminations.

Becker began immediately. A fussy bureaucrat, he had been personnel manager for a large Hamburg department store before the war. The SS uniform, the black boots, and gleaming visor worn rakishly low over the eyes had given a certain menace to Becker's featureless countenance. His responsibility with the SS had been to locate able-bodied prisoners from the concentration camps to work as slave labor in German war industries. He now resembled an unemployed clerk.

"Last week, Thalberg was arrested. The week before, poor Moser went on trial. We have not managed a single emigration in months." His voice had a petulant whine. The others grumbled their agreement.

"Becker makes a point." The second speaker was Karl Staden, a financier who had looted the banks of occupied countries to enrich the Reich's treasury. He was now living under an assumed name and employed as a wine salesman by his brother-in-law. "Is our web functioning? Or are we finished? We deserve to know."

"A little patience, Staden." Kruger spoke with imperturbable serenity.

"Patience? It is well for you to speak of patience, my dear Kruger." The third man's voice had a rude arrogance that grated visibly on Kruger. As a former SS general, Blutig clearly outranked the onetime intelligence officer. Still, he was the most vulnerable among them.

General Blutig had commanded Einsatzgruppen B, one of the "Special Action Groups" that followed the German armies into Russia. Blutig's group had not done so well as Einsatzgruppen A, which had liquidated over 229,000 Jews and Communist Party members. But his men had compiled a respectable second-best record, with over 100,000 executions.

Blutig was the target now of an exhaustive Russian manhunt. He lived disguised as a peasant on his sister's farm near Bamberg.

Kruger looked with poorly concealed contempt at the huge, neckless head, a great potato resting between thick shoulders. Blutig's pose as a peasant, he thought, was an inspired cover.

Only Feuerbach among them had no complaint. He was the youngest, a former SS sergeant in his late twenties, erect, square shouldered with rugged features and closely cropped hair. Feuerbach might have been an impressive figure but for a peculiar lifelessness. The man never spoke and was content simply to sit among these distinguished comrades and do Kruger's bidding. Indeed, it was Feuerbach who had gone into the old woman's house in Muhlbach while Kruger had waited in the car.

"Gentlemen, I am sensitive to your every concern." Kruger was soothing and assured. "General Blutig, as a military man I know that you particularly appreciate the value of the strategic retreat. That is what we have done of late. And gentlemen, do not forget, we are but one corner of the Spiderweb. Should our group fail, a hundred others exist to carry on throughout the Reich. We are as spores braving a cold winter, waiting for the warming spring." He liked the imagery. He smiled. "But let us also remember that within the Spiderweb our ring has a special mission. And, on this point, I have news."

Kruger's small, pursed smile broke into a full grin. He signalled Feuerbach. "Otto. Please set out the glasses."

The stiff giant nearly toppled his chair in his haste. He opened a door to a china closet and seized the stems of five goblets in his long fingers. The other men watched in pleasant expectation.

"Now, the bottle, please, Otto." The man handed it to Kruger, who examined it fondly. "May I point out, gentlemen, Scotch whiskey. Courtesy of my American colleagues." Major Kincaid had arranged PX privileges for Kruger. He poured the gold-brown fluid for each man, then raised his glass.

"Let us drink a toast, for we have reason to celebrate tonight."

They all stood up and lifted their glasses. Kruger led them.

"To the Spiderweb. Fine yet strong. Unseen yet everywhere."

"To the Spiderweb," they chorused, then drained their glasses.

Kruger sat down. "And now to work." He mentioned offhandedly that he had obtained the American plates, without revealing how. Feuerbach's face remained as expressive as stone.

Kruger permitted himself a philosophic aside. "The Führer, in his scrupulous sense of fair play, which the English believe they invented, rejected an early plan to counterfeit American money. 'But we are not at war with the Americans.' That is what that honorable man said. Consequently, by the time we started work on the dollar, the war was virtually over. And so it seems poetic justice that they will become the unwitting financiers of Germany's resurrection." He smiled contentedly. "Ah well. To more practical matters."

"As you can appreciate, the problem has now passed beyond the conceptual stage. Our problems are now logistic. Most crucial is to find a printer. First-rate, trustworthy, not too rapacious. You, Becker, will conduct that search."

Becker nodded self-importantly.

"You, Staden, will devise our channels to the Zurich banking community. I believe you still have useful connections. We will hold the American dollars in our possession as briefly as possible. As you know, under the occupation, we are not legally allowed to possess their money, even if it were legitimate. These notes must be converted quickly into other hard currencies, Swiss francs, Portuguese escudos, Swedish kronor."

"Quite right, Herr Doktor. I know who are still our friends among the Swiss."

"And my assignment?"

Kruger looked into the smug, stupid face of Blutig. "Please, General, we appreciate your dedication. But we dare not risk exposure of a man of your rank in the mere mechanics of this task. Your kind have done quite enough for Germany already. Our sole concern is to get you out of the country as our first exile to be financed with American dollars."

The man grunted something Kruger took to be approval.

"One more thing. I do not know if you are aware, gentlemen, Dr. von Hummel was recently seized in Salzburg carrying five million in gold meant for Spiderweb operations. I need not exaggerate, therefore, how critical the dollar project now becomes. It shall be our salvation." He rose. "And now I thank you for joining me this evening. A productive session, don't you agree?"

A babel of good feeling erupted around the table. They got up and exchanged mutually encouraging words as they prepared to leave. Kruger accompanied them outside, where Feuerbach would drive them to the Nuremberg railroad station in the Daimler-Benz. It was risky, Kruger recognized, but marvelous for morale.

There was a final round of well-wishing and handshakes as they entered the car. At Kruger's suggestion, they had temporarily eschewed the Party salute. He watched as Feuerbach skillfully swung the automobile around and disappeared down the drive. Kruger stood for a moment, deep satisfaction in his face. Then he turned to enter the house.

The rustling came from the stiff foliage of a huge Lebensbaum framing the doorway. The figure tumbled out and Kruger found himself facing the barrel of a pistol.

"Kruger. You are going to die!" The voice was an hysterical falsetto.

Kruger gasped. "Who . . . who are you? What do you want of me?"

"Murderer!" The man moved closer until Kruger saw the protuberant, maddened eyes.

The voice was now shrieking, tremulous. "Pig! Murderer! Now you are going to know Goldhammer's justice!"

A flicker of recognition swept across Kruger's terrorized face. He bolted for the door of the house. Goldhammer ran after him. Kruger pushed open the door, tripped on the doorsill, and flattened against the floor. Goldhammer now stood directly above him. Kruger turned. He could see the tattooed number on the man's wrist. The hand clutching the pistol shook uncontrollably.

His mind raced. He had attempted escape. The man had not fired. Kruger's terror began to ebb. The gun barrel continued to bob wildly before his face.

"Shoot, Jew! Why don't you shoot?" He flung the words out. Kruger rose slowly, first to one knee. Then he was in a crouch and finally straight up, towering over the shivering figure. "What are you waiting for?" He took a step forward and Goldhammer retreated.

"You frightened little fool. You can't shoot. You're not man enough. You're just what we said you were." As he spoke, Kruger continued to edge closer, while Goldhammer backed off. Kruger was now reaching for the gun.

"Oh, God!" Goldhammer cried. "I can't do it." His hand dropped to his side. The gun hung loosely. His shoulders heaved with his sobs. He fell to the ground, crouched in a foetal coil, his face buried in his arm. "I can't be you. I don't want to be you."

Kruger bent over him and delicately lifted the gun from his hand. "Are you crazy? Why are you trying to kill *me?*" He accented the *me* incredulously. He held his body stiffly. The trembling was barely perceptible. "You were the lucky ones. At Oranienburg. Yes. I remember. Privileged Jews."

"Murderer. You sent us to our deaths." Goldhammer's words came between broken sobs. "My wife. My child."

Kruger relaxed slightly. The sweat was cooling on his

brow. "A stupid, useless policy, of course. That madman Himmler's idea. 'The glue of hatred to unite our people.' " He snorted. "I myself never approved."

Goldhammer looked up at him, his mouth hanging open, his eyes wide in dumb horror.

Kruger went on, gesturing with the gun as he spoke almost casually now. "Zealots carrying the Führer's vague abstractions to ridiculous ends. Every movement produces them."

Goldhammer's head jerked convulsively. "You sent us . . . to die . . ." he panted with each word, "and . . . you . . . didn't believe?" The eyes were now rolling.

Kruger gave him a condescending smile. "Ah. How could someone like you understand? The sanctity of an order. Obedience. Duty. A soldier's code. Not one's personal whim." He shook his head hopelessly. "Of course, you couldn't." He motioned with the gun. "Now, get out of here." He gave Goldhammer a nudging, not particularly hard kick in the rump. "Kill Jews? Am I killing you? Get out."

Goldhammer crawled toward the door, his head turned back, fixing Kruger with insane eyes. He pulled himself up, still panting, and began to flee down the drive, all the while gazing over his shoulder, his face a grotesque mask.

13

"YOU KNOW. YOU ARE NOT A GOOD MAN."

Horning's head rested on her small, firm breasts. He looked up to see her wistful smile. She smoothed his hair against his temples.

"I haven't had any complaints before."

"Don't be so coarse. God! You Americans. I mean that you have made me hope again. And that is a bad thing."

She bent her head down and kissed him. Moments before, he had been a searing lover, fusing their bodies with thrusts that skirted violence. Now he was quiet again, remote, as he had been since their return. His silences of late had driven her to an incandescent heat in their lovemaking, as though she thought she could reach him in giving more of herself.

She now looked off pensively. "I had finally accepted what my happiness with Erik was. I don't know how to explain. I wish you understood German. It was like God was playing games with me, teasing me to make me think happiness was my due. I found later that my life with Erik was a lottery. I had won. For no reason. Only by chance. And it was taken away from me just as easily. In time, I accepted that. Disappointments. Ugliness. The lies people live by. The lies my country lived by. The dirty little compromises. That was life. I didn't quarrel with it." She ran her fingers lightly down his chest. "And now you, my darling man, are starting to make me believe in dreams again. And that is bad. Cruel." She kissed his forehead lightly.

Horning pulled away from her, out of the bed, and slumped into a deep, worn chair that reflected the frayed elegance of the hotel room. His head was resting in his hands. It bothered her that she could not see his face. She spoke softly. "Will you ever tell me what is wrong?"

He shook his head imperceptibly.

"Of course. It is your wife." Her voice was resigned.

He got up and sat next to her on the bed. He ran his hand through her hair. It was still damp from their exertions. He smiled sadly. "I told you that's over. It's only a matter of time. Ugly details."

She put her arms around his neck and kissed him hard. "I think I have been too honest. That is possible, too." He did not answer. "I have told you what my life has been since Erik died." Her eyes were downcast and she spoke in a bare whisper. "I left out nothing."

Horning tensed. His hands slipped from her shoulder.

"I know it upset you. Perhaps you despise me." She lowered her eyes.

His jaw tightened. His words came with slow, pounding deliberation. "I told you. I understood. It was the war."

"That's true, my darling." She seized his hand and looked at him, pleadingly. "Your women never knew that kind of war. Do you think they would be so different?"

"Look. We don't have to go through all that again. I said I understood."

He grabbed at his clothes and began to dress quickly. "Yes, it bothered me. It bothers the hell out of me. Not your husband. Poor dead bastard. But the others. I never want to hear about it again!" He was standing over her, shouting. "Christ!" He slumped down on the bed. "I never gave a damn who had a woman before me. But, with you . . ." He shook his head.

She was now on her knees on the bed, her hands clenched tightly before her, trembling. "What does it matter what you were? What I was? I love you now . . . here . . . where I have found you in your life. But you can't accept that." Her voice had become low, despairing.

He spoke with measured deliberation, without looking at her. "I have never known anyone like you. I have never felt . . ." he choked off the sentiment, unspoken.

The gray-green eyes took on a hardness. The throaty voice unveiled a cutting edge. "That is all you can say? Do you take me for one of your conquered tramps? Someone to be had for a few cigarettes, a piece of chocolate? Only the price is higher? Your loving attention for my information?" She was stammering in her fury. "So you can become the great police detective! Is that what it is with us?"

"You came to me first looking for a deal." His voice was accusing. "You can't deny that."

"Because I was frightened. I did not know what was to
become of me. But since that moment, I have never asked you
for anything." Her words were desperate.

He looked at her with a prosecutor's searching regard.
"The Spiderweb. You swore you knew nothing about it. You
swore to me you never told a soul where that bag was.
Yet ..."

"Ahh!" She drove her clenched fist against her mouth to
suppress the shriek. "You can't believe that!" Her cry was
almost hysterical. "Tante Bertha? You could believe I told
them?" She buried her face in the pillow, sobbing inconsolably. Horning moved his hand tentatively toward the heaving,
slender shoulders, then drew back.

She cried for a long time. Horning sat motionless. Then
she was quiet. She sat up, her eyes now empty of expression.
She wiped her tears with the back of her hand. She wrapped a
nightgown around her naked body and moved with heavy
footsteps to the closet. She threw a small suitcase on the bed.
"There is no hope for us."

Horning remained motionless, diverting his eyes as she
silently dressed and packed. He heard the door latch and
turned. He spoke huskily. "Where will you go?"

"What does it matter? You have had all you could take
from me."

"I want to know where you're going!" His voice took on
a sharpness.

"You don't have to be afraid. I won't run away. I
suppose I will return to Dollmann. Your authorities can
always find me there." She closed the door behind her.

14

THE DIRECTOR OF THE SECRET SERVICE NAGGED
at Cyril Patterson like a mother accompanying an unruly child
to the principal's office.

"Do we have the report from Europe yet?"

Patterson was grimly patient. "We sent it to Secretary
Vinson's office a week ago. Remember?"

"Any developments since? I want to be on top of this."

"I was on the transatlantic phone with Horning this
morning. That means we're up to date as of one o'clock their
time. He's working every angle. But there really isn't a clue
now."

"So all we have to offer the Secretary is a dead end."

"Not all. I'm going over myself. Remember?"

"That's right. Good."

Patterson's office as Special Agent in Charge of the Counterfeit Detail was down the long corridor from Director Dawson's. As soon as he had completed his call to Europe, he had gathered his file and walked to Dawson's office. As his steps echoed down the cavernous hallway, he had thought again how much he disliked the lofty ceilings and massive columns lining the interior of the Treasury Building. They shrank a man.

The Director had been waiting for him, noisily snapping the pages of the *Washington Times-Herald*. As Patterson entered, he had leaped up without a greeting.

"Let's go. The Secretary's waiting."

The office of the Secretary of the Treasury looked out on its immediate neighbor, the East Wing of the White House. There was a matching power and assurance in the Secretary's manner. Patterson felt himself and his chief reduced to intruders clambering out of the bowels of the bureaucracy.

The Secretary's white mane and soft Kentuckian accents almost risked caricature. He had long been a power in Congress before his present post. He was not only the President's appointee, but Truman's friend and intimate. Patterson sensed a tough, natural competitor beneath the courtly exterior.

The Secretary glanced briefly at the papers the Secret Service Director handed him. He looked off pensively. He then turned his steady gaze on Dawson. "I need not elaborate to you that removing this threat is important to the economic stability of Western Europe. Right now their economies are shot. The dollar is their bedrock. The prospect of millions, even billions, of spurious dollars floating around over there is a potential calamity. And imagine the disruption and the cost if we have to redesign, reprint, and replace billions of notes in this country to beat the counterfeiters?"

The two men nodded.

"Naturally, I've had to bring this matter up before the President. The Russians are already proving to be bastards. Just as many of us feared. The big worry at the White House is that the engravings might fall into their hands. One final point. The retention of the Counterfeit Detail in Treasury probably depends on solving this case."

Dawson squirmed in his chair.

"That's right." The Secretary shook a finger at the man. "Hoover's already got the President's ear, telling him how the FBI is ready to move in on this case in an instant. "The son of a bitch." The man's profanity had a biblical resonance. "There's nothing he'd like better than to seize another chunk of power. The man's too strong already. And he is not about to enhance his empire at my expense. Not while I am Secretary of the Treasury!"

"Mr. Secretary." Dawson assumed his leathery back-woodsman pose, speaking in a slow cadence that gave his words more assurance than Patterson knew he felt.

"This has not been an easy case. No sir. Not by any means." His voice rose to a quiet indignation. "But I've given thirty years of my life to this service." He paused, his head now shaking with a righteous wrath. "And no poacher from the FBI is going to take our game away!"

The Secretary was now nodding vigorously. "That's it! That's what I want to hear, Dawson."

"Let me say one thing more, sir. We are sending the best man in this country to take control over the investigation, on the scene. Cy here leaves for Germany tomorrow to work with George Horning. Virtually his entire shop back here will be backing them up until this case is broken."

Patterson smiled modestly.

"That's splendid, gentlemen."

They followed the Secretary's lead and rose with him. On the way to the door, he put his arm around Patterson's shoulder.

"Cy, I know your reputation. I couldn't be more pleased that you're going. I just might drop that one on the President at the cabinet meeting this noon." He glanced at his watch and quickly shook their hands as they left.

Patterson was still glowing as they passed by the Treasury Secretary's smiling receptionist. Dawson turned a hard eye on his subordinate.

"Don't screw it up."

*

Chaim Katzman hurried along the street with small, padding steps, asking people to inform the police. He himself would speak to no German in uniform.

He had returned to his flat above the deserted butcher shop and was reading his prayer book with a loud, lamenting wail when two policemen arrived. He refused to acknowledge their presence.

"Never mind," one of them said, after Katzman ignored their questions. He pointed to a light seeping from under the door at the end of the hallway. The first policeman jerked open the door. A cloying sweetness billowed out of the room.

The man lay on his back on the red satin bedspread. His mouth hung slack. The skin was a translucent white around the nostrils and lips. The eyes stared into an infinite void.

One of the policemen went to the tiny gas stove and checked the jets. Old Katzman had already turned them off when he had found Julius Goldhammer dead.

*

Horning watched morosely as the C-47 lumbered across the runway and rolled to a stop on the tarmac. The hatch opened like a gill on a bloated whale. Several officers were first down the ramp. Then he spied the unmistakable, frisky, bowlegged stride of Cyril Patterson. Horning reluctantly rose from the bench in the passenger shed and headed for the plane. He experienced an old, unpleasant memory, the day he had been thrown for a three-yard loss on third-and-one, then had fumbled on the next play. He had given the oafish Stavisky, coming in to take his halfback slot, the same cold regard he now offered the approaching Patterson.

"George. It's so good to see you!" Patterson's face was an ear-to-ear grin. The plane's prop wash fanned his fringe of curls. He set his bags down, pumped Horning's hand, and put an arm around his shoulder. Horning took one of the bags as they headed for the passengers' shed.

"I can't tell you how pleased the chief is with the job you're doing here." He gave Horning a squeeze on the arm. The younger man eyed him fishily.

Once inside the shed, the reduced roar of the airplanes accented Horning's silence. Patterson stopped. They stood face to face. "George. Believe me. I'm here because we always made a hell of a team. Right? Gives me a chance to see Europe, too. Don't forget, I spent my war showing the FBI how to catch bush leaguers who were printing their own rationing stamps. We're still a team. We're working on this thing as full partners."

"Cy. You don't have to apologize." Horning looked into Patterson's caricature face, the huge, hooking nose, the great

chin rushing to meet it, the jutting ears. "I understand. And I
can't blame the Service."

Outside the terminal, they put Patterson's bags into the
trunk of an army sedan that Horning had extracted from
Colonel Ferretti. As they drove from the Unterbiberg field
into Munich, Patterson assumed a wistful air. "George, if we
crack this thing, and soon, it's a hell of a feather in your cap."
He nodded with deliberation. "In *your* cap, I said."

"If we don't?"

"Rough. Rough as hell. And I don't mean for you. I
mean on the Service." He recapped the Treasury Secretary's
words. Patterson's chin slumped to his chest. "I think we
better start by my meeting this Frau Falkenhausen." He did
not see the pain on Horning's face.

*

Kruger was a fastidious man. He had never cared for the
technical side of the Bernhard operation, the clanging, greasy
machinery, the ink-smeared workmen. He had avoided the
print shop at Oranienburg. Now, fate had thrown him again
into this unappealing world. He rejected Becker's invitation to
visit the plant and directed his accomplice instead to meet him
in a small café nearby.

"What do we know about these people?"

"Lehre and Son?" Becker had a self-satisfied smile. "I
could not have done better. Their work is outstanding. They
printed shares for some of the great firms, Siemens, I.G.
Farben. They were practically the government documents
office during the war. Ration cards, occupation scrip, that sort
of thing. Best of all for us, they have this huge plant and far
too little work."

Kruger raised a skeptical brow.

"They were a bit too close to the regime for the Americans." Becker shrugged.

"I see. Now, please tell me. When do we commence production?"

"We are ready at the printing end. The nightshift werkmeister, this fellow Dussendorf, has complete access to the plant. He will do the work during off hours."

"Access to the plant? I should have imagined we had purchased it with what he demanded. Herr Dussendorf is quite clearly not motivated by National Socialism."

Becker looked hurt. "Half of that was necessary for the night watchman."

"And production?"

"Only the manufacture of the paper remains."

Kruger snorted impatiently. "I thought I had solved that problem for you, too?"

"Yes, Herr Doktor, and it was a brilliant and courageous thing you did."

In his work for the Americans, Kruger had noticed the similarity of the paper on which military scrip and actual dollars were printed. He found out that the scrip was produced on a paper stock called twenty-four-pound coupon bond. He had turned several samples over to Becker with instructions to find someone who could acquire it or reproduce it.

"You have a proper sample. What is the problem?"

"The papermaker, Leubke. It seems, how should I put it, he needed some wooing."

"Yes, I am quite aware of the proclivities of your recruit. A drunkard and a pervert. Why do you think I sent our handsome young Feuerbach to deal with him, and with a case of Hock, too?"

"Yes, I saw Feuerbach when he returned. He looked like

a violated virgin." Becker gave a leering laugh, which Kruger
ignored.

"So what is the problem now?"

"None other than time, Herr Doktor. I talked to Leubke just two days ago. He has only just now found the suitable materials. He tells me almost certainly within three weeks."

"Good. It is my intention then to call a meeting of the Nuremberg Spiderweb in three weeks and one day."

*

SS General Blutig was sweating profusely. He still wore the open-necked peasant shirt in which he had been arrested. Sweat poured over thick jowls and into the deep creases of his neck.

"Not even the pleasure of loosening him up a little." The man who spoke was short and broad shouldered, with narrow eyes and impassive, flat Slav features. He wore the uniform of a Soviet army major.

"No. Our brave SS general sang like a diva. But go ahead, if it makes you feel any better." The second man was much older, with a head of gray curls and a lean, seamed face.

Major Yuri Semyonov stood before Blutig with his hands on his hips. The German stared at him through gaping eyes. His mouth hung open. The Russian delivered a powerful blow with the back of his hand. Blutig made an animal-like grunt. Another blow brought blood flowing from the loose, hanging lips.

"What's the point?" Semyonov shrugged his shoulders and turned again to Colonel Kuznetzy. "It's quite extraordinary what this cur has told us."

"Yes. Potentially far more valuable than finding another Nazi neck to stretch."

The long hunt for the Commander of Eisensatzgruppen

B had ended with swift suddenness. Blutig had been found, as the informer promised, on his sister's farm, disguised as a field hand. The Americans had alerted the Russians through the U.N. War Crimes Commission Liaison Office when they received the tip. They had insisted on accompanying the Russians to the farm and making the initial arrest themselves. As soon as Blutig's identity had been established, they abided by the four-power agreement and turned him over to the Russians.

Colonel Kuznetzy signaled to two enlisted guards to take Blutig away. His head hung down, lolling from side to side, as they dragged him from the room. After the door closed, the two officers heard the kicks, the pummelling, and the groans. They laughed.

"How do you suggest we handle this?" Kuznetzy posed the question.

Semyonov's eyes closed to bare slits. He drummed his fingers together. "Of course, we could notify the Americans."

Kuznetzy looked at him, pained. "Comrade. I suggest you put on your other hat. Perhaps it will help you to think more clearly."

Semyonov smiled craftily. "I only wanted your blessing to proceed, Colonel."

"This can be an extraordinary coup, especially for our operations in America." Kuznetzy ran his hand through his curls and shook his head. "Also, certain promotion, if you succeed."

"And perhaps an apartment in the Kalinin Prospect." Semyonov smiled.

"And maybe a transfer to the embassy in Washington, while you are dreaming."

The two men laughed heartily.

"But first let us accomplish the task. Frankly, I don't

have a thought as to how we should proceed. I am only a
schoolteacher in uniform. But, you will stay here in the U.S.
zone and somehow obtain those plates. Continue to use the
war crimes cover. It is quite perfect."

"I will first have to go to the War Crimes Liaison Office
in Munich to have my permit extended to remain in their
zone."

"Fine. I will be returning to Leipzig tomorrow. From
there I will notify Moscow of the plan. Once I have taken that
step, it becomes imperative that you succeed."

"Of course, Colonel."

*

"Did you have any trouble?"

"No, the hotel manager let us into the room. They don't
like the Communists any more than we do. A good deal less, I
suspect."

"Just 'cause the Russkies wash their feet in the toilet
bowls?" Colonel Houlihan laughed loudly and took the folder
without looking up at the young lieutenant. "This everything?" He found it difficult to accept that this "Stanford
smoothie," as he privately referred to Hart Simmons, could
pull off a decent second-story job.

"That's all of it. It looks like some travel orders, a couple
of personal letters, a few names and addresses."

"Anything linking him to the NKVD?"

"Really, Colonel! They're not likely to wear name tags.
But we think it's safe to assume that any Russians sent into
our zone . . ."

"Yeh. Yeh. Can it, Simmons. I'm the one who taught
you that pitch. Remember?"

"Of course, Colonel." He smiled politely. "I hope the

quality of those photostats is readable. We didn't have much time to copy them."

"I stalled the Russian about as long as I could," Houlihan said. "A shrewd little article. They bagged a kraut SS general in our zone. They claim he took care of about one hundred thousand Jews and Commies. Wouldn't you love to be that poor son of a bitch in the Russians' hands? This Semyonov claims he's got a lead on a few accomplices. That's why he says he wants to stay here. I gave him a one-month extension. I want you people to keep an eye on him all the while he's here. Keep me informed."

"It's heating up nicely, isn't it, Colonel?"

"You're goddamned right. They're already giving us a hard time getting into our zone in Berlin. They've set up checkpoints all along the autobahn. I wonder how FDR would like Uncle Joe now?"

"Churchill gave a speech the other day predicting what looks like a protracted period of con . . ."

"Spare me, Simmons. Just let me read this file. You buzz off now."

The young officer saluted and left Houlihan alone.

The colonel looked out the window toward the sun, still high in the afternoon sky. He glanced at his watch, sighed, and reluctantly opened the folder. He shook his head wearily as he studied the pages of cyrillic letters. He would have to pass the file on to the translators in the morning. He was about to set the folder aside when his eyes froze on a creased sheet of paper on which the luckless Blutig had scrawled four names. At the top was "Wolf Kruger, Fuel Administrator, American Military Government, Nuremberg." Houlihan quickly slipped the file folder into his desk drawer. He was breathing deeply.

15

"GEORGE. I NEED TO SEE YOU." HER VOICE SET HIS
blood pounding.

"Are you all right?" He tried for cool detachment.

Erika hesitated. "Yes. I believe so. But I must talk to
you . . ." she paused, "and your Mr. Patterson."

Horning felt a small stab of disappointment. "Sure. Of
course. Meet us in the dining room of the Vier Jahreseitzen,"
he glanced at his watch, "in an hour. Tell that pansy Dollmann you've been ordered by the authorities. If he gives you a

hard time, tell him we'll make it tough on him." He knew her
circumstances.

"Thank you." Her voice was empty. She hung up without another word.

Horning had not expected to hear from her again after the earlier meeting with Patterson on his arrival in Munich. Horning had started to call her a dozen times afterward, but always checked himself. Pride. Lingering mistrust. He did not know. He was grateful she had called, whatever the reason.

At that first encounter with Patterson, Erika had been withdrawn, almost mute. She had barely looked at Horning. Patterson did most of the talking. If he was aware of the current leaping between the other two, he had given no indication.

"Look, Erika. I hope I can call you Erika." Patterson had adopted his most avuncular style. "In the eyes of the U.S. government, you haven't done anything wrong. We aren't out to hurt you. But you can be terribly helpful to us."

She had bowed her head and was quiet while Patterson waited patiently. When she looked up, her eyes were damp. The words came with effort. "I want nothing more to do with this matter. I am sorry. It has cost me so much."

"I know. I do understand. Believe me. If there were any way to spare you . . . But at this point, there is no one else. You are the key to the case." He said it with a tougher voice that somehow disclaimed his earlier assurance of her blamelessness.

"What more can I do?" She had pleaded.

"This man who approached you, before you came to us, Kruger. Where do you think we might find him?"

She had sighed heavily. "I have already gone over this matter with Mr. Horning some weeks ago. There is nothing more I can add. Will you please leave me alone? I must return to the shop."

Three weeks had passed since that barren audience. Then she had made the call to Horning.

She was in the hotel dining room when they arrived, seated at one of the corner tables where afternoon guests had drinks, alone, visibly uncomfortable, under the leering gaze of the waiters. An untouched glass of wine sat before her.

She and Horning regarded each other cautiously. They exchanged no more than a nod. Patterson was expansive and complimented her on choosing the most secure table. He ordered beer for himself and Horning, then looked to Erika expectantly.

She spoke with toneless resignation. "I have been called by an American officer who says that he wants to discuss the case."

"Did he mention our investigation?" Patterson's face wrinkled with curiosity.

"No. And that is what struck me as odd. He made no mention of you."

"Yes. That is strange. Who was he?"

"He identified himself as an officer in your army intelligence. Colonel Houlihan, I believe."

Patterson and Horning exchanged knowing nods. Patterson went on. "How did he find you?" Horning interrupted. "Ferretti's report to G-2, probably."

"What exactly did he want you to do?" Patterson resumed.

"He wants to meet me . . . to ask questions. I did not know what to say. I told him I knew nothing and that I was very busy. Then he said things as if to threaten me if I did not cooperate. I was frightened." She turned her gaze downward. "That is when I called Mr. Horning."

It was quiet at the table. A small contented smile spread across Patterson's face. He winked at Horning, whose eyes were fixed on Erika's bowed head.

"Erika." Patterson spoke with great gentleness. "I want you to meet him."

She looked up, alarm in her face. She reflexively turned to Horning. "Must I? I don't want to."

Horning turned away.

She looked to Patterson. "But you said I had done nothing wrong according to your government."

"That's true, my dear girl. But that's not quite the point." His voice became firmer. "We expect your cooperation. It's essential to us. And don't worry, we will protect you. I want you to call this fellow back. Set up an appointment in an open, safe place. Then let us know what happens."

Erika's shoulders slumped. She nodded without looking at the two men. She gathered up her gloves and quickly departed.

"George." Horning's eyes were following her out. "Hey. George." Patterson gave him a playful punch. "This is it. Our break. The big one."

*

They had agreed on a bench along an open walk near the west entrance to the *Englische Garten*. She told him that she would be wearing a gray walking suit and would carry a small black purse.

"What do you look like?" There had been a coarse, suggestive quality in his question.

"That does not matter. I am sure you will recognize me."

She had kept him waiting half an hour. Houlihan sat on the park bench, arms folded, his eyes darting, his mind musing. Pretty lady skips town and, what do you know, after that, the plates are gone. Smartass Secret Service agent comes looking for them. Finds an old dame croaked in another hick town. All of a sudden, the Russkies are hot for my old pal Kruger and some other krauts. Two and two are starting to look like six. He was smiling.

Erika passed by the bench where he was sitting, pretending not to notice him. He called after her in a gruff whisper. "Over here, sweetheart." Whatever dignity a uniform lent Houlihan was lost in civilian clothes. He looked to her like a hog butcher on his day off. She sat down on the bench.

"Got a little worried about you, princess. It's good for your sake you showed up."

She spoke, staring ahead without looking at him. "It seems a strange way, Colonel, to conduct an official investigation."

"Security, don't you know?"

"Of course." She gave him a sly smile. "Can you tell me why a poor German woman is of such interest to the great government of the United States?"

Houlihan's eyes played over the fine-boned face, then down her body to the calves of her legs. "Let's say I'm putting some pieces together that are making a terrific picture. Except there's one piece missing."

"And you believe I have it?"

He nodded with a confident smile. "And you'll tell me because you're a smart woman."

"And why should I want to help you to complete this picture of yours?"

Houlihan sat up straight. "Because I don't think you're about to obstruct an official investigation by the U.S. Army."

She suppressed a giggle. "Do you know something, Colonel? I don't think you are on, what do you say, an official investigation of the U.S. Army." Her lowered voice mocked his gravity.

Houlihan flushed. He started to speak angrily, then saw her playful smile. He grunted a laugh instead.

"You said yourself that I am an intelligent woman. I'm sure it takes an intelligent man to recognize one."

He eyed her appreciatively. "Suppose you tell me who killed that old lady down in Muhlbach?"

Her smiling mask dissolved. She turned her head aside. After a time, she forced herself to speak. "I cannot say, I do not know."

"All right. Let's come at it this way. Have you been in contact with a man named Wolf Kruger?"

"Yes. Rather, he found me."

"When? How long ago?"

"Within the past six to eight weeks. I cannot be sure."

"How recently before that woman was murdered?"

"The last time, a few days before."

"You never heard from Kruger after that?"

"Never."

Houlihan folded his arms, leaned back his head, and closed his eyes. "Good. Good. That's it." He spoke as though to himself. "It's all in place."

She moved slightly closer to him and managed a coquettish smile. "I suppose, Colonel, like all men, you only pursue a woman until you get what you want." She laughed gaily. "Now, you won't need me any longer."

He eyed her suspiciously, before a slow smile broke across his broad face. "Depends on what you've got in mind."

She picked up her purse and placed it in her lap. "I really must go now. You cleverly found out how to reach me. I hope that the information will not be useless to you in the future." She put out her hand. He took it awkwardly.

Houlihan studied her departing figure with anticipation.

*

Erika met Patterson and Horning, this time in a room in the Europäischer Hotel.

Before her arrival, Patterson had spoken to Horning eagerly. "George, we are going to flush that son of a bitch out. He's on to something. And we're going to find out what it is. We happen to have just the bait to trap him." He gave Horning's knee a slap and laughed.

Horning gnawed at his lip. "Why don't we just take him? Why endanger the woman?"

Patterson shrugged and threw up his hands. "With what? How do we get a grip on him? You're the one who told me it's all guesswork. What those Englishmen told you. Suspicions. No facts. That's not even the important part. If we scare this guy off now, it will break the last thread. Then what will we have?" He looked puzzled. "George. You surprise me."

"Yes." Horning sighed heavily. "You're right. I just don't want to see her hurt."

Patterson gave him a man-to-man grin. "Hey, Georgie boy. Got a little something going? Believe me. Nothing is going to happen to her. That's the last thing I want."

It was then that Erika had arrived. She sat uneasily in the chair Patterson pulled up for her and refused the cigarette he offered.

"Must I go on? It's quite unpleasant. I've told you what it was he wanted from me." She gave a pleading look in Horning's direction.

Patterson took her hand. "Erika. This means so much to

us. If you stop now, the whole case could collapse. If you'll
continue, just a little longer, we can resolve this thing." He
gave her arm a comforting squeeze. "Will you do it at least for
your poor aunt?"

She looked startled and drew back stiffly. "I am doing
this . . ." She looked at Horning, then stopped. Her voice fell
to a hoarse whisper. "I don't know why I am doing it.
Because, I suppose, I am afraid of what will happen to me if I
don't."

"I have told you that you don't have to worry about
that. Have faith in us."

She eyed Patterson wearily. "And then, I suppose, you
will find me a job selling cigarettes in your wonderful PX?"

He looked at her, puzzled, then went on explaining what
he wanted her to do next.

When Patterson finished, she was silent for a time. She
looked again at Horning, who had sat wordlessly throughout.
"George."

He did not answer. She continued to look steadily at
him.

"Yes, Erika." He said it impatiently.

Patterson was now eyeing them both with fresh curiosity.

"Do you want me to do this?" Her gaze was unrelenting.
It disconcerted him. He cleared his throat. "You only have to
do what you want. Whatever you think is right."

"What is right? I have no idea what is right. It would
help me decide if I knew you were willing to let me go
through with this."

Horning got up and stood by the hotel window, hands
jammed into his pockets. The room was utterly quiet. She
turned an emotionless face to Patterson. "Apparently Mr.

Horning thinks that what you are asking of me is quite proper. I value his judgment highly. I will do whatever you want."

*

Kruger glanced again at his watch. "I suppose we shall have to begin without him. No one has any idea what has become of the general?"

They sat around the rustic table of Kruger's bauernstube.

Becker spoke. "None of us can contact him easily, off on that farm. But we did get the message to him of this meeting."

Staden, the former financier now wine merchant, gave Kruger a sympathetic smile. "Is it so critical to have our friend, the general, present, Herr Doktor?"

"It is not so much his presence that pleases me, but his absence that worries me."

They all laughed, except for the tall, stiff Feuerbach, who stared ahead vacantly.

"In any case, let us begin. First, let me say that while much in our poor afflicted country lies in ruin, German technical genius is apparently intact. In short, we have succeeded." Kruger looked around the room triumphantly.

Staden began a sturdy applause. "Wunderbar! Herrlich!" The others joined in.

"We are now ready to move to the next phase. The key is to establish a steady, inconspicuous flow. Therefore, we will make our trips on a phased schedule, always traveling separately. Each man will carry no more than one hundred and twenty-five thousand dollars per trip. With four men, that means we will be carrying half a million dollars into Switzerland each cycle."

Becker raised his hand in the manner of a bright schoolboy. "But, Doctor Kruger, there are five of us when General Blutig is present."

Kruger assumed an exaggerated solemnity. "The general is a figure of such eminence in our movement that we hardly dare reduce him to the status of bank messenger."

They looked at him uncertainly, then laughed.

"General Blutig will accompany me personally on the first journey. We are all familiar with his impatience to find, shall we say, a more agreeable climate. As soon as the transaction has been completed, I will provide Blutig with the financing and other arrangements to join our comrades abroad. The good general will be moving to a Latin paradise."

"Where is that?" Becker asked, in a wistful voice.

"Paraguay."

Staden laughed. "Couldn't we make it Chile? It's even farther."

Kruger smiled. "Please, Staden. A little charity. Now, if we may get back to our work. Each of us will be carrying six thousand two hundred and fifty twenty-dollar bills each trip. We will be supplied with custom-made luggage, courtesy of SD surplus one might say. Concealment should be no problem. A chain of safe houses will lead us over the border. In Zurich you will each have a list of banks with whom we can deal confidently. Herr Staden has seen to that."

The wine salesman smiled smugly.

"You will be supplied with instructions for setting up accounts in various currencies, escudos, pounds, Swiss francs. These accounts will be in the names of fictitious German firms. The names will also be provided to you. Fortunately, the bankers of Zurich have an extraordinary lack of curiosity about their depositors.

"We will meet here in exactly one week. At that time, the funds will be distributed to you for the first wave of our

Swiss invasion. We will continue these efforts as long as the work of the Spiderweb requires financing. In a very real sense, gentlemen, our resources are now virtually unlimited."

Staden began thumping the table. The small party sent up another uneven but spirited cheer.

"I think perhaps a toast is in order." Feuerbach sprang to life before Kruger motioned to him.

Kruger smiled benignly as he poured from a bottle of schnapps. "This time, I believe, a wholly German toast is appropriate."

They raised their glasses. "To the Spiderweb. Fine yet strong. Unseen yet everywhere."

16

COLONEL HOULIHAN PUT THE RECEIVER DOWN
with a pleased smile. She had seemed eager to see him, in fact
had accepted his invitation instantly. He was to meet Erika at
Zur Eiche, The Oaks, outside the city, a place she had
suggested.

"It has, if you will excuse me for saying so, Colonel, not
yet been discovered by our conquerors." He was impressed by
her easy self-assurance.

Zur Eiche was indeed set in a grove of oaks. Outside, a
handsome bower, set with tables, surrounded the restaurant

on three sides. But no guests dared brave the chill April evening. The interior was rustic, but not relentlessly so.

Houlihan was relieved that he had worn civilian clothes. The woman was right. Not an American was visible. The patrons were German, currency manipulators, lawyers, officials who had caught on with the Americans and a few postadolescent playboys from prominent Munich families.

She was not yet there. The unsmiling maitre d' led him to a table for two along a far wall. The guests, as he inched his way through the crowded dining room, eyed him with cold curiosity.

He had finished three glasses of something sweet that tasted of caraway seeds before she arrived. He had not understood the waiter and had communicated by nodding his head at anything.

He had rehearsed a stinging rebuke for her late arrival. But when he saw her, he only smiled foolishly. She peeled off a glove and extended her hand to him.

"It is so good to see you again, Colonel." She held his hand an imperceptible extra second.

His tongue felt thick and clumsy. The waiter appeared and stared at him expectantly. Houlihan stared back wordlessly.

"Please bring me whatever the gentleman is having." She smiled and patted Houlihan's hand.

"Kümmel?" The waiter raised a skeptical brow.

"No, no. Some white wine will be fine, thank you."

An orchestra, ruled by saccharine violins, played a repertoire largely unmolested since the 1930s, which seemed inevitably to return to a song that Erika hummed, *Wenn der weisse Flieder wieder blüht."* The floor was crowded. She prayed that he would not ask her to dance.

Toward the end of a largely silent dinner, she asked with direct innocence, "Have you approached Doctor Kruger?"

Houlihan looked at her guardedly.

"Come now, Colonel. I too, as you say, can place the pieces together."

"What do you say we dance?"

"I had hoped you would ask."

On the dance floor he felt her fingers rubbing softly against his neck. Her waist against his hand felt trim and yielding. The orchestra was again playing "When the White Lilac Blooms Again." Erika hummed along.

She spoke into his ear. "I admire what you are going to do. It requires a real man."

Houlihan pulled her closer and did not detect the stiffening in her body. "What do you think I'm going to do?"

"The intelligent thing."

She endured another chorus. "I would love to have another drink. May we sit down, Colonel?"

"You move so gracefully for such a large man." She settled herself into her chair.

"I don't do much of it." He swirled his drink and emptied it. "Herr Ober." He pulled the waiter by the arm and pointed to the two empty glasses.

"It's not going to be easy. It's a hell of a risk."

"Of course. I understand. Suppose you had a friend? Someone willing to share that risk?"

The guardedness returned to his eyes. "What are we talking about?"

"Colonel." She pinched his hand playfully. "Don't be so suspicious. You know, I could have gone to the Americans already with what I know about, shall we say, your unusual interest in this case. I have not done that. That is not what I want."

"I'm waiting."

"Daniel. May I call you Daniel?"

"Dan."

"Dan. I will tell you something so that you know we can trust each other. I have already been questioned by your authorities."

His mouth tightened. "Army?"

"No. Not your army. I believe it is called the Secret Service."

"What do they know?" He had turned pale. "What did you tell them?"

"Let me tell you this. If you intend to act, you must do it quickly. They know of Kruger, but not yet where to find him. I did not tell them, because I do not know myself. And I have said nothing about our meeting."

Houlihan reached out and crushed her hand in the vise of his own. "If you're playing with me, God help you."

Her face blanched. "Please don't hurt me."

He relaxed his grip. She withdrew the hand and rubbed it with the other. "You are so strong."

"You didn't tell them about me? Why? What's your game?"

She looked at him with a naked directness. "You are soon going to have a great deal of money. When it happens, I want to be with you."

He made a guttural, ugly laugh. "You're damned right. And I'm not doing it by pushing stacks of phony American paper."

She had difficulty following him.

"No, ma'am. Houlihan has a plan. You might say I'm going on the gold standard."

She still looked bewildered.

"Come on. Let's get going."

"Going?"

"That's right. To Nuremberg."

*

The exaggerated caution with which he drove was the only sign that he had been drinking heavily. Houlihan's jeep covered the drive to Nuremberg in three hours. He had allowed her to stop by her room to throw some things into a bag before they left Munich. Her attempt to telephone Patterson and Horning while Houlihan waited outside had not succeeded.

He drove remorselessly, stopping only at checkpoints where MPs exchanged knowing glances along with their salutes on seeing the attractive woman curled in the front seat under the Colonel's raincoat.

On their arrival in Nuremberg at 3 A.M. Houlihan banged on the door of a decayed second-class hotel until the half-sleeping porter appeared. The man agreed to rouse the manager only after Houlihan threatened that he was an American officer with Military Government.

Erika could feel the shabbiness of the room before the lights confirmed it. She collapsed on the bed and felt its chilling dampness. Houlihan flung her skirt back, exposing tapering thighs. The huge body was over her instantly. She resisted as he tore savagely at her garters and pants. He did not struggle with her. He merely reared back and gave her a powerful, cupping blow across the head that sent her sprawling on her back, barely conscious. Then he went on with his work. After a furious burst, he slumped to her side like a felled ox and was soon asleep. He had not bothered to undress.

Erika awakened at noon. Her head throbbed in pain. With careful fingers she explored the sensitive, swollen jaw and lips. She rose from the bed and stood a moment while her head cleared. In the mirror, her face did not look as bad as it felt. She felt an aching void inside her. Houlihan lay on his back like a beached whale, breathing noisily through his mouth.

She dressed quietly. She turned the door handle with elaborate care and slipped out of the room.

When she returned, he was sitting on the edge of the bed, his hands hanging between his legs. He looked up at her dully, but said nothing.

She forced a smile. "I was so hungry. Would you like me to have something sent up for you to eat?"

He shook his head and reached down under the bed for a small canvas bag he had carried into the room the night before. "I need a drink." She went to look for a glass, but he already had the bottle to his lips.

He wiped his mouth. "I've got some heavy work ahead of me tonight." He said it self-pityingly. He stretched back out on the bed and was soon asleep again.

Houlihan spent the rest of the day alternately drinking and sleeping. She later brought him a thin sandwich of stiff, dried ham on gray-colored bread. He ate half of it, cursed the Germans, then fell asleep again.

Erika had failed in two more attempts to telephone Horning and Patterson in Munich from the seamy lobby of the Hotel Franke.

*

Two men emerged from the house into the dark night. They both went to the passenger's side of the Daimler-Benz. The taller man opened the door and allowed the other in. The door closed with a thud. He trotted around to the driver's side. Houlihan watched from the entrance to the drive. As the purr of the automobile approached, he ran quickly back across the road to the vehicle concealed under the trees.

Houlihan cursed his luck, having to tail the powerful automobile in a jeep. He drove frantically, with his lights out, as closely behind as he dared. Inside Nuremberg, he briefly lost his prey and fretted like a thwarted child. Then the huge car reappeared out of a side street, and he resumed the pursuit. The trail led over the tracks of railroad sidings, past bombed-out ruins of German industry on the edge of town. He saw the brake lights of the Daimler-Benz winking. He pulled into the shadow of a half-collapsed brick wall and cut his engine. He could see the two men get out of the car and disappear into the only whole and lighted building in the area.

*

"This is Dussendorf." Becker gestured in the direction of the printer. Kruger did not bother to take the ink-stained hand.

"Is all in order?" Feuerbach stood silent and menacing next to him.

"Yes, Herr Doktor." The printer motioned for Kruger to follow him to the press. "We had a small problem getting a proper match under fluorescent light, but we found that by treating the ink . . ."

Kruger spoke with biting evenness. "I am not interested in your ink."

"Yes, of course." The man nodded submissively. "In any case, you can see we are already printing."

As the sheets floated into the delivery bin, Dussendorf took one out and showed it to Kruger. "They are extraordinary plates. Notice the detail in the . . ."

"Yes. Yes. How long before you will be completed?"

The man reluctantly replaced the sheet. "We have really just started. Perhaps another three hours. Thus far, I have only these sheets printed and cut." He pointed to a small stack of bills on a table. "Here, let me . . ."

The door burst open, crashing against the wall.

"All of you down on the floor." The voice bellowed.

Kruger's head spun to the open doorway where Houlihan stood. The barrel of a pistol pointed directly at the German, who stood paralyzed.

"On the floor, goddamn it! Do you hear me?"

The others looked to Kruger in their confusion. "He says lie on the floor," Kruger muttered in German. They followed Kruger's lead and spread out on the grease-stained cement.

"Take the plate off the machine." Houlihan stood rigid with his legs wide apart. Sweat bathed his face. His teeth were bared in a tight grimace.

Kruger relayed the instruction to the trembling Dussendorf. The printer rose, stopped the press, and freed the metal sheet from the cylinder.

"Where's the reverse plate?"

Again Kruger translated, and Dussendorf took the other plate from the table where the stacks of finished bills rested.

"Tell him to put the plates and those bills in here." Houlihan tossed out his small canvas bag. Dussendorf understood without further instruction.

"Now, tell him to drop it nice and gentle at my feet."

Kruger mumbled something in German. A knowing look passed between him and Dussendorf.

The hurled bag caught Houlihan in the face. Instantly Feuerbach sprang at him. The shot boomed like artillery in the cavernous room. Kruger's body was flung back in a heap. Feuerbach froze before Houlihan. Kruger tried to sit up, his blue eyes locked on a raw red circle in the middle of his chest. He fell back with a thud.

"Goddamn it! If anyone else moves, I'll kill him." Houlihan was edging backwards toward the still open door. The hand holding the gun trembled. His chest heaved and the words came oddly syncopated, as though he were struggling for air. With his free hand, he groped on the floor for the bag, never moving his eyes or the gun from the still rigid Feuerbach.

Then he was gone. They heard the engine of the jeep whine to life. The members of the Spiderweb moved wordlessly around Kruger's body. They stared into the open, disbelieving eyes of the dead man, then at each other. A single tear trickled down Feuerbach's vacant face.

*

Both men seemed smaller in civilian clothes. They sat inside a squalid café patronized by Russian DPs on the edge of Dachau.

"All that fighting. All that bloodshed. And, can you believe it? I don't care so much for their beer." The older man with the gray curls laughed wryly. "It's as though we had conquered Italy and hated the pasta."

The younger man nodded glumly. "Or Paris, and closed the whorehouses."

"Yes. All the same, the schnapps is quite good." Colonel Kuznetzy finished his glass. "Now, Semyonov. Why so melancholy?"

"The man is a scoundrel, a thief."

"Ah. You young fellows. So much more intolerant than us oldtimers. The man is a capitalist. He behaves as a capitalist.

What did you expect? Engels? And, in the end, we shall reap the profit of his greed."

Semyonov regarded the older man hopefully. "But a million dollars in currencies redeemable in gold? It is preposterous, isn't it?"

"Is it? Suppose he had never contacted you at all? Your mission would then have been a complete failure."

"That, too, troubles me. The bastard beat me to the Germans by no more than a day or two."

"The money is nothing. We could print up the equivalent in hours with these engravings." The older man pointed a finger at Semyonov. "The important question is this, for that is what Moscow will want to know. How good is his product?"

"We know from the prisoner Blutig that the engravings were made by the same craftsmen who counterfeited the British notes. And they were undeniable masterpieces."

"I'm well aware. We recovered millions, particularly from traitors who worked as agents for the Nazis. Do you know what we have done with them? We used them to pay the British for horse meat for our occupation troops." He laughed. "We still do!"

"Obviously, I cannot guarantee the quality of their American product."

"Of course not, Semyonov. Here is what we will do. On my return to Leipzig, I will request authority from Moscow for half the sum. A half a million dollars should satisfy a budding plutocrat. If we receive approval, we must set up the transfer as near as possible to our zone. We want to minimize the amount of time we hold those engravings in the U.S. sector. I suggest the border checkpoint on the Nuremberg-Leipzig Autobahn."

"That would be Rudolfstein?"

"Exactly."

*

Horning paced the hotel room. In this moment, he hated Cyril Patterson. He could not bear to face the man after learning of Erika's abrupt call from Nuremberg. He slammed his fists against his forehead and made quiet, guttural cries. He sat on the bed, then was up again, resuming his pacing. If only he had been in the room when she called, and not Patterson. It was too late. He could only will the next hours to pass mercifully.

Horning went to the hideous rococco desk and yanked open the middle drawer. He slammed it back with a curse. He pulled the hollow-ringing side drawers. The last one he pulled clear off its runners and set it hurtling across the room. He searched furiously for his briefcase, snatched some paper from it, and sat down. He could not look at himself in the mirror above the desk. He took out a pen and waited several moments to compose himself. He began to write in rapid, bold strokes.

Dear Sally,

I haven't been fair to you, nor frankly to myself. Yes, a letter is cowardly. What I have to tell you is far easier for me this way. I know that. But the sooner I get the truth out, the sooner you can begin a life that makes more sense than ours.

There is no easier way to tell you. There is someone else, and I know you are too proud to want to go on that way. I want nothing of what has been ours. Whatever we have shared belongs to you, except my freedom. I've got to have that.

I know it's trite as hell to say so. But you will find

someone far better for you than I ever will be. What I am
doing now would only have been a matter of time with us.
The woman I have met and love has only made it happen
sooner, and for the better, someday we will all agree.

I don't know when I will be back. But as soon as I
do . . .

He leaned back breathing deeply as though drained by
the effort. He reread what he had written. He slowly
crumpled the letter and tossed it to the floor. There was a
rueful smile on his face. He had read somewhere, Churchill he
thought maybe, that when you have to kill somebody, you
owe it to them to do it in the kindest possible way. He would
deal with Sally later. But at least the decision had been made.
He would find Patterson downstairs in the dining room
waiting for him, and they would work out their plan.

*

Houlihan had not left the Hotel Franke since the night
he had reappeared with the bulging canvas bag. Erika had
brought food to him in the room. He rarely ate, but drank
steadily. He had made all contacts with Semyonov by telephone from the hotel, rashly demanding service on the few
long-distance lines functioning to Munich, in the name of
U.S. Army Intelligence. His tension demanded frequent physical release. He had taken Erika repeatedly in the three days
they spent in the dim, narrow room, always fitfully, briefly,
joylessly.

On the morning after their arrival, Erika had carried
out his instructions and had ordered the jeep parked out of
sight in the rear of the hotel. The manager had agreed to it for
a pack of cigarettes.

On the day of their departure, they left the hotel before

dawn. By the time they reached the autobahn, the morning was sunlit and the air clean and cool. Houlihan hunched forward, gripping the wheel with both hands, his eyes never leaving the road, his face taut.

They drove through the deep-cut valleys and dolomite hills of the Frankische Schweiz with its unearthly formations sculpted in stone. Erika gazed out at the landscape, so unlike her native Bavaria. Off in the distance, she could see castles crowning steep cliffs. She had put Houlihan out of her mind, until he broke the silence.

"Have you got it straight?"

"What is that?" She did not look at him. "Oh, yes. I believe so."

"Their vehicle will be parked on the right-hand side of the road. It'll have a bunch of returning Russian DPs in the back. A soldier is supposed to be outside, pretending to change the left rear tire. I'll pull up about two hundred feet behind him." He glanced at her. She was still staring ahead. "Do you understand?" She nodded. She was calculating the time before it would be over.

"When you get out, walk halfway to the truck. No more. Even if you have to wait for Semyonov to come to you. In case they try anything funny."

His shirt collar was puckered with sweat. He had opened his jacket and she saw where he wore his shoulder holster.

"Don't give him the bag until he hands you the brief-case. Look in it first. I told him to make sure it's open. Then get back to the jeep as soon as you can."

She nodded. The canvas bag lay on the floor between them.

Just beyond Helmbrechts they passed a sign warning of the approaching Soviet zone, twenty kilometers to the north. There would be no further towns between them and Rudolfstein on the border. Houlihan was visibly tense. Erika felt not calm but oddly detached.

At the ten-kilometer marker he slowed and began searching the roadside. Within minutes, she raised her hand and pointed ahead. They could make out a gray canvas-covered vehicle on the roadside. Beyond it, barely visible, lay the American checkpoint. The Soviet post, Houlihan knew, was approximately a quarter of a mile past the Americans. He turned the jeep onto the dirt shoulder and began creeping up on the Soviet vehicle. He could see a figure crouched behind a rear wheel.

*

Cyril Patterson trained the binoculars down the northbound lane of the autobahn. Horning and an Army officer were bent beside him, staring intently through the observation slot. Horning's face was a gray mask. Patterson gave him a tight smile. "George, it'll work."

They watched from the inside of a battle-scarred pillbox set amidst a field overgrown with weeds. Ten minutes before, they had watched the Soviet truck pull off to the opposite side of the autobahn two hundred yards away and had watched the soldier swing down from the cab.

Behind the pillbox, out of sight, an army staff car waited. A sergeant sat at the wheel poised for Patterson's signal.

"They're coming! Quick. Start the car. You two get out there. Now! As soon as she's out of the jeep, start for the road."

Horning and the officer drew pistols and ran out the rear entrance of the pillbox.

Patterson saw the jeep come to a halt. He could see a female figure emerging. A Soviet officer leaped from the cab of the truck and entered his field of vision. The staff car screeched from behind the pillbox and bounded down a rutted path toward the two figures meeting on the highway.

As she approached the Russian, the woman suddenly bolted across the autobahn and ran toward the car racing to meet her.

Patterson gripped the binoculars until his hands shook. He heard the sharp crack. "Oh God, no!" His voice was a tortured denial. Her body was flung across the highway.

*

Houlihan shoved the pistol back into the holster and leaped from the jeep. He ran toward the crumpled figure. The canvas bag lay open and the wind whipped loose bills along the roadside.

Houlihan snatched the bag and ran for the truck. It was already moving when a hand reached out from the cab and pulled him aboard. The vehicle picked up speed as it rolled toward the American checkpoint, smashing through the wooden barrier and scattering the guards. Shots rang out as the truck bore down on the Russian guard post, where the barrier had already been lifted. The truck cruised into the safety of the Soviet sector.

Patterson ran to the staff car now parked alongside the still figure. Horning knelt at her side, holding her hand. His face was buried in his other hand and his shoulders were shaking. The other men gaped at the woman in stricken silence. Patterson's heavy panting and the wind were now the only sounds. Some bills blew across her blood-stained back. An MP appeared from the checkpoint.

"Sir, we've called an ambulance."

Horning, still holding the limp hand, looked up. His face was shining with tears. He spoke in a voice gone hollow.

"It doesn't matter."

The officer spoke to one of the MPs who had rushed down from the checkpoint. "Did you get the number of the Russian vehicle? We'll have to get a report to U.S. High Commission. Jesus." He shook his head. "Do they really think they can get away with it?"

Patterson had bent down to pick up some bills from the road. He gasped and uttered a small, sharp cry.

The officer spoke. "Sir, what is it? What's the matter?"

He turned a horror-stricken face to Horning. "This poor, beautiful creature. We've killed her. We killed her for nothing." He gazed off toward the Russian zone. "May they do the same to him." His voice was dead, toneless. He held the handful of bills before them with a helpless gesture. "They made plates for counterfeiting gold certificates. That's what he's given them. They haven't been used in our country for years."

23911